The Rivet in Grandfather's Neck

The Rivet in Grandfather's Neck

A Comedy of Limitations

James Branch Cabell

MINT EDITIONS

The Rivet in Grandfather's Neck: A Comedy of Limitations was first published in 1915.

This edition published by Mint Editions 2021.

ISBN 9781513295763 | E-ISBN 9781513297262

Published by Mint Editions®

minteditionbooks.com

Publishing Director: Jennifer Newens
Design & Production: Rachel Lopez Metzger
Project Manager: Micaela Clark
Typesetting: Westchester Publishing Services

Contents

In the middle of the cupboard door was the carved figure of a man. . . He had goat's legs, little horns on his head, and a long beard; the children in the room called him, "Major-General-field-sergeant-commander-Billy-goat's-legs" . . . He was always looking at the table under the looking-glass where stood a very pretty little shepherdess made of china. . . Close by her side stood a little chimney-sweep, as black as coal and also made of china. . . Near to them stood another figure. . . He was an old Chinaman who could nod his head, and used to pretend he was the grandfather of the shepherdess, although he could not prove it. He, however, assumed authority over her, and therefore when "Major-general-field-sergeant-commander-Billy-goat's-legs" asked for the little shepherdess to be his wife, he nodded his head to show that he consented.

Then the little shepherdess cried, and looked at her sweetheart, the chimney-sweep. "I must entreat you," said she, "to go out with me into the wide world, for we cannot stay here." . . . When the chimney-sweep saw that she was quite firm, he said, "My way is through the stove up the chimney." . . . So at last they reached the top of the chimney. . . The sky with all its stars was over their heads. . . They could see for a very long distance out into the wide world, and the poor little shepherdess leaned her head on her chimney-sweep's shoulder and wept. "This is too much," she said, "the world is too large." . . . And so with a great deal of trouble they climbed down the chimney and peeped out. . . There lay the old Chinaman on the floor. . . broken into three pieces. . . "This is terrible," said the shepherdess. "He can be riveted," said the chimney-sweep. . . The family had the Chinaman's back mended and a strong rivet put through his neck; he looked as good as new, but when "Major-General-field-sergeant-commander-Billy-goat's-legs" again asked for the shepherdess to be his wife, the old Chinaman could no longer nod his head.

And so the little china people remained together and were thankful for the rivet in grandfather's neck, and continued to love each other until they were broken to pieces.

PART I

PROPINQUITY

"A singer, eh? . . . Well, well! but when he sings
Take jealous heed lest idiosyncrasies
Entinge and taint too deep his melodies;
See that his lute has no discordant strings
To harrow us; and let his vaporings
Be all of virtue and its victories,
And of man's best and noblest qualities,
And scenery, and flowers, and similar things.

"Thus Bid Our Paymasters Whose Mutterings
Some Few Deride, And Blithely Link Their Rhymes
At random; and, as ever, on frail wings
Of wine-stained paper scribbled with such rhymes
Men mount to heaven, and loud laughter springs
From hell's midpit, whose fuel is such rhymes."

—Paul Verville. *Nascitur*

I

At a very remote period, when editorials were mostly devoted to discussion as to whether the Democratic Convention (shortly to be held in Chicago) would or would not declare in favor of bi-metallism; when golf was a novel form of recreation in America, and people disputed how to pronounce its name, and pedestrians still turned to stare after an automobile; when, according to the fashion notes, "the godet skirts and huge sleeves of the present modes" were already doomed to extinction; when the baseball season had just begun, and some of our people were discussing the national game, and others the spectacular burning of the old Pennsylvania Railway depot at Thirty-third and Market Street in Philadelphia, and yet others the significance of General Fitzhugh Lee's recent appointment as consul-general to Habana: at this remote time, Lichfield talked of nothing except the Pendomer divorce case.

And Colonel Rudolph Musgrave had very narrowly escaped being named as the co-respondent. This much, at least, all Lichfield knew when George Pendomer—evincing unsuspected funds of generosity—permitted his wife to secure a divorce on the euphemistic grounds of "desertion." John Charteris, acting as Rudolph Musgrave's friend, had patched up this arrangement; and the colonel and Mrs. Pendomer, so rumor ran, were to be married very quietly after a decent interval.

Remained only to deliberate whether this sop to the conventions should be accepted as sufficient.

"At least," as Mrs. Ashmeade sagely observed, "we can combine vituperation with common-sense, and remember it is not the first time a Musgrave has figured in an entanglement of the sort. A lecherous race! proverbial flutterers of petticoats! His surname convicts the man unheard and almost excuses him. All of us feel that. And, moreover, it is not as if the idiots had committed any unpardonable sin, for they have kept out of the newspapers."

Her friend seemed dubious, and hazarded something concerning "the merest sense of decency."

"In the name of the Prophet, figs! People—I mean the people who count in Lichfield—are charitable enough to ignore almost any crime which is just a matter of common knowledge. In fact, they are mildly grateful. It gives them something to talk about. But when detraction is printed in the morning paper you can't overlook it without incurring the suspicion of being illiterate and virtueless. That's Lichfield."

"But, Polly—"

"Sophist, don't I know my Lichfield? I know it almost as well as I know Rudolph Musgrave. And so I prophesy that he will not marry Clarice Pendomer, because he is inevitably tired of her by this. He will marry money, just as all the Musgraves do. Moreover, I prophesy that we will gabble about this mess until we find a newer target for our stone throwing, and be just as friendly with the participants to their faces as we ever were. So don't let me hear any idiotic talk about whether or no *I* am going to receive her—"

"Well, after all, she was born a Bellingham. We must remember that."

"Wasn't I saying I knew my Lichfield?" Mrs. Ashmeade placidly observed.

AND TIME, INDEED, ATTESTED HER to be right in every particular.

Yet it must be recorded that at this critical juncture chance rather remarkably favored Colonel Musgrave and Mrs. Pendomer, by giving Lichfield something of greater interest to talk about; since now, just in the nick of occasion, occurred the notorious Scott Musgrave murder. Scott Musgrave—a fourth cousin once removed of the colonel's, to be quite accurate—had in the preceding year seduced the daughter of a village doctor, a negligible "half-strainer" up country at Warren; and her two brothers, being irritated, picked this particular season to waylay him in the street, as he reeled homeward one night from the Commodores' Club, and forthwith to abolish Scott Musgrave after the primitive methods of their lower station in society.

These details, indeed, were never officially made public, since a discreet police force "found no clues"; for Fred Musgrave (of King's Garden), as befitted the dead man's well-to-do brother, had been at no little pains to insure constabulary shortsightedness, in preference to having the nature of Scott Musgrave's recreations unsympathetically aired. Fred Musgrave thereby afforded Lichfield a delectable opportunity (conversationally and abetted by innumerable "they *do* say's") to accredit the murder, turn by turn, to every able-bodied person residing within stone's throw of its commission. So that few had time, now, to talk of Rudolph Musgrave and Clarice Pendomer; for it was not in Lichfieldian human nature to discuss a mere domestic imbroglio when here, also in the Musgrave family, was a picturesque and gory assassination to lay tongue to.

So Colonel Musgrave was duly reëlected that spring to the librarianship of the Lichfield Historical Association, and the name of Mrs. George Pendomer was not stricken from the list of patronesses of the Lichfield German Club, but was merely altered to "Mrs. Clarice Pendomer."

At the bottom of his heart Colonel Musgrave was a trifle irritated that his self-sacrifice should be thus unrewarded by martyrdom. Circumstances had enabled him to assume, and he had gladly accepted, the blame for John Charteris's iniquity, rather than let Anne Charteris know the truth about her husband and Clarice Pendomer. The truth would have killed Anne, the colonel believed; and besides, the colonel had enjoyed the performance of a picturesque action.

And having acted as a hero in permitting himself to be pilloried as a libertine, it was preferable of course not to have incurred ostracism thereby. His common-sense conceded this; and yet, to Colonel Musgrave, it could not but be evident that Destiny was hardly rising to the possibilities of the situation.

II

Concerning Colonel Musgrave one finds the ensuing account in a publication of the period devoted to biographies of more or less prominent Americans. It is reproduced unchanged, because these memoirs were—in the old days—compiled by the person whom they commemorated. The custom was a worthy one, since the value of an autobiography is determined by the nature of its superfluities and falsehoods.

"MUSGRAVE, RUDOLPH VARTREY, editor; *b.* Lichfield, Sill., Mar. 14, 1856; *s.* William Sebastian and Martha (Allardyce) M; *g. s.* Theodorick Q.M., gov. of Sill. 1805–8, judge of the General Ct., 1808–11, judge Supreme Ct. of Appeals, 1811–50 and pres. Supreme Ct. of Appeals, 1841–50; grad. King's Coll. and U. of Sill. Corr. sec. Lichfield Hist. Soc., and editor Sill. Mag. of Biog. since 1890; dir. Traders Nat. Bank, Sill.; mem. Soc. of the Sons of Col. Govs., pres. Sill. Soc. of Protestant Martyrs, comdr. Sill. Mil. Order of Lost Battles, mem. exec. bd. Sill. Hist. Assn. for the Preservation of Ruins. Democrat, Episcopalian, unmarried. *Author*: Colonial Lichfield, 1892; Right on the Scaffold, 1893; Secession and the South, 1894; Chart of the Descendants of Zenophon Perkins, 1894; Recollections of a Gracious Era, 1895; Notes as to the Vartreys of Westphalia, 1896. Has also written numerous pamphlets on hist., biog. and geneal. subjects. *Address*: Lichfield, Sill."

For Colonel Musgrave was by birth the lineal head of all the Musgraves of Matocton, which is in Lichfield, as degrees are counted there, equivalent to what being born a marquis would mean in England. Handsome and trim and affable, he defied chronology by looking ten years younger than he was known to be. For at least a decade he had been invaluable to Lichfield matrons alike against the entertainment of an "out-of-town girl," the management of a cotillion and the prevention of unpleasant pauses among incongruous dinner companies.

In short, he was by all accounts the social triumph of his generation; and his military title, won by four years of arduous service at receptions and parades while on the staff of a former Governor of the State, this seasoned bachelor carried off with plausibility and distinction.

The story finds him "Librarian and Corresponding Secretary" of the Lichfield Historical Association, which office he had held for some six years. The salary was small, and the colonel had inherited little; but his sister, Miss Agatha Musgrave, who lived with him, was a notable housekeeper. He increased his resources in a gentlemanly fashion by genealogical research, directed mostly toward the rehabilitation of ambiguous pedigrees; and for the rest, no other man could have fulfilled more gracefully the main duty of the Librarian, which was to exhibit the Association's collection of relics to hurried tourists "doing" Lichfield.

His "Library manner" was modeled upon that which an eighteenth century portrait would conceivably possess, should witchcraft set the canvas breathing.

III

Also the story finds Colonel Musgrave in the company of his sister on a warm April day, whilst these two sat upon the porch of the Musgrave home in Lichfield, and Colonel Musgrave waited until it should be time to open the Library for the afternoon. And about them birds twittered cheerily, and the formal garden flourished as gardens thrive nowhere except in Lichfield, and overhead the sky was a turkis-blue, save for a few irrelevant clouds which dappled it here and there like splashes of whipped cream.

Yet, for all this, the colonel was ill-at-ease; and care was on his brow, and venom in his speech.

"And one thing," Colonel Musgrave concluded, with decision, "I wish distinctly understood, and that is, if she insists on having young men loafing about her—as, of course, she will—she will have to entertain them in the garden. I won't have them in the house, Agatha. You remember that Langham girl you had here last Easter?" he added, disconsolately—"the one who positively littered up the house with young men, and sang idiotic jingles to them at all hours of the night about the Bailey family and the correct way to spell chicken? She drove me to the verge of insanity, and I haven't a doubt that this Patricia person will be quite as obstreperous. So, please mention it to her, Agatha—casually, of course—that, in Lichfield, when one is partial to either vocal exercise or amorous daliance, the proper scene of action is the garden. I really cannot be annoyed by her."

"But, Rudolph," his sister protested, "you forget she is engaged to the Earl of Pevensey. An engaged girl naturally wouldn't care about meeting any young men."

"H'm!" said the colonel, drily.

Ensued a pause, during which the colonel lighted yet another cigarette.

Then, "I have frequently observed," he spoke, in absent wise, "that all young women having that peculiarly vacuous expression about the eyes—I believe there are misguided persons who describe such eyes as being 'dreamy,'—are invariably possessed of a fickle, unstable and coquettish temperament. Oh, no! You may depend upon it, Agatha, the fact that she contemplates purchasing the right to support a peculiarly disreputable member of the British peerage will not hinder her in the least from making advances to all the young men in the neighborhood."

Miss Musgrave was somewhat ruffled. She was a homely little woman with nothing of the ordinary Musgrave comeliness. Candor even compels the statement that in her pudgy swarthy face there was a droll suggestion of the pug-dog.

"I am sure," Miss Musgrave remonstrated, with placid dignity, "that you know nothing whatever about her, and that the reports about the earl have probably been greatly exaggerated, and that her picture shows her to be an unusually attractive girl. Though it is true," Miss Musgrave conceded after reflection, "that there are any number of persons in the House of Lords that I wouldn't in the least care to have in my own house, even with the front parlor all in linen as it unfortunately is. So awkward when you have company! And the Bible does bid us not to put our trust in princes, and, for my part, I never thought that photographs could be trusted, either."

"Scorn not the nobly born, Agatha," her brother admonished her, "nor treat with lofty scorn the well-connected. The very best people are sometimes respectable. And yet," he pursued, with a slight hiatus of thought, "I should not describe her as precisely an attractive-looking girl. She seems to have a lot of hair,—if it is all her own, which it probably isn't,—and her nose is apparently straight enough, and I gather she is not absolutely deformed anywhere; but that is all I can conscientiously say in her favor. She is artificial. Her hair, now! It has a—well, you would not call it exactly a crinkle or precisely a wave, but rather somewhere between the two. Yes, I think I should describe it as a ripple. I fancy it must be rather like the reflection of a sunset in—a duck-pond, say, with a faint wind ruffling the water. For I gather that her hair is of some light shade,—induced, I haven't a doubt, by the liberal use of peroxides. And this ripple, too, Agatha, it stands to reason, must be the result of coercing nature, for I have never seen it in any other woman's hair. Moreover," Colonel Musgrave continued, warming somewhat to his subject, "there is a dimple—on the right side of her mouth, immediately above it,—which speaks of the most frivolous tendencies. I dare say it comes and goes when she talks,—winks at you, so to speak, in a manner that must be simply idiotic. That foolish little cleft in her chin, too—"

But at this point, his sister interrupted him.

"I hadn't a notion," said she, "that you had even looked at the photograph. And you seem to have it quite by heart, Rudolph,—and some people admire dimples, you know, and, at any rate, her mother had red hair, so Patricia isn't really responsible. I decided that it would be foolish to use the best mats tonight. We can save them for Sunday supper, because I am only going to have eggs and a little cold meat, and not make company of her."

For no apparent reason, Rudolph Musgrave flushed.

"I inspected it—quite casually—last night. Please don't be absurd, Agatha! If we were threatened with any other direful visitation—influenza, say, or the seventeen-year locust,—I should naturally read up on the subject in order to know what to expect. And since Providence has seen fit to send us a visitor rather than a visitation—though, personally, I should infinitely prefer the influenza, as interfering in less degree with my comfort,—I have, of course, neglected no opportunity of finding out what we may reasonably look forward to. I fear the worst, Agatha. For I repeat, the girl's face is, to me, absolutely unattractive!"

The colonel spoke with emphasis, and flung away his cigarette, and took up his hat to go.

And then, "I suppose," said Miss Musgrave, absently, "you will be falling in love with her, just as you did with Anne Charteris and Aline Van Orden and all those other minxes. I *would* like to see you married, Rudolph, only I couldn't stand your having a wife."

"I! I!" sputtered the colonel. "I think you must be out of your head! I fall in love with that chit! Good Lord, Agatha, you are positively idiotic!"

And the colonel turned on his heel, and walked stiffly through the garden. But, when half-way down the path, he wheeled about and came back.

"I beg your pardon, Agatha," he said, contritely, "it was not my intention to be discourteous. But somehow—somehow, dear, I don't quite see the necessity for my falling in love with anybody, so long as I have you."

And Miss Musgrave, you may be sure, forgave him promptly; and afterward—with a bit of pride and an infinity of love in her kind, homely face,—her eyes followed him out of the garden on his way to open the Library. And she decided in her heart that she had the dearest and best and handsomest brother in the universe, and that she must remember to tell him, accidentally, how becoming his new hat was. And then, at some unspoken thought, she smiled, wistfully.

"She would be a very lucky girl if he did," said Miss Musgrave, apropos of nothing in particular; and tossed her grizzly head.

"An earl, indeed!" said Miss Musgrave.

IV

And this is how it came about:

Patricia Vartrey (a second cousin once removed of Colonel Rudolph Musgrave's), as the older inhabitants of Lichfield will volubly attest, was always a person who did peculiar things. The list of her eccentricities is far too lengthy here to be enumerated; but she began it by being born with red hair—Titian reds and auburns were undiscovered euphemisms in those days—and, in Lichfield, this is not regarded as precisely a lady-like thing to do; and she ended it, as far as Lichfield was concerned, by eloping with what Lichfield in its horror could only describe, with conscious inadequacy, as "a quite unheard-of person."

Indisputably the man was well-to-do already; and from this nightmarish topsy-turvidom of Reconstruction the fellow visibly was plucking wealth. Also young Stapylton was well enough to look at, too, as Lichfield flurriedly conceded.

But it was equally undeniable that he had made his money through a series of commercial speculations distinguished both by shiftiness and daring, and that the man himself had been until the War a wholly negligible "poor white" person,—an overseer, indeed, for "Wild Will" Musgrave, Colonel Musgrave's father, who was of course the same Lieutenant-Colonel William Sebastian Musgrave, C.S.A., that met his death at Gettysburg.

This upstart married Patricia Vartrey, for all the chatter and whispering, and carried her away from Lichfield, as yet a little dubious as to what recognition, if any, should be accorded the existence of the Stapyltons. And afterward (from a notoriously untruthful North, indeed) came rumors that he was rapidly becoming wealthy; and of Patricia Vartrey's death at her daughter's birth; and of the infant's health and strength and beauty, and of her lavish upbringing,—a Frenchwoman, Lichfield whispered, with absolutely nothing to do but attend upon the child.

And then, little by little, a new generation sprang up, and, little by little, the interest these rumors waked became more lax; and it was brought about, at last, by the insidious transitions of time, that Patricia Vartrey was forgotten in Lichfield. Only a few among the older men remembered her; some of them yet treasured, as these fogies so often do, a stray fan or an odd glove; and in bycorners of sundry time-toughened hearts there lurked the memory of a laughing word or of a glance or of some such casual bounty, that Patricia Vartrey had accorded these hearts' owners when the world was young.

But Agatha Musgrave, likewise, remembered the orphan cousin who had been reared with her. She had loved Patricia Vartrey; and, in due time, she wrote to Patricia's daughter,—in stately, antiquated phrases that astonished the recipient not a little,—and the girl had answered. The correspondence flourished. And it was not long before Miss Musgrave had induced her young cousin to visit Lichfield.

Colonel Rudolph Musgrave, be it understood, knew nothing of all this until the girl was actually on her way. And now, she was to arrive that afternoon, to domicile herself in his quiet house for two long weeks—this utter stranger, look you!—and upset his comfort, ask him silly questions, expect him to talk to her, and at the end of her visit, possibly, present him with some outlandish gimcrack made of cardboard and pink ribbons, in which she would expect him to keep his papers. The Langham girl did that.

It is honesty's part to give you the man no better than he was. Lichfield at large had pampered him; many women had loved him; and above all, Miss Agatha had spoiled him. After fifteen years of being the pivot about which the economy of a household revolves, after fifteen years of being the inevitable person whose approval must be secured before any domestic alteration, however trivial, may be considered, no mortal man may hope to remain a paragon of unselfishness.

Colonel Musgrave joyed in the society of women. But he classed them—say, with the croquettes adorned with pink paper frills which were then invariably served at the suppers of the Lichfield German Club,—as acceptable enough, upon a conscious holiday, but wholly incongruous with the slippered ease of home. When you had an inclination for feminine society, you shaved and changed your clothes and thought up an impromptu or so against emergency, and went forth to seek it. That was natural; but to have a petticoated young person infesting your house, hourly, was as preposterous as ice-cream soda at breakfast.

The metaphor set him off at a tangent. He wondered if this Patricia person could not (tactfully) be induced to take her bath after breakfast, as Agatha did? after he had his? Why, confound the girl, he was not responsible for there being only one bathroom in the house! It was necessary for him to have his bath and be at the Library by nine o'clock. This interloper must be made to understand as much.

The colonel reached the Library undecided as to whether Miss Stapylton had better breakfast in her room, or if it would be entirely proper for her to come to the table in one of those fluffy lace-trimmed garments such as Agatha affected at the day's beginning?

The question was a nice one. It was not as though servants were willing to be bothered with carrying trays to people's rooms; he knew what Agatha had to say upon that subject. It was not as though he were the chit's first cousin, either. He almost wished himself in the decline of life, and free to treat the girl paternally.

And so he fretted all that afternoon.

Then, too, he reflected that it would be very awkward if Agatha should be unwell while this Patricia person was in the house. Agatha in her normal state was of course the kindliest and cheeriest gentlewoman in the universe, but any physical illness appeared to transform her nature disastrously. She had her "attacks," she "felt badly" very often nowadays, poor dear; and how was a Patricia person to be expected to make allowances for the fact that at such times poor Agatha was unavoidably a little cross and pessimistic?

V

Yet Colonel Musgrave strolled into his garden, later, with a tolerable affectation of unconcern. Women, after all, he assured himself, were necessary for the perpetuation of the species; and, resolving for the future to view these weakly, big-hipped and slope-shouldered makeshifts of Nature's with larger tolerance, he cocked his hat at a devil-may-carish angle, and strode up the walk, whistling jauntily and having, it must be confessed, to the unprejudiced observer very much the air of a sheep in wolf's clothing.

"At worst," he was reflecting, "I can make love to her. They, as a rule, take kindlily enough to that; and in the exercise of hospitality a host must go to all lengths to divert his guests. Failure is not permitted. . ."

Then she came to him.

She came to him across the trim, cool lawn, leisurely, yet with a resilient tread that attested the vigor of her slim young body. She was all in white, diaphanous, ethereal, quite incredibly incredible; but as she passed through the long shadows of the garden—fire-new, from the heart of the sunset, Rudolph Musgrave would have sworn to you,—the lacy folds and furbelows and semi-transparencies that clothed her were now tinged with gold, and now, as a hedge or flower-bed screened her from the horizontal rays, were softened into multitudinous graduations of grays and mauves and violets.

"Failure is not permitted," he was repeating in his soul. . .

"You're Cousin Rudolph, aren't you?" she asked. "How perfectly entrancing! You see until today I always thought that if I had been offered the choice between having cousins or appendicitis I would have preferred to be operated on."

And Rudolph Musgrave noted, with a delicious tingling somewhere about his heart, that her hair was really like the reflection of a sunset in rippling waters,—only many times more beautiful, of course,—and that her mouth was an inconsiderable trifle, a scrap of sanguine curves, and that her eyes were purple glimpses of infinity.

Then he observed that his own mouth was giving utterance to divers irrelevant and foolish sounds, which eventually resolved themselves into the statement he was glad to see her. And immediately afterward the banality of this remark brought the hot blood to his face and, for the rest of the day, stung him and teased him, somewhere in the background of his mind, like an incessant insect.

Glad, indeed!

Before he had finished shaking hands with Patricia Stapylton, it was all over with the poor man.

"Er—h'm!" quoth he.

"Only," Miss Stapylton was meditating, with puckered brow, "it would be unseemly for me to call you Rudolph—"

"You impertinent minx!" cried he, in his soul; "I should rather think it would be!"

"—and Cousin Rudolph sounds exactly like a dried-up little man with eyeglasses and crows' feet and a gentle nature. I rather thought you were going to be like that, and I regard it as extremely hospitable of you not to be. You are more like—like what now?" Miss Stapylton put her head to one side and considered the contents of her vocabulary,—"you are like a viking. I shall call you Olaf," she announced, when she had reached a decision.

This, look you, to the most dignified man in Lichfield,—a person who had never borne a nickname in his life. You must picture for yourself how the colonel stood before her, big, sturdy and blond, and glared down at her, and assured himself that he was very indignant; like Timanthes, the colonel's biographer prefers to draw a veil before the countenance to which art is unable to do justice.

Then, "I have no admiration for the Northmen," Rudolph Musgrave declared, stiffly. "They were a rude and barbarous nation, proverbially addicted to piracy and intemperance."

"My goodness gracious!" Miss Stapylton observed,—and now, for the first time, he saw the teeth that were like grains of rice upon a pink rose petal. Also, he saw dimples. "And does one mean all that by a viking?"

"The vikings," he informed her—and his Library manner had settled upon him now to the very tips of his fingers—"were pirates. The word is of Icelandic origin, from *vik*, the name applied to the small inlets along the coast in which they concealed their galleys. I may mention that Olaf was not a viking, but a Norwegian king, being the first Christian monarch to reign in Norway."

"Dear me!" said Miss Stapylton; "how interesting!"

Then she yawned with deliberate cruelty.

"However," she concluded, "I shall call you Olaf, just the same."

"Er—h'm!" said the colonel.

And this stuttering boor (he reflected) was Colonel Rudolph Musgrave, confessedly the social triumph of his generation! This imbecile, without a syllable to say for himself, without a solitary adroit word within tongue's reach, wherewith to annihilate the hussy, was a Musgrave of Matocton!

And she did. To her he was "Olaf" from that day forth.

Rudolph Musgrave called her, "You." He was nettled, of course, by her forwardness—"Olaf," indeed!—yet he found it, somehow, difficult to bear this fact in mind continuously.

For while it is true our heroes and heroines in fiction no longer fall in love at first sight, Nature, you must remember, is too busily employed with other matters to have much time to profit by current literature. Then, too, she is not especially anxious to be realistic. She prefers to jog along in the old rut, contentedly turning out chromolithographic sunrises such as they give away at the tea stores, contentedly staging the most violent and improbable melodramas; and—sturdy old Philistine that she is—she even now permits her children to fall in love in the most primitive fashion.

She is not particularly interested in subtleties and soul analyses; she merely chuckles rather complacently when a pair of eyes are drawn, somehow, to another pair of eyes, and an indescribable something is altered somewhere in some untellable fashion, and the world, suddenly, becomes the most delightful place of residence in all the universe. Indeed, it is her favorite miracle, this. For at work of this sort the old Philistine knows that she is an adept; and she has rejoiced in the skill of her hands, with a sober workmanly joy, since Cain first went a-wooing in the Land of Nod.

So Colonel Rudolph Musgrave, without understanding what had happened to him, on a sudden was strangely content with life.

It was at supper—dinner, in Lichfield, when not a formal entertainment, is eaten at two in the afternoon—that he fell a-speculating as to whether Her eyes, after all, could be fitly described as purple.

Wasn't there a grayer luminosity about them than he had at first suspected?—wasn't the cool glow of them, in a word, rather that of sunlight falling upon a wet slate roof?

It was a delicate question, an affair of nuances, of almost imperceptible graduations; and in debating a matter of such nicety, a man must necessarily lay aside all petty irritation, such as being nettled by an irrational nickname, and approach the question with unbiased mind.

He did. And when, at last, he had come warily to the verge of decision, Miss Musgrave in all innocence announced that they would excuse him if he wished to get back to his work.

He discovered that, somehow, the three had finished supper; and, somehow, he presently discovered himself in his study, where eight o'clock had found him every evening for the last ten years, when he was not about his social diversions. An old custom, you will observe, is not lightly broken.

VI

Subsequently: "I have never approved of these international marriages," said Colonel Musgrave, with heat. "It stands to reason, she is simply marrying the fellow for his title. *(The will of Jeremiah Brown, dated 29 November, 1690, recorded 2 February, 1690–1, mentions his wife Eliza Brown and appoints her his executrix.)* She can't possibly care for him. *(This, then, was the second wife of Edward Osborne of Henrico, who, marrying him 15 June, 1694, died before January, 1696–7.)* But they are all flibbertigibbets, every one of them. *(She had apparently no children by either marriage—)* And I dare say she is no better than the rest."

Came a tap on the door. Followed a vision of soft white folds and furbelows and semi-transparencies and purple eyes and a pouting mouth.

"I am become like a pelican in the wilderness, Olaf," the owner of these vanities complained. "Are you very busy? Cousin Agatha is about her housekeeping, and I have read the afternoon paper all through,—even the list of undelivered letters and the woman's page,—and I just want to see the Gilbert Stuart picture," she concluded,—exercising, one is afraid, a certain economy in regard to the truth.

This was a little too much. If a man's working-hours are not to be respected—if his privacy is to be thus invaded on the flimsiest of pretexts,—why, then, one may very reasonably look for chaos to come again. This, Rudolph Musgrave decided, was a case demanding firm and instant action. Here was a young person who needed taking down a peg or two, and that at once.

But he made the mistake of looking at her first. And after that, he lied glibly. "Good Lord, no! I am not in the least busy now. In fact, I was just about to look you two up."

"I was rather afraid of disturbing you." She hesitated; and a lucent mischief woke in her eyes. "You are so patriarchal, Olaf," she lamented. "I felt like a lion venturing into a den of Daniels. But if you cross your heart you aren't really busy—why, then, you can show me the Stuart, Olaf."

It is widely conceded that Gilbert Stuart never in his after work surpassed the painting which hung then in Rudolph Musgrave's study,—the portrait of the young Gerald Musgrave, afterward the friend of Jefferson and Henry, and, still later, the author of divers bulky tomes, pertaining for the most part to ethnology. The boy smiles at you from the canvas, smiles ambiguously,—smiles with a woman's mouth, set above a resolute chin, however,—and with a sort of humorous sadness in his eyes. These latter are of a dark shade of blue—purple, if you will,—and his hair is tinged with red.

"Why, he took after me!" said Miss Stapylton. "How thoughtful of him, Olaf!"

And Rudolph Musgrave saw the undeniable resemblance. It gave him a queer sort of shock, too, as he comprehended, for the first time, that the faint blue vein on that lifted arm held Musgrave blood,—the same blood which at this thought quickened. For any person guided by appearances, Rudolph Musgrave considered, would have surmised that the vein in question contained celestial ichor or some yet diviner fluid.

"It is true," he conceded, "that there is a certain likeness."

"And he is a very beautiful boy," said Miss Stapylton, demurely. "Thank you, Olaf; I begin to think you are a dangerous flatterer. But he is only a boy, Olaf! And I had always thought of Gerald Musgrave as a learned person with a fringe of whiskers all around his face—like a centerpiece, you know."

The colonel smiled. "This portrait was painted early in life. Our kinsman was at that time, I believe, a person of rather frivolous tendencies. Yet he was not quite thirty when he first established his reputation by his monograph upon *The Evolution of Marriage*. And afterwards, just prior to his first meeting with Goethe, you will remember—"

"Oh, yes!" Miss Stapylton assented, hastily; "I remember perfectly. I know all about him, thank you. And it was that beautiful boy, Olaf, that young-eyed cherub, who developed into a musty old man who wrote musty old books, and lived a musty, dusty life all by himself, and never married or had any fun at all! How *horrid*, Olaf!" she cried, with a queer shrug of distaste.

"I fail," said Colonel Musgrave, "to perceive anything—ah—horrid in a life devoted to the study of anthropology. His reputation when he died was international."

"But he never had any fun, you jay-bird! And, oh, Olaf! Olaf! that boy could have had so much fun! The world held so much for him! Why, Fortune is only a woman, you know, and what woman could have refused him anything if he had smiled at her like that when he asked for it?"

Miss Stapylton gazed up at the portrait for a long time now, her hands clasped under her chin. Her face was gently reproachful.

"Oh, boy dear, boy dear!" she said, with a forlorn little quaver in her voice, "how *could* you be *so* foolish? *Didn't* you know there was something better in the world than grubbing after musty old tribes and customs and folk-songs? Oh, precious child, how could you?"

Gerald Musgrave smiled back at her, ambiguously; and Rudolph Musgrave laughed. "I perceive," said he, "you are a follower of Epicurus. For my part, I must have fetched my ideals from the tub of the Stoic. I can conceive of no nobler life than one devoted to furthering the cause of science."

She looked up at him, with a wan smile. "A barren life!" she said: "ah, yes, his was a wasted life! His books are all out-of-date now, and nobody reads them, and it is just as if he had never been. A barren life, Olaf! And that beautiful boy might have had so much fun—Life is queer, isn't it, Olaf?"

Again he laughed, "The criticism," he suggested, "is not altogether original. And Science, no less than War, must have her unsung heroes. You must remember," he continued, more seriously, "that any great work must have as its foundation the achievements of unknown men. I fancy that Cheops did not lay every brick in his pyramid with his own hand; and I dare say Nebuchadnezzar employed a few helpers when he was laying out his hanging gardens. But time cannot chronicle these lesser men. Their sole reward must be the knowledge that they have aided somewhat in the unending work of the world."

Her face had altered into a pink and white penitence which was flavored with awe.

"I—I forgot," she murmured, contritely; "I—forgot you were—like him—about your genealogies, you know. Oh, Olaf, I'm very silly! Of course, it is tremendously fine and—and nice, I dare say, if you like it,—to devote your life to learning, as you and he have done. I forgot, Olaf. Still, I am sorry, somehow, for that beautiful boy," she ended, with a disconsolate glance at the portrait.

VII

Long after Miss Stapylton had left him, the colonel sat alone in his study, idle now, and musing vaguely. There were no more addenda concerning the descendants of Captain Thomas Osborne that night.

At last, the colonel rose and threw open a window, and stood looking into the moonlit garden. The world bathed in a mist of blue and silver. There was a breeze that brought him sweet, warm odors from the garden, together with a blurred shrilling of crickets and the conspiratorial conference of young leaves.

"Of course, it is tremendously fine and—and nice, if you like it," he said, with a faint chuckle. "I wonder, now, if I do like it?"

He was strangely moved. He seemed, somehow, to survey Rudolph Musgrave and all his doings with complete and unconcerned aloofness. The man's life, seen in its true proportions, dwindled into the merest flicker of a match; he had such a little while to live, this Rudolph Musgrave! And he spent the serious hours of this brief time writing notes and charts and pamphlets that perhaps some hundred men in all the universe might care to read—pamphlets no better and no more accurate than hundreds of other men were writing at that very moment.

No, the capacity for originative and enduring work was not in him; and this incessant compilation of dreary footnotes, this incessant rummaging among the bones of the dead—did it, after all, mean more to this Rudolph Musgrave than one full, vivid hour of life in that militant world yonder, where men fought for other and more tangible prizes than the mention of one's name in a genealogical journal?

He could not have told you. In his heart, he knew that a thorough digest of the Wills and Orders of the Orphans' Court of any county must always rank as a useful and creditable performance; but, from without, the sounds and odors of Spring were calling to him, luring him, wringing his very heart, bidding him come forth into the open and crack a jest or two before he died, and stare at the girls a little before the match had flickered out.

At this time he heard a moaning noise. The colonel gave a shrug, sighed, and ascended to his sister's bedroom. He knew that Agatha must be ill; and that there is no more efficient quietus to wildish meditations than the heating of hot-water bottles and the administration of hypnotics he had long ago discovered.

PART II

RENASCENCE

"As one imprisoned that hath lain alone
And dreamed of sunlight where no vagrant gleam
Of sunlight pierces, being freed, must deem
This too but dreaming, and must dread the sun
Whose glory dazzles,—even as such-an-one
Am I whose longing was but now supreme
For this high hour, and, now it strikes, esteem
I do but dream long dreamed-of goals are won.

"Phyllis, I am not worthy of thy love.
I pray thee let no kindly word be said
Of me at all, for in the train thereof,
Whenas yet-parted lips, sigh-visited,
End speech and wait, mine when I will to move,
Such joy awakens that I grow afraid."

—Thomas Rowland. *Triumphs of Phyllis*

I

They passed with incredible celerity, those next ten days—those strange, delicious, topsy-turvy days. To Rudolph Musgrave it seemed afterward that he had dreamed them away in some vague Lotus Land—in a delectable country where, he remembered, there were always purple eyes that mocked you, and red lips that coaxed you now, and now cast gibes at you.

You felt, for the most part of your stay in this country, flushed and hot and uncomfortable and unbelievably awkward, and you were mercilessly bedeviled there; but not for all the accumulated wealth of Samarkand and Ind and Ophir would you have had it otherwise. Ah, no, not otherwise in the least trifle. For now uplifted to a rosy zone of acquiescence, you partook incuriously at table of nectar and ambrosia, and noted abroad, without any surprise, that you trod upon a more verdant grass than usual, and that someone had polished up the sun a bit; and, in fine, you snatched a fearful joy from the performance of the most trivial functions of life.

Yet always he remembered that it could not last; always he remembered that in the autumn Patricia was to marry Lord Pevensey. She sometimes gave him letters to mail which were addressed to that nobleman. He wondered savagely what was in them; he posted them with a vicious shove; and, for the time, they caused him acute twinges of misery. But not for long; no, for, in sober earnest, if some fantastic sequence of events had made his one chance of winning Patricia Stapylton dependent on his spending a miserable half-hour in her company, Rudolph Musgrave could not have done it.

As for Miss Stapylton, she appeared to delight in the cloistered, easy-going life of Lichfield. The quaint and beautiful old town fell short in nothing of her expectations, in spite of the fact that she had previously read John Charteris's tales of Lichfield,—"those effusions which" (if the *Lichfield Courier-Herald* is to be trusted) "have builded, by the strength and witchery of record and rhyme, romance and poem, a myriad-windowed temple in Lichfield's honor—exquisite, luminous, and enduring—for all the world to see."

Miss Stapylton appeared to delight in the cloistered easy-going life of Lichfield,—that town which was once, as the outside world has half-forgotten now, the center of America's wealth, politics and culture, the town to which Europeans compiling "impressions" of America devoted one of their longest chapters in the heyday of Elijah Pogram and Jefferson Brick. But the War between the States has changed all that, and Lichfield endures today only as a pleasant backwater.

Very pleasant, too, it was in the days of Patricia's advent. There were strikingly few young men about, to be sure; most of them on reaching maturity had settled in more bustling regions. But many maidens remained whom memory delights to catalogue,—tall, brilliant Lizzie Allardyce, the lovely and cattish Marian Winwood, to whom Felix Kennaston wrote those wonderful love-letters which she published when he married Kathleen Saumarez, the rich Baugh heiresses from Georgia, the Pride twins, and Mattie Ferneyhaugh, whom even rival beauties loved, they say, and other damsels by the score,—all in due time to be wooed and won, and then to pass out of the old town's life.

Among the men of Rudolph Musgrave's generation—those gallant oldsters who were born and bred, and meant to die, in Lichfield,—Patricia did not lack for admirers. Tom May was one of them, of course; rarely a pretty face escaped the tribute of at least one proposal from Tom May. Then there was Roderick Taunton, he with the leonine mane, who spared her none of his forensic eloquence, but found Patricia less tractable than the most stubborn of juries. Bluff Walter Thurman, too, who was said to know more of Dickens, whist and criminal law than any other man living, came to worship at her shrine, as likewise did huge red-faced Ashby Bland, famed for that cavalry charge which history-books tell you that he led, and at which he actually was not present, for reasons all Lichfield knew and chuckled over. And Courtney Thorpe and Charles Maupin, doctors of the flesh and the spirit severally, were others among the rivals who gathered about Patricia at decorous festivals when, candles lighted, the butler and his underlings came with trays of delectable things to eat, and the "nests" of tables were set out, and pleasant chatter abounded.

And among Patricia's attendants Colonel Musgrave, it is needless to relate, was preëminently pertinacious. The two found a deal to talk about, somehow, though it is doubtful if many of their comments were of sufficient importance or novelty to merit record. Then, also, he often read aloud to her from lovely books, for the colonel read admirably and did not scruple to give emotional passages their value. *Trilby*, published the preceding spring in book form, was one of these books, for all this was at a very remote period; and the *Rubaiyat* was another, for that poem was as yet unhackneyed and hardly wellknown enough to be parodied in those happy days.

Once he read to her that wonderful sad tale of Hans Christian Andersen's which treats of the china chimney-sweep and the shepherdess, who eloped from their bedizened tiny parlor-table, and were frightened by the vastness of the world outside, and crept ignominiously back to their fit home. "And so," the colonel ended, "the little china people remained together, and were thankful for the rivet in grandfather's neck, and continued to love each other until they were broken to pieces."

"It was really a very lucky thing," Patricia estimated, "that the grandfather had a rivet in his neck and couldn't nod to the billy-goat-legged person to take the shepherdess away into his cupboard. I don't doubt the little china people were glad of it. But after climbing so far—and seeing the stars,—I think they ought to have had more to be glad for." Her voice was quaintly wistful.

"I will let you into a secret—er—Patricia. That rivet was made out of the strongest material in the whole universe. And the old grandfather was glad, at bottom, he had it in his neck so that he couldn't nod and separate the shepherdess from the chimney-sweep."

"Yes,—I guess he had been rather a rip among the bric-à-brac in his day and sympathized with them?"

"No, it wasn't just that. You see these little china people had forsaken their orderly comfortable world on the parlor table to climb very high. It was a brave thing to do, even though they faltered and came back after a while. It is what we all want to do, Patricia—to climb toward the stars,—even those of us who are too lazy or too cowardly to attempt it. And when others try it, we are envious and a little uncomfortable, and we probably scoff; but we can't help admiring, and there is a rivet in the neck of all of us which prevents us from interfering. Oh, yes, we little china people have a variety of rivets, thank God, to prevent too frequent nodding and too cowardly a compromise with baseness,—rivets that are a part of us and force us into flashes of upright living, almost in spite of ourselves, when duty and inclination grapple. There is always the thing one cannot do for the reason that one is constituted as one is. That, I take it, is the real rivet in grandfather's neck and everybody else's."

He spoke disjointedly, vaguely, but the girl nodded. "I think I understand, Olaf. Only, it is a two-edged rivet—to mix metaphors—and keeps us stiffnecked against all sorts of calls. No, I am not sure that the thing one cannot do because one is what one is, proves to be always a cause for international jubilations and fireworks on the lawn."

II

Thus Lichfield, as to its staid trousered citizenry, fell prostrate at Miss Stapylton's feet, and as to the remainder of its adults, vociferously failed to see anything in the least remarkable in her appearance, and avidly took and compared notes as to her personal apparel.

"You have brought Asmodeus into Lichfield," Colonel Musgrave one day rebuked Miss Stapylton, as they sat in the garden. "The demon of pride and dress is rampant everywhere—er—Patricia. Even Agatha does her hair differently now; and in church last Sunday I counted no less than seven duplicates of that blue hat of yours."

Miss Stapylton was moved to mirth. "Fancy your noticing a thing like that!" said she. "I didn't know you were even aware I had a blue hat."

"I am no judge," he conceded, gravely, "of such fripperies. I don't pretend to be. But, on the other hand, I must plead guilty to deriving considerable harmless amusement from your efforts to dress as an example and an irritant to all Lichfield."

"You wouldn't have me a dowd, Olaf?" said she, demurely. "I have to be neat and tidy, you know. You wouldn't have me going about in a continuous state of unbuttonedness and black bombazine like Mrs. Rabbet, would you?"

Rudolph Musgrave debated as to this. "I dare say," he at last conceded, cautiously, "that to the casual eye your appearance is somewhat—er—more pleasing than that of our rector's wife. But, on the other hand—"

"Olaf, I am embarrassed by such fulsome eulogy. Mrs. Rabbet isn't a day under forty-nine. And you consider me *somewhat* better-looking than she is!"

He inspected her critically, and was confirmed in his opinion.

"Olaf"—coaxingly—"do you really think I am as ugly as that?"

"Pouf!" said the colonel airily; "I dare say you are well enough."

"Olaf"—and this was even more cajoling—"do you know you've never told me what sort of a woman you most admire?"

"I don't admire any of them," said Colonel Musgrave, stoutly. "They are too vain and frivolous—especially the pink-and-white ones," he added, unkindlily.

"Cousin Agatha has told me all about your multifarious affairs of course. She depicts you as a sort of cardiacal buccaneer and visibly gloats over the tale of your enormities. She is perfectly dear about it. But have you never—*cared*—for any woman, Olaf?"

Precarious ground, this! His eyes were fixed upon her now. And hers, for doubtless sufficient reasons, were curiously intent upon anything in the universe rather than Rudolph Musgrave.

"Yes," said he, with a little intake of the breath; "yes, I cared once."

"And—she cared?" asked Miss Stapylton.

She happened, even now, not to be looking at him.

"She!" Rudolph Musgrave cried, in real surprise. "Why, God bless my soul, of course she didn't! She didn't know anything about it."

"You never told her, Olaf?"—and this was reproachful. Then Patricia said: "Well! and did she go down in the cellar and get the wood-ax or was she satisfied just to throw the bric-à-brac at you?"

And Colonel Musgrave laughed aloud.

"Ah!" said he; "it would have been a brave jest if I had told her, wouldn't it? She was young, you see, and wealthy, and—ah, well, I won't deceive you by exaggerating her personal attractions! I will serve up to you no praises of her sauced with lies. And I scorn to fall back on the stock-in-trade of the poets,—all their silly metaphors and similes and suchlike nonsense. I won't tell you that her complexion reminded me of roses swimming in milk, for it did nothing of the sort. Nor am I going to insist that her eyes had a fire like that of stars, or proclaim that Cupid was in the habit of lighting his torch from them. I don't think he was. I would like to have caught the brat taking any such liberties with those innocent, humorous, unfathomable eyes of hers! And they didn't remind me of violets, either," he pursued, belligerently, "nor did her mouth look to me in the least like a rosebud, nor did I have the slightest difficulty in distinguishing between her hands and lilies. I consider these hyperbolical figures of speech to be idiotic. Ah, no!" cried Colonel Musgrave, warming to his subject—and regarding it, too, very intently; "ah, no, a face that could be patched together at the nearest florist's would not haunt a man's dreams o'nights, as hers does! I haven't any need for praises sauced with lies! I spurn hyperbole. I scorn exaggeration. I merely state calmly and judicially that she was God's masterpiece,—the most beautiful and adorable and indescribable creature that He ever made."

She smiled at this. "You should have told her, Olaf," said Miss Stapylton. "You should have told her that you cared."

He gave a gesture of dissent. "She had everything," he pointed out, "everything the world could afford her. And, doubtless, she would have been very glad to give it all up for me, wouldn't she?—for me, who haven't youth or wealth or fame or anything? Ah, I dare say she would have been delighted to give up the world she knew and loved,—the world that loved her,—for the privilege of helping me digest old county records!"

And Rudolph Musgrave laughed again, though not mirthfully.

But the girl was staring at him, with a vague trouble in her eyes. "You should have told her, Olaf," she repeated.

And at this point he noted that the arbutus-flush in her cheeks began to widen slowly, until, at last, it had burned back to the little pink ears, and had merged into the coppery glory of her hair, and had made her, if such a thing were possible—which a minute ago it manifestly was not,—more beautiful and adorable and indescribable than ever before.

"Ah, yes!" he scoffed, "Lichfield would have made a fitting home for her. She would have been very happy here, shut off from the world with us,—with us, whose forefathers have married and intermarried with one another until the stock is worthless, and impotent for any further achievement. For here, you know, we have the best blood in America, and—for utilitarian purposes—that means the worst blood. Ah, we may prate of our superiority to the rest of the world,—and God knows, we do!—but, at bottom, we are worthless. We are worn out, I tell you! we are effete and stunted in brain and will-power, and the very desire of life is gone out of us! We are contented simply to exist in Lichfield. And she—"

He paused, and a new, fierce light came into his eyes. "She was so beautiful!" he said, half-angrily, between clenched teeth.

"You are just like the rest of them, Olaf," she lamented, with a hint of real sadness. "You imagine you are in love with a girl because you happen to like the color of her eyes, or because there is a curve about her lips that appeals to you. That isn't love, Olaf, as we women understand it. Ah, no, a girl's love for a man doesn't depend altogether upon his fitness to be used as an advertisement for somebody's ready-made clothing."

"You fancy you know what you are talking about," said Rudolph Musgrave, "but you don't. You don't realize, you see, how beautiful she—was."

And this time, he nearly tripped upon the tense, for her hand was on his arm, and, in consequence, a series of warm, delicious little shivers was running about his body in a fashion highly favorable to extreme perturbation of mind.

"You should have told her, Olaf," she said, wistfully. "Oh, Olaf, Olaf, why didn't you tell her?"

She did not know, of course, how she was tempting him; she did not know, of course, how her least touch seemed to waken every pulse in his body to an aching throb, and set hope and fear a-drumming in his breast. Obviously, she did not know; and it angered him that she did not.

"She would have laughed at me," he said, with a snarl; "how she would have laughed!"

"She wouldn't have laughed, Olaf." And, indeed, she did not look as if she would.

"But much you know of her!" said Rudolph Musgrave, morosely. "She was just like the rest of them, I tell you! She knew how to stare a man out of countenance with big purple eyes that were like violets with the dew on them, and keep her paltry pink-and-white baby face all pensive and sober, till the poor devil went stark, staring mad, and would have pawned his very soul to tell her that he loved her! She knew! She did it on purpose. She would look pensive just to make an ass of you! She—"

And here the colonel set his teeth for a moment, and resolutely drew back from the abyss.

"She would not have cared for me," he said, with a shrug. "I was not exactly the sort of fool she cared for. What she really cared for was a young fool who could dance with her in this silly new-fangled gliding style, and send her flowers and sweet-meats, and make love to her glibly—and a petticoated fool who would envy her fine feathers,—and, at last, a knavish fool who would barter his title for her money. She preferred fools, you see, but she would never have cared for a middle-aged penniless fool like me. And so," he ended, with a vicious outburst of mendacity, "I never told her, and she married a title and lived unhappily in gilded splendor ever afterwards."

"You should have told her, Olaf," Miss Stapylton persisted; and then she asked, in a voice that came very near being inaudible: "Is it too late to tell her now, Olaf?"

The stupid man opened his lips a little, and stood staring at her with hungry eyes, wondering if it were really possible that she did not hear the pounding of his heart; and then his teeth clicked, and he gave a despondent gesture.

"Yes," he said, wearily, "it is too late now."

Thereupon Miss Stapylton tossed her head. "Oh, very well!" said she; "only, for my part, I think you acted very foolishly, and I don't see that you have the least right to complain. I quite fail to see how you could have expected her to marry you—or, in fact, how you can expect any woman to marry you,—if you won't, at least, go to the trouble of asking her to do so!"

Then Miss Stapylton went into the house, and slammed the door after her.

III

Nor was that the worst of it. For when Rudolph Musgrave followed her—as he presently did, in a state of considerable amaze,—his sister informed him that Miss Stapylton had retired to her room with an unaccountable headache.

And there she remained for the rest of the evening. It was an unusually long evening.

Yet, somehow, in spite of its notable length—affording, as it did, an excellent opportunity for undisturbed work,—Colonel Musgrave found, with a pricking conscience, that he made astonishingly slight progress in an exhaustive monograph upon the fragmentary Orderly Book of an obscure captain in a long-forgotten regiment, which if it had not actually served in the Revolution, had at least been demonstrably granted money "for services," and so entitled hundreds of aspirants to become the Sons (or Daughters) of various international disagreements.

Nor did he see her at breakfast—nor at dinner.

IV

A curious little heartache accompanied Colonel Musgrave on his way home that afternoon. He had not seen Patricia Stapylton for twenty-four hours, and he was just beginning to comprehend what life would be like without her. He did not find the prospect exhilarating.

Then, as he came up the orderly graveled walk, he heard, issuing from the little vine-covered summer-house, a loud voice. It was a man's voice, and its tones were angry.

"No! no!" the man was saying; "I'll agree to no such nonsense, I tell you! What do you think I am?"

"I think you are a jackass-fool," Miss Stapylton said, crisply, "and a fortune-hunter, and a sot, and a travesty, and a whole heap of other things I haven't, as yet had time to look up in the dictionary. And I think—I think you call yourself an English gentleman? Well, all I have to say is God pity England if her gentlemen are of your stamp! There isn't a costermonger in all Whitechapel who would dare talk to me as you've done! I would like to snatch you bald-headed, I would like to kill you—And do you think, now, if you were the very last man left in all the *world* that I would—No, don't you try to answer me, for I don't wish to hear a single word you have to say. Oh, oh! how *dare* you!"

"Well, I've had provocation enough," the man's voice retorted, sullenly. "Perhaps, I have cut up a bit rough, Patricia, but, then, you've been talkin' like a fool, you know. But what's the odds? Let's kiss and make up, old girl."

"Don't touch me!" she panted; "ah, don't you *dare!*"

"You little devil! you infernal little vixen? You'll jilt me, will you?"

"Let me go!" the girl cried, sharply. Rudolph Musgrave went into the summer-house.

The man Colonel Musgrave found there was big and loose-jointed, with traces of puffiness about his face. He had wheat-colored hair and weakish-looking, pale blue eyes. One of his arms was about Miss Stapylton, but he released her now, and blinked at Rudolph Musgrave.

"And who are you, pray?" he demanded, querulously. "What do you want, anyhow? What do you mean by sneakin' in here and tappin' on a fellow's shoulder—like a damn' woodpecker, by Jove! I don't know you."

There was in Colonel Musgrave's voice a curious tremor, when he spoke; but to the eye he was unruffled, even faintly amused.

"I am the owner of this garden," he enunciated, with leisurely distinctness, "and it is not my custom to permit gentlewomen to be insulted in it. So I am afraid I must ask you to leave it."

"Now, see here," the man blustered, weakly, "we don't want any heroics, you know. See here, you're her cousin, ain't you? By God, I'll leave it to you, you know! She's treated me badly, don't you understand. She's a jilt, you know. She's playin' fast and loose—"

He never got any further, for at this point Rudolph Musgrave took him by the coat-collar and half-dragged, half-pushed him through the garden, shaking him occasionally with a quiet emphasis. The colonel was angry, and it was a matter of utter indifference to him that they were trampling over flower-beds, and leaving havoc in their rear.

But when they had reached the side-entrance, he paused and opened it, and then shoved his companion into an open field, where a number of cows, fresh from the evening milking, regarded them with incurious eyes. It was very quiet here, save for the occasional jangle of the cow-bells and the far-off fifing of frogs in the marsh below.

"It would have been impossible, of course," said Colonel Musgrave, "for me to have offered you any personal violence as long as you were, in a manner, a guest of mine. This field, however, is the property of Judge Willoughby, and here I feel at liberty to thrash you."

Then he thrashed the man who had annoyed Patricia Stapylton.

That thrashing was, in its way, a masterpiece. There was a certain conscientiousness about it, a certain thoroughness of execution—a certain plodding and painstaking carefulness, in a word, such as is possible only to those who have spent years in guiding fat-witted tourists among the antiquities of the Lichfield Historical Association.

"You ought to exercise more," Rudolph Musgrave admonished his victim, when he had ended. "You are entirely too flabby now, you know. That path yonder will take you to the hotel, where, I imagine, you are staying. There is a train leaving Lichfield at six-fifteen, and if I were you, I would be very careful not to miss that train. Good-evening. I am sorry to have been compelled to thrash you, but I must admit I have enjoyed it exceedingly."

Then he went back into the garden.

V

In the shadow of a white lilac-bush, Colonel Musgrave paused with an awed face.

"Good Lord!" said he, aghast at the notion; "what would Agatha say if she knew I had been fighting like a drunken truck-driver! Or, rather, what would she refrain from saying! Only, she wouldn't believe it of me. And, for the matter of that," Rudolph Musgrave continued, after a moment's reflection, "I wouldn't have believed it of myself a week ago. I think I am changing, somehow. A week ago I would have fetched in the police and sworn out a warrant; and, if the weather had been as damp as it is, I would have waited to put on my rubbers before I would have done that much."

VI

He found her still in the summer-house, expectant of him, it seemed, her lips parted, her eyes glowing. Rudolph Musgrave, looking down into twin vivid depths, for a breathing-space, found time to rejoice that he had refused to liken them to stars. Stars, forsooth!—and, pray, what paltry sun, what irresponsible comet, what pallid, clinkered satellite, might boast a purple splendor such as this? For all asterial scintillations, at best, had but a clap-trap glitter; whereas the glow of Patricia's eyes was a matter worthy of really serious attention.

"What have you done with him, Olaf?" the girl breathed, quickly.

"I reasoned with him," said Colonel Musgrave. "Oh, I found him quite amenable to logic. He is leaving Lichfield this evening, I think."

Thereupon Miss Stapylton began to laugh. "Yes," said she, "you must have remonstrated very feelingly. Your tie's all crooked, Olaf dear, and your hair's all rumpled, and there's dust all over your coat. You would disgrace a rag-bag. Oh, I'm glad you reasoned—that way! It wasn't dignified, but it was dear of you, Olaf. Pevensey's a beast."

He caught his breath at this. "Pevensey!" he stammered; "the Earl of Pevensey!—the man you are going to marry!"

"Dear me, no!" Miss Stapylton answered, with utmost unconcern; "I would sooner marry a toad. Why, didn't you know, Olaf? I thought, of course, you knew you had been introducing athletics and better manners among the peerage! That sounds like a bill in the House of Commons, doesn't it?" Then Miss Stapylton laughed again, and appeared to be in a state of agreeable, though somewhat nervous, elation. "I wrote to him two days ago," she afterward explained, "breaking off the engagement. So he came down at once and was very nasty about it."

"You—you have broken your engagement," he echoed, dully; and continued, with a certain deficiency of finesse, "But I thought you wanted to be a countess?"

"Oh, you boor, you vulgarian!" the girl cried, "Oh, you do put things so crudely, Olaf! You are hopeless."

She shook an admonitory forefinger in his direction, and pouted in the most dangerous fashion.

"But he always seemed so nice," she reflected, with puckered brows, "until today, you know. I thought he would be eminently suitable. I liked him tremendously until—" and here, a wonderful, tender change came into her face, a wistful quaver woke in her voice—"until I found there was someone else I liked better."

"Ah!" said Rudolph Musgrave.

So, that was it—yes, that was it! Her head was bowed now—her glorious, proud little head,—and she sat silent, an abashed heap of fluffy frills and ruffles, a tiny bundle of vaporous ruchings and filmy tucks and suchlike vanities, in the green dusk of the summer-house.

But he knew. He had seen her face grave and tender in the twilight, and he knew.

She loved some man—some lucky devil! Ah, yes, that was it! And he knew the love he had unwittingly spied upon to be august; the shamed exultance of her face and her illumined eyes, the crimson banners her cheeks had flaunted,—these were to Colonel Musgrave as a piece of sacred pageantry; and before it his misery was awed, his envy went posting to extinction.

Thus the stupid man reflected, and made himself very unhappy over it.

Then, after a little, the girl threw back her head and drew a deep breath, and flashed a tremulous smile at him.

"Ah, yes," said she; "there are better things in life than coronets, aren't there, Olaf?"

You should have seen how he caught up the word!

"Life!" he cried, with a bitter thrill of speech; "ah, what do I know of life? I am only a recluse, a dreamer, a visionary! You must learn of life from the men who have lived, Patricia. I haven't ever lived. I have always chosen the coward's part. I have chosen to shut myself off from the world, to posture in a village all my days, and to consider its trifles as of supreme importance. I have affected to scorn that brave world yonder where a man is proven. And, all the while, I was afraid of it, I think. I was afraid of you before you came."

At the thought of this Rudolph Musgrave laughed as he fell to pacing up and down before her.

"Life!" he cried, again, with a helpless gesture; and then smiled at her, very sadly. "'Didn't I know there was something better in life than grubbing after musty tribes and customs and folk-songs?'" he quoted. "Why, what a question to ask of a professional genealogist! Don't you realize, Patricia, that the very bread I eat is, actually, earned by the achievements of people who have been dead for centuries? and in part, of course, by tickling the vanity of living snobs? That constitutes a nice trade for an able-bodied person as long as men are paid for emptying garbage-barrels—now, doesn't it? And yet it is not altogether for the pay's sake I do it," he added, haltingly. "There really is a fascination about the work. You are really working out a puzzle,—like a fellow solving a chess-problem. It isn't really work, it is amusement. And when you are establishing a royal descent, and tracing back to czars and Plantagenets and Merovingians, and making it all seem perfectly plausible, the thing is sheer impudent, flagrant art, and *you* are the artist—" He broke off here and shrugged. "No, I could hardly make you understand. It doesn't matter. It is enough that I have bartered youth and happiness and the very power of living for the privilege of grubbing in old county records."

He paused. It is debatable if he had spoken wisely, or had spoken even in consonance with fact, but his outburst had, at least, the saving grace of sincerity. He was pallid now, shaking in every limb, and in his heart was a dull aching. She seemed so incredibly soft and little and childlike, as she looked up at him with troubled eyes.

"I—I don't quite understand," she murmured. "It isn't as if you were an old man, Olaf. It isn't as if—"

But he had scarcely heard her. "Ah, child, child!" he cried, "why did you come to waken me? I was content in my smug vanities. I was content in my ignorance. I could have gone on contentedly grubbing through my musty, sleepy life here, till death had taken me, if only you had not shown me what life might mean! Ah, child, child, why did you waken me?"

"I?" she breathed; and now the flush of her cheeks had widened, wondrously.

"You! you!" he cried, and gave a wringing motion of his hands, for the self-esteem of a complacent man is not torn away without agony. "Who else but you? I had thought myself brave enough to be silent, but still I must play the coward's part! That woman I told you of—that woman I loved—was you! Yes, you, you!" he cried, again and again, in a sort of frenzy.

And then, on a sudden, Colonel Musgrave began to laugh.

"It is very ridiculous, isn't it?" he demanded of her. "Yes, it is very—very funny. Now comes the time to laugh at me! Now comes the time to lift your brows, and to make keen arrows of your eyes, and of your tongue a little red dagger! I have dreamed of this moment many and many a time. So laugh, I say! Laugh, for I have told you that I love you. You are rich, and I am a pauper—you are young, and I am old, remember,—and I love you, who love another man! For the love of God, laugh at me and have done—laugh! for, as God lives, it is the bravest jest I have ever known!"

But she came to him, with a wonderful gesture of compassion, and caught his great, shapely hands in hers.

"I—I knew you cared," she breathed. "I have always known you cared. I would have been an idiot if I hadn't. But, oh, Olaf, I didn't know you cared so much. You frighten me, Olaf," she pleaded, and raised a tearful face to his. "I am very fond of you, Olaf dear. Oh, don't think I am not fond of you." And the girl paused for a breathless moment. "I think I might have married you, Olaf," she said, half-wistfully, "if—if it hadn't been for one thing."

Rudolph Musgrave smiled now, though he found it a difficult business. "Yes," he assented, gravely, "I know, dear. If it were not for the other man—that lucky devil! Yes, he is a very, very lucky devil, child, and he constitutes rather a big 'if,' doesn't he?"

Miss Stapylton, too, smiled a little. "No," said she, "that isn't quite the reason. The real reason is, as I told you yesterday, that I quite fail to see how you can expect any woman to marry you, you jay-bird, if you won't go to the trouble of asking her to do so."

And, this time, Miss Stapylton did not go into the house.

VII

When they went in to supper, they had planned to tell Miss Agatha of their earth-staggering secret at once. But the colonel comprehended, at the first glimpse of his sister, that the opportunity would be ill-chosen.

The meal was an awkward half-hour. Miss Agatha, from the head of the table, did very little talking, save occasionally to evince views of life that were both lachrymose and pugnacious. And the lovers talked with desperate cheerfulness, so that there might be no outbreak so long as Pilkins—preëminently ceremonious among butlers, and as yet inclined to scoff at the notion that the Musgraves of Matocton were not divinely entrusted to his guardianship,—was in the room.

Coming so close upon the heels of his high hour, this contretemps of Agatha's having one of her "attacks," seemed more to Rudolph Musgrave than a man need rationally bear with equanimity. Perhaps it was a trifle stiffly that he said he did not care for any raspberries.

His sister burst into tears.

"That's all the thanks I get. I slave my life out, and what thanks do I get for it? I never have any pleasure, I never put my foot out of the house except to go to market,—and what thanks do I get for it? That's what I want you to tell me with the first raspberries of the season. That's what I want! Oh, I don't wonder you can't look me in the eye. And I wish I was dead! that's what I wish!"

Colonel Musgrave did not turn at once toward Patricia, when his sister had stumbled, weeping, from the dining-room.

"I—I am so sorry, Olaf," said a remote and tiny voice.

Then he touched her hand with his finger-tips, ever so lightly. "You must not worry about it, dear. I daresay I was unpardonably brusque. And Agatha's health is not good, so that she is a trifle irritable at times. Why, good Lord, we have these little set-to's ever so often, and never give them a thought afterwards. That is one of the many things the future Mrs. Musgrave will have to get accustomed to, eh? Or does that appalling prospect frighten you too much?"

And Patricia brazenly confessed that it did not. She also made a face at him, and accused Rudolph Musgrave of trying to crawl out of marrying her, which proceeding led to frivolities unnecessary to record, but found delectable by the participants.

VIII

Colonel Musgrave was alone. He had lifted his emptied coffee-cup and he swished the lees gently to and fro. He was curiously intent upon these lees, considered them in the light of a symbol. . .

Then a comfortable, pleasant-faced mulattress came to clear the supper-table. Virginia they called her. Virginia had been nurse in turn to all the children of Rudolph Musgrave's parents; and to the end of her life she appeared to regard the emancipation of the South's negroes as an irrelevant vagary of certain "low-down" and probably "ornery" Yankees—as an, in short, quite eminently "tacky" proceeding which very certainly in no way affected her vested right to tyrannize over the Musgrave household.

"Virginia," said Colonel Musgrave, "don't forget to make up a fire in the kitchen-stove before you go to bed. And please fill the kettle before you go upstairs, and leave it on the stove. Miss Agatha is not well tonight."

"Yaas, suh. I unnerstan', suh," Virginia said, sedately.

Virginia filled her tray, and went away quietly, her pleasant yellow face as imperturbable as an idol's.

PART III
TERTIUS

"It is in many ways made plain to us
That love must grow like any common thing,
Root, bud, and leaf, ere ripe for garnering
The mellow fruitage front us; even thus
Must Helena encounter Theseus
Ere Paris come, and every century
Spawn divers queens who die with Antony
But live a great while first with Julius.

"Thus I have spoken the prologue of a play
Wherein I have no part, and laugh, and sit
Contented in the wings, whilst you portray
An amorous maid with gestures that befit
This lovely rôle,—as who knows better, pray,
Than I that helped you in rehearsing it?"

—Horace Symonds. *Civic Voluntaries*

I

When the Presidential campaign was at its height; when in various sections of the United States "the boy orator of La Platte" was making invidious remarks concerning the Republican Party, and in Canton (Ohio) Mr. M.A. Hanna was cheerfully expressing his confidence as to the outcome of it all; when the Czar and the Czarina were visiting President Faure in Paris "amid unparalleled enthusiasm"; and when semi-educated people were appraising, with a glibness possible to ignorance only, the literary achievements of William Morris and George du Maurier, who had just died: at this remote time, Roger Stapylton returned to Lichfield.

For in that particular October Patricia's father, an accommodating physician having declared old Roger Stapylton's health to necessitate a Southern sojourn, leased the Bellingham mansion in Lichfield. It happened that, by rare good luck, Tom Bellingham—of the Bellinghams of Assequin, not the Bellinghams of Bellemeade, who indeed immigrated after the War of 1812 and have never been regarded as securely established from a social standpoint,—was at this time in pecuniary difficulties on account of having signed another person's name to a cheque.

Roger Stapylton refurnished the house in the extreme degree of Lichfieldian elegance. Colonel Musgrave was his mentor throughout the process; and the oldest families of Lichfield very shortly sat at table with the former overseer, and not at all unwillingly, since his dinners were excellent and an infatuated Rudolph Musgrave—an axiom now in planning any list of guests,—was very shortly to marry the man's daughter.

In fact, the matter had been settled; and Colonel Musgrave had received from Roger Stapylton an exuberantly granted charter of courtship.

This befell, indeed, upon a red letter day in Roger Stapylton's life. The banker was in business matters wonderfully shrewd, as divers transactions, since the signing of that half-forgotten contract whereby he was to furnish a certain number of mules for the Confederate service, strikingly attested: but he had rarely been out of the country wherein his mother bore him; and where another nabob might have dreamed of an earl, or even have soared aspiringly in imagination toward a marchioness-ship for his only child, old Stapylton retained unshaken faith in the dust-gathering creed of his youth.

He had tolerated Pevensey, had indeed been prepared to purchase him much as he would have ordered any other expensive trinket or knickknack which Patricia desired. But he had never viewed the match with enthusiasm.

Now, though, old Stapylton exulted. His daughter—half a Vartrey already—would become by marriage a Musgrave of Matocton, no less. Pat's carriage would roll up and down the oak-shaded avenue from which he had so often stepped aside with an uncovered head, while gentlemen and ladies cantered by; and it would be Pat's children that would play about the corridors of the old house at whose doors he had lived so long,—those awe-inspiring corridors, which he had very rarely entered, except on Christmas Day and other recognized festivities, when, dressed to the nines, the overseer and his uneasy mother were by immemorial custom made free of the mansion, with every slave upon the big plantation.

"They were good days, sir," he chuckled. "Heh, we'll stick to the old customs. We'll give a dinner and announce it at dessert, just as your honored grandfather did your Aunt Constantia's betrothal—"

For about the Musgraves of Matocton there could be no question. It was the old man's delight to induce Rudolph Musgrave to talk concerning his ancestors; and Stapylton soon had their history at his finger-tips. He could have correctly blazoned every tincture in their armorial bearings and have explained the origin of every rampant, counter-changed or couchant beast upon the shield.

He knew it was the *Bona Nova* in the November of 1619,—for the first Musgrave had settled in Virginia, prior to his removal to Lichfield,—which had the honor of transporting the forebear of this family into America. Stapylton could have told you offhand which scions of the race had represented this or that particular county in the House of Burgesses, and even for what years; which three of them were Governors, and which of them had served as officers of the State Line in the Revolution; and, in fine, was more than satisfied to have his daughter play Penelophon to Colonel Musgrave's debonair mature Cophetua.

In a word, Roger Stapylton had acquiesced to the transferal of his daughter's affections with the peculiar equanimity of a properly reared American parent. He merely stipulated that, since his business affairs prevented an indefinite stay in Lichfield, Colonel Musgrave should presently remove to New York City, where the older man held ready for him a purely ornamental and remunerative position with the Insurance Company of which Roger Stapylton was president.

But upon this point Rudolph Musgrave was obdurate.

He had voiced, and with sincerity, as you may remember, his desire to be proven upon a larger stage than Lichfield afforded. Yet the sincerity was bred of an emotion it did not survive. Today, unconsciously, Rudolph Musgrave was reflecting that he was used to living in Lichfield, and would appear to disadvantage in a new surrounding, and very probably would not be half so comfortable.

Aloud he said, in firm belief that he spoke truthfully: "I cannot conscientiously give up the Library, sir. I realize the work may not seem important in your eyes. Indeed, in anybody's eyes it must seem an inadequate outcome of a man's whole life. But it unfortunately happens to be the only kind of work I am capable of doing. And—if you will pardon me, sir,—I do not think it would be honest for me to accept this generous salary and give nothing in return."

But here Patricia broke in.

Patricia agreed with Colonel Musgrave in every particular. Indeed, had Colonel Musgrave proclaimed his intention of setting up in life as an assassin, Patricia would readily have asserted homicide to be the most praiseworthy of vocations. As it was, she devoted no little volubility and emphasis and eulogy to the importance of a genealogist in the eternal scheme of things; and gave her father candidly to understand that an inability to appreciate this fact was necessarily indicative of a deplorably low order of intelligence.

Musgrave was to remember—long afterward—how glorious and dear this brightly-colored, mettlesome and tiny woman had seemed to him in the second display of temper he witnessed in Patricia. It was a revelation of an additional and as yet unsuspected adorability.

Her father, though, said: "Pat, I've suspected for a long time it was foolish of me to have a red-haired daughter." Thus he capitulated,—and with an ineffable air of routine.

Colonel Musgrave was, in a decorous fashion, the happiest of living persons.

II

Colonel Musgrave was, in a decorous fashion, the happiest of living persons. . .

As a token of this he devoted what little ready money he possessed to renovating Matocton, where he had not lived for twenty years. He rarely thought of money, not esteeming it an altogether suitable subject for a gentleman's meditations. And to do him justice, the reflection that old Stapylton's wealth would some day be at Rudolph Musgrave's disposal was never more than an agreeable minor feature of Patricia's entourage whenever, as was very often, Colonel Musgrave fell to thinking of how adorable Patricia was in every particular.

Yet there were times when he thought of Anne Charteris as well. He had not seen her for a whole year now, for the Charterises had left Lichfield shortly after the Pendomer divorce case had been settled, and were still in Europe.

This was the evening during which Roger Stapylton had favorably received his declaration; and Colonel Musgrave was remembering the time that he and Anne had last spoken with a semblance of intimacy—that caustic time when Anne Charteris had interrupted him in high words with her husband, and circumstances had afforded to Rudolph Musgrave no choice save to confess, to this too-perfect woman, of all created beings, his "true relations" with Clarice Pendomer.

Even as yet the bitterness of that humiliation was not savorless. . .

It seemed to him that he could never bear to think of the night when Anne had heard his stammerings through, and had merely listened, and in listening had been unreasonably beautiful. So Godiva might have looked on Peeping Tom, with more of wonder than of loathing, just at first. . .

It had been very hard to bear. But it seemed necessary. The truth would have hurt Anne too much. . .

He noted with the gusto of a connoisseur how neatly the dénouement of this piteous farce had been prepared. His rage with Charteris; Anne's overhearing, and misinterpretation of, a dozen angry words; that old affair with Clarice—immediately before her marriage (one of how many pleasurable gallantries? the colonel idly wondered, and regretted that he had no Leporello to keep them catalogued for consultation)—and George Pendomer's long-smoldering jealousy of Rudolph Musgrave: all fitted in as neatly as the bits of a puzzle.

It had been the simplest matter in the world to shield John Charteris. Yet, the colonel wished he could be sure it was an unadulterated desire of protecting Anne which had moved him. There had been very certainly an enjoyment all the while in reflecting how nobly Rudolph Musgrave was behaving for the sake of "the only woman he had ever loved." Yes, one had undoubtedly phrased it thus—then, and until the time one met Patricia.

But Anne was different, and in the nature of things must always be a little different, from all other people—even Patricia Stapylton.

Always in reverie the colonel would come back to this,—that Anne could not be thought of, quite, in the same frame of mind wherein one appraised other persons. Especially must he concede this curious circumstance whenever, as tonight, he considered divers matters that had taken place quite long enough ago to have been forgotten.

It was a foolish sort of a reverie, and scarcely worth the setting down. It was a reverie of the kind that everyone, and especially everyone's wife, admits to be mawkish and unprofitable; and yet, somehow, the next still summer night, or long sleepy Sunday afternoon, or, perhaps, some cheap, jigging and heartbreaking melody, will set a carnival of old loves and old faces awhirl in the brain. One grows very sad over it, of course, and it becomes apparent that one has always been ill-treated by the world; but the sadness is not unpleasant, and one is quite willing to forgive.

Yes,—it was a long, long time ago. It must have been a great number of centuries. Matocton was decked in its spring fripperies of burgeoning, and the sky was a great, pale turquoise, and the buttercups left a golden dust high up on one's trousers. One had not become entirely accustomed to long trousers then, and one was rather proud of them. One was lying on one's back in the woods, where the birds were astir and eager to begin their house-building, and twittered hysterically over the potentialities of straws and broken twigs.

Overhead, the swelling buds of trees were visible against the sky, and the branches were like grotesque designs on a Japanese plate. There was a little clump of moss, very cool and soft, that just brushed one's cheek.

One was thinking—really thinking—for the first time in one's life; and, curiously enough, one was thinking about a girl, although girls were manifestly of no earthly importance.

But Anne Willoughby was different. Even at the age when girls seemed feckless creatures, whose aimings were inexplicable, both as concerned existence in general, and, more concretely, as touched gravel-shooters and snowballs, and whose reasons for bursting into tears were recondite, one had perceived the difference. One wondered about it from time to time.

Gradually, there awoke an uneasy self-conscious interest as to all matters that concerned her, a mental pricking up of the ears when her name was mentioned.

One lay awake o' nights, wondering why her hair curled so curiously about her temples, and held such queer glowing tints in its depths when sunlight fell upon it. One was uncomfortable and embarrassed and Briarean-handed in her presence, but with her absence came the overwhelming desire of seeing her again.

After a little, it was quite understood that one was in love with Anne Willoughby. . .

It was a matter of minor importance that her father was the wealthiest man in Fairhaven, and that one's mother was poor. One would go away into foreign lands after a while, and come back with a great deal of money,—lakes of rupees and pieces of eight, probably. It was very simple.

But Anne's father had taken an unreasonable view of the matter, and carried Anne off to a terrible aunt, who returned one's letters unopened. That was the end of Anne Willoughby.

Then, after an interval—during which one fell in and out of love assiduously, and had upon the whole a pleasant time,—Anne Charteris had come to Lichfield. One had found that time had merely added poise and self-possession and a certain opulence to the beauty which had caused one's voice to play fantastic tricks in conference with Anne Willoughby,—ancient, unforgotten conferences, wherein one had pointed out the many respects in which she differed from all other women, and the perfect feasibility of marrying on nothing a year.

Much as one loved Patricia, and great as was one's happiness, men did not love as boys did, after all. . .

"'Ah, Boy, it is a dream for life too high,'" said Colonel Musgrave, in his soul. "And now let's think of something sensible. Let's think about the present political crisis, and what to give the groomsmen, and how much six times seven is. Meanwhile, you are not the fellow in *Aux Italiens*, you know; you are not bothered by the faint, sweet smell of any foolish jasmine-flower, you understand, or by any equally foolish hankerings after your lost youth. You are simply a commonplace, every-day sort of man, not thoroughly hardened as yet to being engaged, and you are feeling a bit pulled down tonight, because your liver or something is out of sorts."

Upon reflection, Colonel Musgrave was quite sure that he was happy; and that it was only his liver or something which was upset. But, at all events, the colonel's besetting infirmity was always to shrink from making changes; instinctively he balked against commission of any action which would alter his relations with accustomed circumstances or persons. It was very like Rudolph Musgrave that even now, for all the glow of the future's bright allure, his heart should hark back to the past and its absurd dear memories, with wistfulness.

And he found it, as many others have done, but cheerless sexton's work, this digging up of boyish recollections. One by one, they come to light—the brave hopes and dreams and aspirations of youth; the ruddy life has gone out of them; they have shriveled into an alien, pathetic dignity. They might have been one's great-grandfather's or Hannibal's or Adam's; the boy whose life was swayed by them is quite as dead as these.

Amaryllis is dead, too. Perhaps, you drop in of an afternoon to talk over old happenings. She is perfectly affable. She thinks it is time you were married. She thinks it very becoming, the way you have stoutened. And, no, they weren't at the Robinsons'; that was the night little Amaryllis was threatened with croup.

Then, after a little, the lamps of welcome are lighted in her eyes, her breath quickens, her cheeks mount crimson flags in honor of her lord, her hero, her conqueror.

It is Mr. Grundy, who is happy to meet you, and hopes you will stay to dinner. He patronizes you a trifle; his wife, you see, has told him all about that boy who is as dead as Hannibal. You don't mind in the least; you dine with Mr. and Mrs. Grundy, and pass a very pleasant evening.

Colonel Musgrave had dined often with the Charterises.

III

And then some frolic god, *en route* from homicide by means of an unloaded pistol in Chicago for the demolishment of a likely ship off Palos, with the coöperancy of a defective pistonrod, stayed in his flight to bring Joe Parkinson to Lichfield.

It was Roger Stapylton who told the colonel of this advent, as the very apex of jocularity.

"For you remember the Parkinsons, I suppose?"

"The ones that had a cabin near Matocton? Very deserving people, I believe."

"And *their* son, sir, wants to marry my daughter," said Mr. Stapylton,—"*my* daughter, who is shortly to be connected by marriage with the Musgraves of Matocton! I don't know what this world will come to next."

It was a treat to see him shake his head in deprecation of such anarchy.

Then Roger Stapylton said, more truculently: "Yes, sir! on account of a boy-and-girl affair five years ago, this half-strainer, this poor-white trash, has actually had the presumption, sir,—but I don't doubt that Pat has told you all about it?"

"Why, no," said Colonel Musgrave. "She did not mention it this afternoon. She was not feeling very well. A slight headache. I noticed she was not inclined to conversation."

It had just occurred to him, as mildly remarkable, that Patricia had never at any time alluded to any one of those countless men who must have inevitably made love to her.

"Though, mind you, I don't say anything against Joe. He's a fine young fellow. Paid his own way through college. Done good work in Panama and in Alaska too. But—confound it, sir, the boy's a fool! Now I put it to you fairly, ain't he a fool?" said Mr. Stapylton.

"Upon my word, sir, if his folly has no other proof than an adoration of your daughter," the colonel protested, "I must in self-defense beg leave to differ with you."

Yes, that was it undoubtedly. Patricia had too high a sense of honor to exhibit these defeated rivals in a ridiculous light, even to him. It was a revelation of an additional and as yet unsuspected adorability.

Then after a little further talk they separated. Colonel Musgrave left that night for Matocton in order to inspect the improvements which were being made there. He was to return to Lichfield on the ensuing Wednesday, when his engagement to Patricia was to be announced—"just as your honored grandfather did your Aunt Constantia's betrothal."

Meanwhile Joe Parkinson, a young man much enamored, who fought the world by ordinary like Hal o' the Wynd, "for his own hand," was seeing Patricia every day.

IV

Colonel Musgrave remained five days at Matocton, that he might put his house in order against his nearing marriage. It was a pleasant sight to see the colonel stroll about the paneled corridors and pause to chat with divers deferential workmen who were putting the last touches there, or to observe him mid-course in affable consultation with gardeners anent the rolling of a lawn or the retrimming of a rosebush, and to mark the bearing of the man so optimistically colored by goodwill toward the solar system.

He joyed in his old home,—in the hipped roof of it, the mullioned casements, the wide window-seats, the high and spacious rooms, the geometrical gardens and broad lawns, in all that was quaint and beautiful at Matocton,—because it would be Patricia's so very soon, the lovely frame of a yet lovelier picture, as the colonel phrased it with a flight of imagery.

Gravely he inspected all the portraits of his feminine ancestors that he might decide, as one without bias, whether Matocton had ever boasted a more delectable mistress. Equity—or in his fond eyes at least,—demanded a negative. Only in one of these canvases, a counterfeit of Miss Evelyn Ramsay, born a Ramsay of Blenheim, that had married the common great-great-grandfather of both the colonel and Patricia—Major Orlando Musgrave, an aide-de-camp to General Charles Lee in the Revolution,—Rudolph Musgrave found, or seemed to find, dear likenesses to that demented seraph who was about to stoop to his unworthiness.

He spent much time before this portrait. Yes, yes! this woman had been lovely in her day. And this bright, roguish shadow of her was lovely, too, eternally postured in white patnet, trimmed with a vine of rose-colored satin leaves, a pink rose in her powdered hair and a huge ostrich plume as well.

Yet it was an adamantean colonel that remarked:

"My dear, perhaps it is just as fortunate as not that you have quitted Matocton. For I have heard tales of you, Miss Ramsay. Oh, no! I honestly do not believe that you would have taken kindlily to any young person—not even in the guise of a great-great-grand-daughter,—to whom you cannot hold a candle, madam. A fico for you, madam," said the most undutiful of great-great-grandsons.

Let us leave him to his roseate meditations. Questionless, in the woman he loved there was much of his own invention: but the circumstance is not unhackneyed; and Colonel Musgrave was in a decorous fashion the happiest of living persons.

Meanwhile Joe Parkinson, a young man much enamored, who fought the world by ordinary, like Hal o' the Wynd "for his own hand," was seeing Patricia every day.

V

Joe Parkinson—tall and broad-shouldered, tanned, resolute, chary of speech, decisive in gesture, having close-cropped yellow hair and frank, keen eyes like amethysts,—was the one alien present when Colonel Musgrave came again into Roger Stapylton's fine and choicely-furnished mansion.

This was on the evening Roger Stapylton gave the long-anticipated dinner at which he was to announce his daughter's engagement. As much indeed was suspected by most of his dinner-company, so carefully selected from the aristocracy of Lichfield; and the heart of the former overseer, as these handsome, courtly and sweet voiced people settled according to their rank about his sumptuous table, was aglow with pride.

Then Rudolph Musgrave turned to his companion and said softly: "My dear, you are like a wraith. What is it?"

"I have a headache," said Patricia. "It is nothing."

"You reassure me," the colonel gaily declared, "for I had feared it was a heartache—"

She faced him. Desperation looked out of her purple eyes. "It is," the girl said swiftly.

"Ah—?" Only it was an intake of the breath, rather than an interjection. Colonel Musgrave ate his fish with deliberation. "Young Parkinson?" he presently suggested.

"I thought I had forgotten him. I didn't know I cared—I didn't know I *could* care so much—" And there was a note in her voice which thrust the poor colonel into an abyss of consternation.

"Remember that these people are your guests," he said, in perfect earnest.

"—and I refused him this afternoon for the last time, and he is going away tomorrow—"

But here Judge Allardyce broke in, to tell Miss Stapylton of the pleasure with which he had *nolle prosequied* the case against Tom Bellingham.

"A son of my old schoolmate, ma'am," the judge explained. "A Bellingham of Assequin. Oh, indiscreet of course—but, God bless my soul! when were the Bellinghams anything else? The boy regretted it as much as anybody."

And she listened with almost morbid curiosity concerning the finer details of legal intricacy.

Colonel Musgrave was mid-course in an anecdote which the lady upon the other side of him found wickedly amusing.

He was very gay. He had presently secured the attention of the company at large, and held it through a good half-hour; for by common consent Rudolph Musgrave was at his best tonight, and Lichfield found his best worth listening to.

"Grinning old popinjay!" thought Mr. Parkinson; and envied him and internally noted, and with an unholy fervor cursed, the adroitness of intonation and the discreetly modulated gesture with which the colonel gave to every point of his merry-Andrewing its precise value.

The colonel's mind was working busily on matters oddly apart from those of which he talked. He wanted this girl next to him—at whom he did not look. He loved her as that whippersnapper yonder was not capable of loving anyone. Young people had these fancies; and they outlived them, as the colonel knew of his own experience. Let matters take their course unhindered, at all events by him. For it was less his part than that of any other man alive to interfere when Rudolph Musgrave stood within a finger's reach of, at worst, his own prosperity and happiness.

He would convey no note to Roger Stapylton. Let the banker announce the engagement. Let the young fellow go to the devil. Colonel Musgrave would marry the girl and make Patricia, at worst, content. To do otherwise, even to hesitate, would be the emptiest quixotism. . .

Then came the fatal thought, "But what a gesture!" To fling away his happiness—yes, even his worldly fortune,—and to do it smilingly! Patricia must, perforce, admire him all her life.

Then as old Stapylton stirred in his chair and broke into a wide premonitory smile, Colonel Musgrave rose to his feet. And of that company Clarice Pendomer at least thought of how like he was to the boy who had fought the famous duel with George Pendomer some fifteen years ago.

Ensued a felicitous speech. Rudolph Musgrave was familiar with his audience. And therefore:

Colonel Musgrave alluded briefly to the pleasure he took in addressing such a gathering. He believed no other State in the Union could have afforded an assembly of more distinguished men and fairer women. But the fact was not unnatural; they might recall the venerable saying that blood will tell? Well, it was their peculiar privilege to represent today that sturdy stock which, when this great republic was in the pangs of birth, had with sword and pen and oratory discomfited the hirelings of England and given to history the undying names of several Revolutionary patriots,—all of whom he enumerated with the customary pause after each cognomen to allow for the customary applause.

And theirs, too, was the blood of those heroic men who fought more recently beneath the stars and bars, as bravely, he would make bold to say, as Leonidas at Thermopylae, in defense of their loved Southland. Right, he conceded, had not triumphed here. For hordes of brutal soldiery had invaded the fertile soil, the tempest of war had swept the land and left it desolate. The South lay battered and bruised, and pros trate in blood, the "Niobe of nations," as sad a victim of ingratitude as King Lear.

The colonel touched upon the time when buzzards, in the guise of carpet-baggers, had battened upon the recumbent form; and spoke slightingly of divers persons of antiquity as compared with various Confederate leaders, whose names were greeted with approving nods and ripples of polite enthusiasm.

But the South, and in particular the grand old Commonwealth which they inhabited, he stated, had not long sat among the ruins of her temples, like a sorrowing priestess with veiled eyes and a depressed soul, mourning for that which had been. Like the fabled Phoenix, she had risen from the ashes of her past. Today she was once more to be seen in her hereditary position, the brightest gem in all that glorious galaxy of States which made America the envy of every other nation. Her battlefields converted into building lots, tall factories smoked where once a holocaust had flamed, and where cannon had roared you heard today the tinkle of the school bell. Such progress was without a parallel.

Nor was there any need for him, he was assured, to mention the imperishable names of their dear homeland's poets and statesmen of today, the orators and philanthropists and prominent business-men who jostled one another in her splendid, new asphalted streets, since all were quite familiar to his audience,—as familiar, he would venture to predict, as they would eventually be to the most cherished recollections of Macaulay's prophesied New Zealander, when this notorious antipodean should pay his long expected visit to the ruins of St. Paul's.

In fine, by a natural series of transitions, Colonel Musgrave thus worked around to "the very pleasing duty with which our host, in view of the long and intimate connection between our families, has seen fit to honor me"—which was, it developed, to announce the imminent marriage of Miss Patricia Stapylton and Mr. Joseph Parkinson.

It may conservatively be stated that everyone was surprised.

Old Stapylton had half risen, with a purple face.

The colonel viewed him with a look of bland interrogation.

There was silence for a heart-beat.

Then Stapylton lowered his eyes, if just because the laws of caste had triumphed, and in consequence his glance crossed that of his daughter, who sat motionless regarding him. She was an unusually pretty girl, he thought, and he had always been inordinately proud of her. It was not pride she seemed to beg him muster now. Patricia through that moment was not the fine daughter the old man was sometimes half afraid of. She was, too, like a certain defiant person—oh, of an incredible beauty, such as women had not any longer!—who had hastily put aside her bonnet and had looked at a young Roger Stapylton in much this fashion very long ago, because the minister was coming downstairs, and they would presently be man and wife,—provided always her pursuing brothers did not arrive in time. . .

Old Roger Stapylton cleared his throat.

Old Roger Stapylton said, half sheepishly: "My foot's asleep, that's all. I beg everybody's pardon, I'm sure. Please go on"—he had come within an ace of saying "Mr. Rudolph," and only in the nick of time did he continue, "Colonel Musgrave."

So the colonel continued in time-hallowed form, with happy allusions to Mr. Parkinson's anterior success as an engineer before he came "like a young Lochinvar to wrest away his beautiful and popular fiancée from us fainthearted fellows of Lichfield"; touched of course upon the colonel's personal comminglement of envy and rage, and so on, as an old bachelor who saw too late what he had missed in life; and concluded by proposing the health of the young couple.

This was drunk with all the honors.

VI

Upon what Patricia said to the colonel in the drawing-room, what Joe Parkinson blurted out in the hall, and chief of all, what Roger Stapylton asseverated to Rudolph Musgrave in the library, after the other guests had gone, it is unnecessary to dwell in this place. To each of these in various fashions did Colonel Musgrave explain such reasons as, he variously explained, must seem to any gentleman sufficient cause for acting as he had done; but most candidly, and even with a touch of eloquence, to Roger Stapylton.

"You are like your grandfather, sir, at times," the latter said, inconsequently enough, when the colonel had finished.

And Rudolph Musgrave gave a little bowing gesture, with an entire gravity. He knew it was the highest tribute that Stapylton could pay to any man.

"She's a daughter any father might be proud of," said the banker, also. He removed his cigar from his mouth and looked at it critically. "She's rather like her mother sometimes," he said carelessly. "Her mother made a runaway match, you may remember—Damn' poor cigar, this. But no, you wouldn't, I reckon. I had branched out into cotton then and had a little place just outside of Chiswick—"

So that, all in all, Colonel Musgrave returned homeward not entirely dissatisfied.

VII

The colonel sat for a long while before his fire that night. The room seemed less comfortable than he had ever known it. So many of his books and pictures and other furnishings had been already carried to Matocton that the walls were a little bare. Also there was a formidable pile of bills upon the table by him,—from contractors and upholsterers and furniture-houses, and so on, who had been concerned in the late renovation of Matocton,—the heralds of a host he hardly saw his way to dealing with.

He had flung away a deal of money that evening, with something which to him was dearer. Had you attempted to condole with him he would not have understood you.

"But what would you have had a gentleman do, sir?" Colonel Musgrave would have said, in real perplexity.

Besides, it was, in fact, not sorrow that he felt, rather it was contentment, when he remembered the girl's present happiness; and what alone depressed the colonel's courtly affability toward the universe at large was the queer, horrible new sense of being somehow out of touch with yesterday's so comfortable world, of being out-moded, of being almost old.

"Eh, well!" he said; "I am of a certain age undoubtedly."

By an odd turn the colonel thought of how his friends of his own class and generation had honestly admired the after-dinner speech which he had made that evening. And he smiled, but very tenderly, because they were all men and women whom he loved.

"The most of us have known each other for a long while. The most of us, in fact, are of a certain age. . . I think no people ever met the sorry problem that we faced. For we were born the masters of a leisured, ordered world; and by a tragic quirk of destiny were thrust into a quite new planet, where we were for a while the inferiors, and after that just the competitors of yesterday's slaves.

"We couldn't meet the new conditions. Oh, for the love of heaven, let us be frank, and confess that we have not met them as things practical go. We hadn't the training for it. A man who has not been taught to swim may rationally be excused for preferring to sit upon the bank; and should he elect to ornament his idleness with protestations that he is self-evidently an excellent swimmer, because once upon a time his progenitors were the only people in the world who had the slightest conception of how to perform a natatorial masterpiece, the thing is simply human nature. Talking chokes nobody, worse luck.

"And yet we haven't done so badly. For the most part we have sat upon the bank our whole lives long. We have produced nothing—after all—which was absolutely earth-staggering; and we have talked a deal of clap-trap. But meanwhile we have at least enhanced the comeliness of our particular sand-bar. We have lived a courteous and tranquil and independent life thereon, just as our fathers taught us. It may be—in the final outcome of things—that will be found an even finer pursuit than the old one of producing Presidents.

"Besides, we have produced ourselves. We have been gentlefolk in spite of all, we have been true even in our iniquities to the traditions of our race. No, I cannot assert that these traditions always square with ethics or even with the Decalogue, for we have added a very complex Eleventh Commandment concerning honor. And for the rest, we have defiantly embroidered life, and indomitably we have converted the commonest happening of life into a comely thing. We have been artists if not artizans."

There was upon the table a large photograph in sepia of Patricia Stapylton. He studied this now. She was very beautiful, he thought.

"'Nor thou detain her vesture's hem'—" said the colonel aloud. "Oh, that infernal Yankee understood, even though he was born in Boston!" And this as coming from a Musgrave of Matocton, may fairly be considered as a sweeping tribute to the author of *Give All to Love*.

Colonel Musgrave was intent upon the portrait. . . So! she had chosen at last between himself and this young fellow, a workman born of workmen, who went about the world building bridges and canals and tunnels and such, in those far countries which were to Colonel Musgrave just so many gray or pink or fawn-colored splotches on the map. It seemed to Colonel Musgrave almost an allegory.

So Colonel Musgrave filled a glass with the famed Lafayette madeira of Matocton, and solemnly drank yet another toast. He loved to do, as you already know, that which was colorful.

"To this new South," he said. "To this new South that has not any longer need of me or of my kind.

"To this new South! She does not gaze unwillingly, nor too complacently, upon old years, and dares concede that but with loss of manliness may any man encroach upon the heritage of a dog or of a trotting-horse, and consider the exploits of an ancestor to guarantee an innate and personal excellence.

"For to her all former glory is less a jewel than a touchstone, and with her portion of it daily she appraises her own doing, and without vain speech. And her high past she values now, in chief, as fit foundation of that edifice whereon she labors day by day, and with augmenting strokes."

AND YET—"IT MAY BE HE will serve you better. But, oh, it isn't possible that he should love you more than I," said Colonel Musgrave of Matocton.

The man was destined to remember that utterance—and, with the recollection, to laugh not altogether in either scorn or merriment.

PART IV
APPRECIATION

"You have chosen; and I cry content thereto,
And cry your pardon also, and am reproved
In that I took you for a woman I loved
Odd centuries ago, and would undo
That curious error. Nay, your eyes are blue,
Your speech is gracious, but you are not she,
And I am older—and changed how utterly!—
I am no longer I, you are not you.

"Time, destined as we thought but to befriend
And guerdon love like ours, finds you beset
With joys and griefs I neither share nor mend
Who am a stranger; and we two are met
Nor wholly glad nor sorry; and the end
Of too much laughter is a faint regret."

—R.E. Townsend. *Sonnets for Elena*

I

Next morning Rudolph Musgrave found the world no longer an impassioned place, but simply a familiar habitation,—no longer the wrestling-ground of big emotions, indeed, but undoubtedly a spot, whatever were its other pretensions to praise, wherein one was at home. He breakfasted on ham and eggs, in a state of tolerable equanimity; and mildly wondered at himself for doing it.

The colonel was deep in a heraldic design and was whistling through his teeth when Patricia came into the Library. He looked up, with the outlines of a frown vanishing like pencilings under the india-rubber of professional courtesy,—for he was denoting *or* at the moment, which is fussy work, as it consists exclusively of dots.

Then his chair scraped audibly upon the floor as he pushed it from him. It occurred to Rudolph Musgrave after an interval that he was still half-way between sitting and standing, and that his mouth was open. . .

He could hear a huckster outside on Regis Avenue. The colonel never forgot the man was crying "Fresh oranges!"

"He kissed me, Olaf. Yes, I let him kiss me, even after he had asked me if he could. No sensible girl would ever do that, of course. And then I knew—"

Patricia was horribly frightened.

"And afterwards the jackass-fool made matters worse by calling me 'his darling.' There is no more hateful word in the English language than 'darling.' It sounds like castor-oil tastes, or a snail looks after you have put salt on him."

The colonel deliberated this information; and he appeared to understand.

"So Parkinson has gone the way of Pevensey,—and of I wonder how many others? Well, may Heaven be very gracious to us both!" he said. "For I am going to do it."

Then composedly he took up the telephone upon his desk and called Roger Stapylton.

"I want you to come at once to Dr. Rabbet's,—yes, the rectory, next door to St. Luke's. Patricia and I are to be married there in half an hour. We are on our way to the City Hall to get the license now. . . No, she might change her mind again, you see. . . I have not the least notion how it happened. I don't care. . . Then you will have to be rude to him or else not see your only daughter married. . . Kindly permit me to repeat, sir, that I don't care about that or anything else. And for the rest, Patricia was twenty-one last December."

The colonel hung up the receiver. "And now," he said, "we are going to the City Hall."

"Are you?" said Patricia, with courteous interest. "Well, my way lies uptown. I have to stop in at Greenberg's and get a mustard plaster for the parrot."

He had his hat by this. "It isn't cool enough for me to need an overcoat, is it?"

"I think you must be crazy," she said, sharply.

"Of course I am. So I am going to marry you."

"Let me go—! Oh, and I had thought you were a gentleman—."

"I fear that at present I am simply masculine." He became aware that his hands, in gripping both her shoulders, were hurting the girl.

"Come now," he continued, "will you go quietly or will I have to carry you?"

She said, "And you would, too—." She spoke in wonder, for Patricia had glimpsed an unguessed Rudolph Musgrave.

His hands went under her arm-pits and he lifted her like a feather. He held her thus at arm's length.

"You—you adorable whirligig!" he laughed. "I am a stronger animal than you. It would be as easy for me to murder you as it would be for you to kill one of those flies on the window-pane. Do you quite understand that fact, Patricia?"

"Oh, but you are an idiot—."

"In wanting you, my dear?"

"Please put me down."

She thoroughly enjoyed her helplessness. He saw it, long before he lowered her.

"Why, not so much in that," said Miss Stapylton, "because inasmuch as I am a woman of superlative charm, of course you can't help yourself. But how do you know that Dr. Rabbet may not be somewhere else, harrying a defenseless barkeeper, or superintending the making of dress-shirt protectors for the Hottentots, or doing something else clerical, when we get to the rectory?"

After an irrelevant interlude she stamped her foot.

"I don't care what you say, I won't marry an atheist. If you had the least respect for his cloth, Olaf, you would call him up and arrange—

Oh, well! whatever you want to arrange—and permit me to powder my nose without being bothered, because I don't want people to think you are marrying a second helping to butter, and I never did like that Baptist man on the block above, anyhow. And besides," said Patricia, as with the occurrence of a new view-point, "think what a delicious scandal it will create!"

II

Patricia spoke the truth. By supper-time Lichfield had so industriously embroidered the Stapylton dinner and the ensuing marriage with hypotheses and explanations and unparented rumors that none of the participants in the affair but could advantageously have exchanged reputations with Benedict Arnold or Lucretia Borgia, had Lichfield believed a tithe of what Lichfield was repeating.

A duel was of course anticipated between Mr. Parkinson and Colonel Musgrave, and the colonel indeed offered, through Major Wadleigh, any satisfaction which Mr. Parkinson might desire.

The engineer, with garnishments of profanity, considered dueling to be a painstakingly-described absurdity and wished "the old popinjay" joy of his bargain.

Lichfield felt that only showed what came of treating poor-white trash as your equals, and gloried in the salutary moral.

III

Meanwhile the two originators of so much Lichfieldian diversion were not unhappy.

But indeed it were irreverent even to try to express the happiness of their earlier married life. . .

They were an ill-matched couple in so many ways that no long-headed person could conceivably have anticipated—in the outcome—more than decorous tolerance of each other. For apart from the disparity in age and tastes and rearing, there was always the fact to be weighed that in marrying the only child of a wealthy man Rudolph Musgrave was making what Lichfield called "an eminently sensible match"—than which, as Lichfield knew, there is no more infallible recipe for discord.

In this case the axiom seemed, after the manner of all general rules, to bulwark itself with an exception. Colonel Musgrave continued to emanate an air of contentment which fell perilously short of fatuity; and that Patricia was honestly fond of him was evident to the most impecunious of Lichfield's bachelors.

True, curtains had been lifted, a little by a little. Patricia could hardly have told you at what exact moment it was that she discovered Miss Agatha—who continued of course to live with them—was a dipsomaniac. Very certainly Rudolph Musgrave was not Patricia's informant; it is doubtful if the colonel ever conceded his sister's infirmity in his most private meditations; so that Patricia found the cause of Miss Agatha's "attacks" to be an open secret of which everyone in the house seemed aware and of which by tacit agreement nobody ever spoke. It bewildered Patricia, at first, to find that as concerned Lichfield at large any over-indulgence in alcohol by a member of the Musgrave family was satisfactorily accounted for by the matter-of-course statement that the Musgraves usually "drank,"—just as the Allardyces notoriously perpetuated the taint of insanity, and the Townsends were proverbially unable "to let women alone," and the Vartreys were deplorably prone to dabble in literature. These things had been for a long while just as they were today; and therefore (Lichfield estimated) they must be reasonable.

Then, too, Patricia would have preferred to have been rid of the old mulatto woman Virginia, because it was through Virginia that Miss Agatha furtively procured intoxicants. But Rudolph Musgrave would not consider Virginia's leaving. "Virginia's faithfulness has been proven by too many years of faithful service" was the formula with which he dismissed the suggestion. . . Afterward Patricia learned from Miss Agatha of the wrong that had been done Virginia by Olaf's uncle, Senator Edward Musgrave, the noted ante-bellum orator, and understood that Olaf—without, of course, conceding it to himself, because that was Olaf's way—was trying to make reparation. Patricia respected the sentiment, and continued to fret under its manifestation.

Miss Agatha also told Patricia of how the son of Virginia and Senator Musgrave had come to a disastrous end—"lynched in Texas, I believe, only it may not have been Texas. And indeed when I come to think of it, I don't believe it was, because I know we first heard of it on a Monday, and Virginia couldn't do the washing that week and I had to send it out. And for the usual crime, of course. It simply shows you how much better off the darkies were before the War," Miss Agatha said.

Patricia refrained from comment, not being willing to consider the deduction strained. For love is a contagious infection; and loving Rudolph Musgrave so much, Patricia must perforce love any person whom he loved as conscientiously as she would have strangled any person with whom he had flirted.

And yet, to Patricia, it was beginning to seem that Patricia Musgrave was not living, altogether, in that Lichfield which John Charteris has made immortal—"that nursery of Free Principles" (according to the *Lichfield Courier-Herald*) "wherein so many statesmen, lieutenants-general and orators were trained to further the faith of their fathers, to thrill the listening senates, draft constitutions, and bruise the paws of the British lion."

IV

It may be remembered that Lichfield had asked long ago, "But who, pray, are the Stapyltons?" It was characteristic of Colonel Musgrave that he went about answering the question without delay. The Stapletons—for "Stapylton" was a happy innovation of Roger Stapylton's dead wife—the colonel knew to have been farmers in Brummell County, and Brummell Courthouse is within an hour's ride, by rail, of Lichfield.

So he set about his labor of love.

And in it he excelled himself. The records of Brummell date back to 1750 and are voluminous; but Rudolph Musgrave did not overlook an item in any Will Book, or in any Orders of the Court, that pertained, however remotely, to the Stapletons. Then he renewed his labors at the courthouse of the older county from which Brummell was formed in 1750, and through many fragmentary, evil-odored and unindexed volumes indefatigably pursued the family's fortune back to the immigration of its American progenitor in 1619,—and, by the happiest fatality, upon the same *Bona Nova* which enabled the first American Musgrave to grace the Colony of Virginia with his presence. It could no longer be said that the wife of a Musgrave of Matocton lacked an authentic and tolerably ancient pedigree.

The colonel made a book of his Stapyltonian researches which he vaingloriously proclaimed to be the stupidest reading within the ample field of uninteresting printed English. Patricia was allowed to see no word of it until the first ten copies had come from the printer's, very splendid in green "art-vellum" and stamped with the Stapylton coat-of-arms in gold.

She read the book. "It is perfectly superb," was her verdict. "It is as dear as remembered kisses after death and as sweet as a plaintiff in a breach-of-promise suit. Only I would have preferred it served with a few kings and dukes for parsley. The Stapletons don't seem to have been anything but perfectly respectable mediocrities."

The colonel smiled. At the bottom of his heart he shared Patricia's regret that the Stapylton pedigree was unadorned by a potentate, because nobody can stay unimpressed by a popular superstition, however crass the thing may be. But for all this, an appraisal of himself and his own achievements profusely showed high lineage is not invariably a guarantee of excellence; and so he smiled and said:

"There are two ends to every stick. It was the Stapletons and others of their sort, rather than any soft-handed Musgraves, who converted a wilderness, a little by a little, into the America of today. The task was tediously achieved, and without ostentation; and always the ship had its resplendent figure-head, as always it had its hidden, nay! grimy, engines, which propelled the ship. And, however direfully America may differ from Utopia, to have assisted in the making of America is no mean distinction. We Musgraves and our peers, I sometimes think, may possibly have been just gaudy autumn leaves which happened to lie in the path of a high wind. And to cut a gallant figure in such circumstances does not necessarily prove the performer to be a *rara avis*, even though he rides the whirlwind quite as splendidly as any bird existent."

Patricia fluttered, and as lightly and irresponsibly as a wren might have done, perched on his knee.

"No! there is really something in heredity, after all. Now, you are a Musgrave in every vein of you. It always seems like a sort of flippancy for you to appear in public without a stock and a tarnished gilt frame with most of the gilt knocked off and a catalogue-number tucked in the corner." Patricia spoke without any regard for punctuation. "And I am so unlike you. I am only a Stapylton. I do hope you don't mind my being merely a Stapylton, Olaf, because if only I wasn't too modest to even think of alluding to the circumstance, I would try to tell you about the tiniest fraction of how much a certain ravishingly beautiful half-strainer loves you, Olaf, and the consequences would be deplorable."

"My dear—" he began.

"Ouch!" said Patricia; "you are tickling me. You don't shave half as often as you used to, do you? No, nowadays you think you have me safe and don't have to bother about being attractive. If I had a music-box I could put your face into it and play all sorts of tunes, only I prefer to look at it. You are a slattern and a jay-bird and a joy forever. And besides, the first Stapleton seems to have blundered somehow into the House of Burgesses, so that entitles me to be a Colonial Dame on my father's side, too, doesn't it, Olaf?"

The colonel laughed. "Madam Vanity!" said he, "I repeat that to be descended of a line of czars or from a house of emperors is, at the worst, an empty braggartism, or, at best—upon the plea of heredity—a handy palliation for iniquity; and to be descended of sturdy and honest and clean-blooded folk is beyond doubt preferable, since upon quite similar grounds it entitles one to hope that even now, 'when their generation is gone, when their play is over, when their panorama is withdrawn in tatters from the stage of the world,' there may yet survive of them 'some few actions worth remembering, and a few children who have retained some happy stamp from the disposition of their parents.'"

Patricia—with eyes widened in admiration at his rhetoric,—had turned an enticing shade of pink.

"I am glad of that," she said.

She snuggled so close he could not see her face now. She was to all appearances attempting to twist the top-button from his coat.

"I am very glad that it entitles one to hope—about the children—Because—"

The colonel lifted her a little from him. He did not say anything. But he was regarding her half in wonder and one-half in worship.

She, too, was silent. Presently she nodded.

He kissed her as one does a very holy relic.

It was a moment to look back upon always. There was no period in Rudolph Musgrave's life when he could not look back upon this instant and exult because it had been his.

Only, Patricia found out afterward, with an inexplicable disappointment, that her husband had not been talking extempore, but was freely quoting his "Compiler's Foreword" just as it figured in the printed book.

One judges this posturing, so inevitable of detection, to have been as significant of much in Rudolph Musgrave as was the fact of its belated discovery characteristic of Patricia.

Yet she had read this book about her family from purely normal motives: first, to make certain how old her various cousins were; secondly, to gloat over any traces of distinction such as her ancestry afforded; thirdly, to note with what exaggerated importance the text seemed to accredit those relatives she did not esteem, and mentally to annotate each page with unprintable events "which *everybody* knew about"; and fourthly, to reflect, as with a gush of steadily augmenting love, how dear and how unpractical it was of Olaf to have concocted these date-bristling pages—so staunch and blind in his misguided gratitude toward those otherwise uninteresting people who had rendered possible the existence of a Patricia.

V

Matters went badly with Patricia in the ensuing months. Her mother's blood told here, as Colonel Musgrave saw with disquietude. He knew the women of his race had by ordinary been unfit for childbearing; indeed, the daughters of this famous house had long, in a grim routine, perished, just as Patricia's mother had done, in their first maternal essay. There were many hideous histories the colonel could have told you of, unmeet to be set down, and he was familiar with this talk of pelvic anomalies which were congenital. But he had never thought of Patricia, till this, as being his kinswoman, and in part a Musgrave.

And even now the Stapylton blood that was in her pulled Patricia through long weeks of anguish. Surgeons dealt with her very horribly in a famed Northern hospital, whither she had been removed. By her obdurate request—and secretly, to his own preference, since it was never in his power to meet discomfort willingly—Colonel Musgrave had remained in Lichfield. Patricia knew that officious people would tell him her life could be saved only by the destruction of an unborn boy.

She never questioned her child would be a boy. She knew that Olaf wanted a boy.

"Oh, even more than he does me, daddy. And so he mustn't know, you see, until it is all over. Because Olaf is such an ill-informed person that he really believes he prefers me."

"Pat," her father inconsequently said, "I'm proud of you! And—and, by God, if I *want* to cry, I guess I am old enough to know my own mind! And I'll help you in this if you'll only promise not to die in spite of what these damn' doctors say, because you're *mine*, Pat, and so you realize a bargain is a bargain."

"Yes—I am really yours, daddy. It is just my crazy body that is a Musgrave," Patricia explained. "The real me is an unfortunate Stapylton who has somehow got locked up in the wrong house. It is not a desirable residence, you know, daddy. No modern improvements, for instance. But I have to live in it! . . . Still, I have not the least intention of dying, and I solemnly promise that I won't."

So these two hoodwinked Rudolph Musgrave, and brought it about by subterfuge that his child was born. At most he vaguely understood that Patricia was having rather a hard time of it, and steadfastly drugged this knowledge by the performance of trivialities. He was eating a cucumber sandwich at the moment young Roger Musgrave came into the world, and by that action very nearly accomplished Patricia's death.

VI

And the gods cursed Roger Stapylton with such a pride in, and so great a love for, his only grandson that the old man could hardly bear to be out of the infant's presence. He was frequently in Lichfield nowadays; and he renewed his demands that Rudolph Musgrave give up the exhaustively-particularized librarianship, so that "the little coot" would be removed to New York and all three of them be with Roger Stapylton always.

Patricia had not been well since little Roger's birth.

It was a peaked and shrewish Patricia, rather than Rudolph Musgrave, who fought out the long and obstinate battle with Roger Stapylton.

She was jealous at the bottom of her heart. She would not have anyone, not even her father, be too fond of what was preëminently hers; the world at large, including Rudolph Musgrave, was at liberty to adore her boy, as was perfectly natural, but not to meddle: and in fine, Patricia was both hysterical and vixenish whenever a giving up of the Library work was suggested.

The old man did not quarrel with her. And with Roger Stapylton's loneliness in these days, and the long thoughts it bred, we have nothing here to do. But when he died, stricken without warning, some five years after Patricia's marriage, his will was discovered to bequeath practically his entire fortune to little Roger Musgrave when the child should come of age; and to Rudolph Musgrave, as Patricia's husband, what was a reasonable income when judged by Lichfield's unexacting standards rather than by Patricia's anticipations. In a word, Patricia found that she and the colonel could for the future count upon a little more than half of the income she had previously been allowed by Roger Stapylton.

"It isn't fair!" she said. "It's monstrous! And all because you were so obstinate about your picayune Library!"

"Patricia—" he began.

"Oh, I tell you it's absurd, Olaf! The money logically ought to have been left to me. And here I will have to come to you for every penny of *my* money. And Heaven knows I have had to scrimp enough to support us all on what I used to have—Olaf," Patricia said, in another voice, "Olaf! why, what is it, dear?"

"I was reflecting," said Colonel Musgrave, "that, as you justly observe, both Agatha and I have been practically indebted to you for our support these past five years—"

VII

It must be enregistered, not to the man's credit, but rather as a simple fact, that it was never within Colonel Musgrave's power to forget the incident immediately recorded.

He forgave; when Patricia wept, seeing how leaden-colored his handsome face had turned, he forgave as promptly and as freely as he was learning to pardon the telling of a serviceable lie, or the perpetration of an occasional barbarism in speech, by Patricia. For he, a Musgrave of Matocton, had married a Stapylton; he had begun to comprehend that their standards were different, and that some daily conflict between these standards was inevitable.

And besides, as it has been veraciously observed, the truth of an insult is the barb which prevents its retraction. Patricia spoke the truth: Rudolph Musgrave and all those rationally reliant upon Rudolph Musgrave for support, had lived for some five years upon the money which they owed to Patricia. He saw about him other scions of old families who accepted such circumstances blithely: but, he said, he was a Musgrave of Matocton; and, he reflected, in the kingdom of the blind the one-eyed is necessarily very unhappy.

He did not mean to touch a penny of such moneys as Roger Stapylton had bequeathed to him; for the colonel considered—now—it was a man's duty personally to support his wife and child and sister. And he vigorously attempted to discharge this obligation, alike by virtue of his salary at the Library, and by spasmodic raids upon his tiny capital, and—chief of all—by speculation in the Stock Market.

Oddly enough, his ventures were through a long while—for the most part—successful. Here he builded a desperate edifice whose foundations were his social talents; and it was with quaint self-abhorrence he often noted how the telling of a smutty jest or the insistence upon a manifestly superfluous glass of wine had purchased from some properly tickled magnate a much desiderated "tip."

And presently these tips misled him. So the colonel borrowed from "Patricia's account."

And on this occasion he guessed correctly.

And then he stumbled upon such a chance for reinvestment as does not often arrive. And so he borrowed a trifle more in common justice to Patricia. . .

VIII

When those then famous warriors, Colonel Gaynor and Captain Green, were obstinately fighting extradition in Quebec; when in Washington the Senate was wording a suitable resolution wherewith to congratulate Cuba upon that island's brand-new independence; and when Messieurs Fitzsimmons and Jeffries were making amicable arrangements in San Francisco to fight for the world's championship:—at this remote time, in Chicago (on the same day, indeed, that in this very city Mr. S.E. Gross was legally declared the author of a play called Cyrano de Bergerac), the Sons of the Colonial Governors opened their tenth biennial convention. You may depend upon it that Colonel Rudolph Musgrave represented the Lichfield chapter.

It was two days later the telegram arrived. It read:

Agatha very ill come to me roger in perfect health.

—Patricia

He noted how with Stapyltonian thrift Patricia telegraphed ten words precisely. . .

And when he had reached home, late in the evening, the colonel, not having taken his bunch of keys with him, laid down his dress-suit case on the dark porch, and reached out one hand to the door-bell. He found it muffled with some flimsy, gritty fabric. He did not ring.

Upon the porch was a rustic bench. He sat upon it for a quarter of an hour—precisely where he had first talked with Agatha about Patricia's first coming to Lichfield. . . Once the door of a house across the street was opened, with a widening gush of amber light wherein he saw three women fitting wraps about them. One of them was adjusting a lace scarf above her hair.

"No, we're not a *bit* afraid—Just around the corner, you know—*Such* a pleasant evening—" Their voices carried far in the still night.

Rudolph Musgrave was not thinking of anything. Presently he went around through the side entrance, and thus came into the kitchen, where the old mulattress, Virginia, was sitting alone. The room was very hot. . . In Agatha's time supper would have been cooked upon the gas-range in the cellar, he reflected. . . Virginia had risen and made as though to take his dress-suit case, her pleasant yellow face as imperturbable as an idol's.

"No—don't bother, Virginia," said Colonel Musgrave.

He met Patricia in the dining-room, on her way to the kitchen. She had not chosen—as even the most sensible of us will instinctively decline to do—to vex the quiet of a house wherein death was by ringing a bell.

Holding his hand in hers, fondling it as she talked, Patricia told how three nights before Miss Agatha had been "queer, you know," at supper. Patricia had not liked to leave her, but it was the night of the Woman's Club's second Whist Tournament. And Virginia had promised to watch Miss Agatha. And, anyhow, Miss Agatha had gone to bed before Patricia left the house, and *anybody* would have thought she was going to sleep all night. And, in fine, Patricia's return at a drizzling half-past eleven had found Miss Agatha sitting in the garden, in her night-dress only, weeping over fancied grievances—and Virginia asleep in the kitchen. And Agatha had died that afternoon of pneumonia.

Even in the last half-stupor she was asking always when would Rudolph come? Patricia told him. . .

Rudolph Musgrave did not say anything. Without any apparent emotion he put Patricia aside, much as he did the dress-suit case which he had forgotten to lay down until Patricia had ended her recital.

He went upstairs—to the front room, Patricia's bedroom. Patricia followed him.

Agatha's body lay upon the bed, with a sheet over all. The undertaker's skill had arranged everything with smug and horrible tranquillity.

Rudolph Musgrave remembered he was forty-six years old; and when in all these years had there been a moment when Agatha—the real Agatha—had not known that what he had done was self-evidently correct, because otherwise Rudolph would not have done it?

"I trust you enjoyed your whist-game, Patricia."

"Well, I couldn't help it. I'm not running a sanitarium. I wasn't responsible for her eternal drinking."

The words skipped out of either mouth like gleeful little devils.

Then both were afraid, and both were as icily tranquil as the thing upon the bed. You could not hear anything except the clock upon the mantel. Colonel Musgrave went to the mantel, opened the clock, and with an odd deliberation removed the pendulum from its hook. Followed one metallic gasp, as of indignation, and then silence.

He spoke, still staring at the clock, his back turned to Patricia. "You must be utterly worn out. You had better go to bed."

He shifted by the fraction of an inch the old-fashioned "hand-colored" daguerreotype of his father in Confederate uniform. "Please don't wear that black dress again. It is no cause for mourning that we are rid of an encumbrance."

Behind him, very far away, it seemed, he heard Patricia wailing, "Olaf—!"

Colonel Musgrave turned without any haste. "Please go," he said, and appeared to plead with her. "You must be frightfully tired. I am sorry that I was not here. I seem always to evade my responsibilities, somehow—"

Then he began to laugh. "It *is* rather amusing, after all. Agatha was the most noble person I have ever known. The—this habit of hers to which you have alluded was not a part of her. And I loved Agatha. And I suppose loving is not altogether dependent upon logic. In any event, I loved Agatha. And when I came back to her I had come home, somehow—wherever she might be at the time. That has been true, oh, ever since I can remember—"

He touched the dead hand now. "Please go!" he said, and he did not look toward Patricia. "For Agatha loved me better than she did God, you know. The curse was born in her. She had to pay for what those dead, soft-handed Musgraves did. That is why her hands are so cold now. She had to pay for the privilege of being a Musgrave, you see. But then we cannot always pick and choose as to what we prefer to be."

"Oh, yes, of course, it is all my fault. Everything is my fault. But God knows what would have become of you and your Agatha if it hadn't been for me. Oh! oh!" Patricia wailed. "I was a child and I hadn't any better sense, and I married you, and you've been living off my money ever since! There hasn't been a Christmas present or a funeral wreath bought in this house since I came into it I didn't pick out and pay for out of my own pocket. And all the thanks I get for it is this perpetual fault-finding, and I wish I was dead like this poor saint here. She spent her life slaving for you. And what thanks did she get for it? Oh, you ought to go down on your knees, Rudolph Musgrave—!"

"Please leave," he said.

"I will leave when I feel like it, and not a single minute before, and you might just as well understand as much. You *have* been living off my money. Oh, you needn't go to the trouble of lying. And she did too. And she hated me, she always hated me, because I had been fool enough to marry you, and she carried on like a lunatic more than half the time, and I always pretended not to notice it, and this is my reward for trying to behave like a lady."

Patricia tossed her head. "Yes, and you needn't look at me as if I were some sort of a bug you hadn't ever seen before and didn't approve of, because I've seen you try that high-and-mighty trick too often for it to work with me."

Patricia stood now beneath the Stuart portrait of young Gerald Musgrave. She had insisted, long ago, that it be hung in her own bedroom—"because it was through that beautiful boy we first got really acquainted, Olaf." The boy smiles at you from the canvas, smiles ambiguously, as the colonel now noted.

"I think you had better go," said Colonel Musgrave. "Please go, Patricia, before I murder you."

She saw that he was speaking in perfect earnest.

IX

Rudolph Musgrave sat all night beside the body. He had declined to speak with innumerable sympathetic cousins—Vartreys and Fentons and Allardyces and Musgraves, to the fifth and sixth remove—who had come from all quarters, with visiting-cards and low-voiced requests to be informed "if there is anything we can possibly do."

Rudolph Musgrave sat all night beside the body. He had not any strength for anger now, and hardly for grief, Agatha had been his charge; and the fact that he had never plucked up courage to allude to her practises was now an enormity in which he could not quite believe. His cowardice and its fruitage confronted him, and frightened him into a panic frenzy of remorse.

Agatha had been his charge; and he had entrusted the stewardship to Patricia. Between them—that Patricia might have her card-game, that he might sit upon a platform for an hour or two with a half-dozen other pompous fools—they had let Agatha die. There was no mercy in him for Patricia or for himself. He wished Patricia had been a man. Had any man—an emperor or a coal-heaver, it would not have mattered—spoken as Patricia had done within the moment, here, within arm's reach of the poor flesh that had been Agatha's, Rudolph Musgrave would have known his duty. But, according to his code, it was not permitted to be discourteous to a woman. . .

He caught himself with grotesque meanness wishing that Agatha had been there,—privileged by her sex where he was fettered,—she who was so generous of heart and so fiery of tongue at need; and comprehension that Agatha would never abet or adore him any more smote him anew.

And chance reserved for him more poignant torture. Next day, while Rudolph Musgrave was making out the list of honorary pall-bearers, the postman brought a letter which had been forwarded from Chicago. It was from Agatha, written upon the morning of that day wherein later she had been, as Patricia phrased it, "queer, you know."

He found it wildly droll to puzzle out those "crossed" four sheets of trivialities written in an Italian hand so minute and orderly that the finished page suggested a fly-screen. He had so often remonstrated with Agatha about her penuriousness as concerned stationery.

"Selina Brice & the Rev'd Henry Anstruther, who now has a church in Seattle, have announced their engagement. Stanley Haggage has gone to Alabama to marry Leonora Bright, who moved from here a year ago. They are both as poor as church mice, & I think marriage in such a case an unwise step for anyone. It brings cares & anxieties enough any way, without starting out with poverty to increase and render deeper every trouble. . ."

Such was the tenor of Agatha's last letter, of the last self-expression of that effigy upstairs who (you could see) knew everything and was not discontent.

Here the dead spoke, omniscient; and told you that Stanley Haggage had gone to Alabama, and that marriage brought new cares and anxieties.

"I cannot laugh," said Rudolph Musgrave, aloud. "I know the jest deserves it. But I cannot laugh, because my upper lip seems to be made of leather and I can't move it. And, besides, I loved Agatha to a degree which only You and I have ever known of. She never understood quite how I loved her. Oh, won't You make her understand just how I loved her? For Agatha is dead, because You wanted her to be dead, and I have never told her how much I loved her, and now I cannot ever tell her how much I loved her. Oh, won't You please show me that You have made her understand? or else have me struck by lightning? or do *anything*. . . ?"

Nothing was done.

X

And afterward Rudolph Musgrave and his wife met amicably, and without reference to their last talk. Patricia wore black-and-white for some six months, and Colonel Musgrave accepted the compromise tacitly. All passed with perfect smoothness between them; and anyone in Lichfield would have told you that the Musgraves were a model couple.

She called him "Rudolph" now.

"Olaf is such a silly-sounding nickname for two old married people, you know," Patricia estimated.

The colonel negligently said that he supposed it did sound odd.

"Only I don't think Clarice Pendomer would care about coming," he resumed,—for the two were discussing an uncompleted list of the people Patricia was to invite to their first house-party.

"And for heaven's sake, why not? We always have her to everything."

He could not tell her it was because the Charterises were to be among their guests. So he said: "Oh, well—!"

"Mrs. C.B. Pendomer, then"—Patricia wrote the name with a flourish. "Oh, you jay-bird, I'm not jealous. Everybody knows you never had any more morals than a tom-cat on the back fence. It's a lucky thing the boy didn't take after you, isn't it? He doesn't, not a bit. No, Harry Pendomer is the puniest black-haired little wretch, whereas your other son, sir, resembles his mother and is in consequence a ravishingly beautiful person of superlative charm—"

He was staring at her so oddly that she paused. So Patricia was familiar with that old scandal which linked his name with Clarice Pendomer's! He was wondering if Patricia had married him in the belief that she was marrying a man who, appraised by any standards, had acted infamously.

"I was only thinking you had better ask Judge Allardyce, Patricia. You see, he is absolutely certain not to come—"

THIS YEAR THE MUSGRAVES HAD decided not to spend the spring alone together at Matocton, as they had done the four preceding years.

"It looks so silly," as Patricia pointed out.

And, besides, a house-party is the most economical method,—as she also pointed out, being born a Stapylton—of paying off your social obligations, because you can always ask so many people who, you know, have made other plans, and cannot accept.

"So we will invite Judge Allardyce, of course," said Patricia. "I had forgotten his court met in June. Oh, and Peter Blagden too. It had slipped my mind his uncle was dead. . ."

"I learned this morning Mrs. Haggage was to lecture in Louisville on the sixteenth. She was reading up in the Library, you see—"

"Rudolph, you are the lodestar of my existence. I will ask her to come on the fourteenth and spend a week. I never could abide the hag, but she has such a—There! I've made a big blot right in the middle of 'darling,' and spoiled a perfectly good sheet of paper! . . . You'd better mail it at once, though, because the evening-paper may have something in it about her lecture."

XI

Rudolph—"

"Why—er—yes, dear?"

This was after supper, and Patricia was playing solitaire. Her husband was reading the paper.

"Agatha told me all about Virginia, you know—"

Here Colonel Musgrave frowned. "It is not a pleasant topic."

"You jay-bird, you behave entirely too much as if you were my grandfather. As I was saying, Agatha told me all about your uncle and Virginia," Patricia hurried on. "And how she ran away afterwards, and hid in the woods for three days, and came to your father's plantation, and how your father bought her, and how her son was born, and how her son was lynched—"

"Now, really, Patricia! Surely there are other matters which may be more profitably discussed."

"Of course. Now, for instance, why is the King of Hearts the only one that hasn't a moustache?" Patricia peeped to see what cards lay beneath that monarch, and upon reflection moved the King of Spades into the vacant space. She was a devotee of solitaire and invariably cheated at it.

She went on, absently: "But don't you see? That colored boy was your own first cousin, and he was killed for doing exactly what his father had done. Only they sent the father to the Senate and gave him columns of flubdub and laid him out in state when he died—and they poured kerosene upon the son and burned him alive. And I believe Virginia thinks that wasn't fair."

"What do you mean?"

"I honestly believe Virginia hates the Musgraves. She is only a negro, of course, but then she was a mother once—Oh, yes! all I need is a black eight—" Patricia demanded, "Now look at your brother Hector—the awfully dissipated one that died of an overdose of opiates. When it happened wasn't Virginia taking care of him?"

"Of course. She is an invaluable nurse."

"And nobody else was here when Agatha went out into the rain. Now, what if she had just let Agatha go, without trying to stop her? It would have been perfectly simple. So is this. All I have to do is to take them off now."

Colonel Musgrave negligently returned to his perusal of the afternoon paper. "You are suggesting—if you will overlook my frankness—the most deplorable sort of nonsense, Patricia."

"I know exactly how Balaam felt," she said, irrelevantly, and fell to shuffling the cards. "You don't, and you won't, understand that Virginia is a human being. In any event, I wish you would get rid of her."

"I couldn't decently do that," said Rudolph Musgrave, with careful patience. "Virginia's faithfulness has been proven by too many years of faithful service. Nothing more strikingly attests the folly of freeing the negro than the unwillingness of the better class of slaves to leave their former owners—"

"Now you are going to quote a paragraph or so from your Gracious Era. As if I hadn't read everything you ever wrote! You are a fearful humbug in some ways, Rudolph."

"And you are a red-headed rattlepate, madam. But seriously, Patricia, you who were reared in the North are strangely unwilling to concede that we of the South are after all best qualified to deal with the Negro Problem. We know the negro as you cannot ever know him."

"You! Oh, God ha' mercy on us!" mocked Patricia. "There wasn't any Negro Problem hereabouts, you beautiful idiot, so long as there were any negroes. Why, today there is hardly one full-blooded negro in Lichfield. There are only a thousand or so of mulattoes who share the blood of people like your Uncle Edward. And for the most part they take after their white kin, unfortunately. And there you have the Lichfield Negro Problem in a nutshell. It is a venerable one and fully set forth in the Bible. You needn't attempt to argue with me, because you are a ninnyhammer, and I am a second Nestor. The Holy Scriptures are perfectly explicit as to what happens to the heads of the children and their teeth too."

"I wish you wouldn't jest about such matters—"

"Because it isn't lady-like? But, Rudolph, you know perfectly well that I am not a lady."

"My dear!" he cried, in horror that was real, "and what on earth have I said even to suggest—"

"Oh, not a syllable; it isn't at all the sort of thing that your sort *says* . . . And I am not your sort. I don't know that I altogether wish I were. But *if* I were, it would certainly make things easier," Patricia added sharply.

"My dear—!" he again protested.

"Now, candidly, Rudolph"—relinquishing the game, she fell to shuffling the cards—"just count up the number of times this month that my—oh, well! I really don't know what to call it except my deplorable omission in failing to be born a lady—has seemed to you to yank the very last rag off the gooseberry-bush?"

He scoffed. "What nonsense! Although, of course, Patricia—"

She nodded, mischief in her brightly-colored tiny face. "Yes, that is just your attitude, you beautiful idiot."

"—although, of course—now, quite honestly, Patricia, I have occasionally wished that you would not speak of sacred and—er, physical and sociological matters in exactly the tone in which—well! in which you sometimes do speak of them. It may sound old-fashioned, but I have always believed that decency is quite as important in mental affairs as it is in physical ones, and that as a consequence, a gentlewoman should always clothe her thoughts with at least the same care she accords her body. Oh, don't misunderstand me! Of course it doesn't do any harm, my dear, between us. But outside—you see, for people to know that you think about such things must necessarily give them a false opinion of you."

Patricia meditated.

She said, with utter solemnity, "Anathema maranatha! oh, hell to damn! may the noses of all respectable people be turned upside down and jackasses dance eternally upon their grandmothers' graves!"

"Patricia—!" cried a shocked colonel.

"I mean every syllable of it. No, Rudolph; *I* can't help it if the vinaigretted beauties of your boyhood were unabridged dictionaries of prudery. You see, I know almost all the swearwords there are. And I read the newspapers, and medical books, and even the things that boys chalk up on fences. In consequence I am not a bit whiteminded, because if you use your mind at all it gets more or less dingy, just like using anything else."

He could not help but laugh, much as he disapproved. Patricia fluttered and, as a wren might have done, perched presently upon his knee.

"Rudolph, can't you laugh more often, and not devote so much time to tracing out the genealogies of those silly people, and being so tediously beautiful and good?" she asked, and with a hint of seriousness. "Rudolph, you don't know how I would adore you if you would rob a church or cut somebody's throat in an alley, and tell me all about it because you knew I wouldn't betray you. You are so infernally respectable in everything you do! How did you come to bully me that day at the

Library? It seems almost as if those two were different people. . . doesn't it, Rudolph?"

"My dear," the colonel said whimsically, "I am afraid we are rather like the shepherdess and the chimney-sweep of the fable I read you very long ago. We climbed up so far that we could see the stars, once, very long ago, Patricia, and we have come back to live upon the parlor table. I suppose it happens to all the little china people."

She took his meaning. Each was aware of an odd sense of intimacy. "Everything we have to be glad for now, Rudolph, is the rivet in grandfather's neck. It is rather a fiasco, isn't it?"

"Eh, there are all sorts of rivets, Patricia. And the thing one cannot do because one is what one is, need not be necessarily a cause for grief."

XII

It was excellent to see Jack Charteris again, as Colonel Musgrave did within a few days of this. Musgrave was unreasonably fond of the novelist and frankly confessed it would be as preposterous to connect Charteris with any of the accepted standards of morality as it would be to judge an artesian-well from the standpoint of ethics.

Anne was not yet in Lichfield. She had broken the journey to visit a maternal grand-aunt and some Virginia cousins, in Richmond, Charteris explained, and was to come thence to Matocton.

"And so you have acquired a boy and, by my soul, a very handsome wife, Rudolph?"

"It is sufficiently notorious," said Colonel Musgrave. "Yes, we are quite absurdly happy." He laughed and added: "Patricia—but you don't know her droll way of putting things—says that the only rational complaint I can advance against her is her habit of rushing into a hospital every month or so and having a section or two of her person removed by surgeons. It worries me,—only, of course, it is not the sort of thing you can talk about. And, as Patricia says, it *is* an unpleasant thing to realize that your wife is not leaving you through the ordinary channels of death or of type-written decrees of the court, but only in vulgar fractions, as it were—"

"Please don't be quite so brutal, Rudolph. It is not becoming in a Musgrave of Matocton to speak of women in any tone other than the most honeyed accents of chivalry."

"Oh, I was only quoting Patricia," the colonel largely said, "and—er—Jack," he continued. "By the way, Jack, Clarice Pendomer will be at Matocton—"

"I rejoice in her good luck," said Charteris, equably.

"—and—well! I was wondering—?"

"I can assure you that there will be no—trouble. That skeleton is safely locked in its closet, and the key to that closet is missing—more thanks to you. You acted very nobly in the whole affair, Rudolph. I wish I could do things like that. As it is, of course, I shall always detest you for having been able to do it."

Charteris said, thereafter: "I shall always envy you, though, Rudolph. No other man I know has ever attained the good old troubadourish ideal of *domnei*—that love which rather abhors than otherwise the notion of possessing its object. I still believe it was a distinct relief to a certain military officer, whose name we need not mention, when Anne decided not to marry you."

The colonel grinned, a trifle consciously. "Well, Anne meant youth, you comprehend, and all the things we then believed in, Jack. It would have been decidedly difficult to live up to such a contract, and—as it were—to fulfil every one of the implied specifications!"

"And yet"—here Charteris flicked his cigarette—"Anne ruled in the stead of Aline Van Orden. And Aline, in turn, had followed Clarice Pendomer. And before the coming of Clarice had Pauline Romeyne, whom time has converted into Polly Ashmeade, reigned in the land—"

"Don't be an ass!" the colonel pleaded; and then observed, inconsequently: "I can't somehow quite realize Aline is dead. Lord, Lord, the letters that I wrote to her! She sent them all back, you know, in genuine romantic fashion, after we had quarreled. I found those boyish ravings only the other day in my father's desk at Matocton, and skimmed them over. I shall read them through some day and appropriately meditate over life's mysteries that are too sad for tears."

He meditated now.

"It wouldn't be quite equitable, Jack," the colonel summed it up, "if the Aline I loved—no, I don't mean the real woman, the one you and all the other people knew, the one that married the enterprising brewer and died five years ago—were not waiting for me somewhere. I can't express just what I mean, but you will understand, I know—?"

"That heaven is necessarily run on a Mohammedan basis? Why, of course," said Mr. Charteris. "Heaven, as I apprehend it, is a place where we shall live eternally among those ladies of old years who never condescended actually to inhabit any realm more tangible than that of our boyish fancies. It is the obvious definition; and I defy you to evolve a more enticing allurement toward becoming a deacon."

"You romancers are privileged to talk nonsense anywhere," the colonel estimated, "and I suppose that in the Lichfield you have made famous, Jack, you have a double right."

"Ah, but I never wrote a line concerning Lichfield. I only wrote about the Lichfield whose existence you continue to believe in, in spite of the fact that you are actually living in the real Lichfield," Charteris returned. "The vitality of the legend is wonderful."

He cocked his head to one side—an habitual gesture with Charteris—and the colonel noted, as he had often done before, how extraordinarily reminiscent Jack was of a dried-up, quizzical black parrot. Said Charteris:

"I love to serve that legend. I love to prattle of 'ole Marster' and 'ole Miss,' and throw in a sprinkling of 'mockin'-buds' and 'hants' and 'horg-killing time,' and of sweeping animadversions as to all 'free niggers'; and to narrate how 'de quality use ter cum'—you spell it c-u-m because that looks so convincingly like dialect—'ter de gret hous.' Those are the main ingredients. And, as for the unavoidable love-interest—" Charteris paused, grinned, and pleasantly resumed: "Why, jes arter dat, suh, a hut Yankee cap'en, whar some uv our folks done shoot in de laig, wuz lef on de road fer daid—a quite notorious custom on the part of all Northern armies—un Young Miss had him fotch up ter de gret hous, un nuss im same's he one uv de fambly, un dem two jes fit un argufy scanlous un never spicion huccum dey's in love wid each othuh till de War's ovuh. And there you are! I need not mention that during the tale's progress it is necessary to introduce at least one favorable mention of Lincoln, arrange a duel 'in de low grouns' immediately after day-break, and have the family silver interred in the back garden, because these points will naturally suggest themselves."

"Jack, Jack!" the colonel cried, "it is an ill bird that fouls its own nest."

"But, believe me, I don't at heart," said Charteris, in a queer earnest voice. "There is a sardonic imp inside me that makes me jeer at the commoner tricks of the trade—and yet when I am practising that trade, when I am writing of those tender-hearted, brave and gracious men and women, and of those dear old darkies, I very often write with tears in my eyes. I tell you this with careful airiness because it is true and because it would embarrass me so horribly if you believed it."

Then he was off upon another tack. "And wherein, pray, have I harmed Lichfield by imagining a dream city situated half way between Atlantis and Avalon and peopled with superhuman persons—and by having called this city Lichfield? The portrait did not only flatter Lichfield, it flattered human nature. So, naturally, it pleased everybody. Yes, that, I take it, is the true secret of romance—to induce the momentary delusion that humanity is a superhuman race, profuse in aspiration, and prodigal in the exercise of glorious virtues and stupendous vices. As a matter of fact, all human passions are depressingly chicken-hearted, I find. Were it not for the police court records, I would pessimistically insist that all of us elect to love one person and to hate another with very much the same enthusiasm that we display in expressing a preference for rare roast beef as compared with the outside slice. Oh, really, Rudolph, you have no notion how salutary it is to the self-esteem of us romanticists to run across, even nowadays, an occasional breach of the peace. For then sometimes—when the coachman obligingly cuts the butler's throat in the back-alley, say—we actually presume to think for a moment that our profession is almost as honest as that of making counterfeit money. . ."

The colonel did not interrupt his brief pause of meditation. Then the novelist said:

"Why, no; if I were ever really to attempt a tale of Lichfield, I would not write a romance but a tragedy. I think that I would call my tragedy *Futility*, for it would mirror the life of Lichfield with unengaging candor; and, as a consequence, people would complain that my tragedy lacked sustained interest, and that its participants were inconsistent; that it had no ordered plot, no startling incidents, no high endeavors, and no especial aim; and that it was equally deficient in all time-hallowed provocatives of either laughter or tears. For very few people would understand that a life such as this, when rightly viewed, is the most pathetic tragedy conceivable."

"Oh, come, now, Jack! come, recollect that your reasoning powers are almost as worthy of employment as your rhetorical abilities! We are not quite so bad as that, you know. We may be a little behind the times in Lichfield; we certainly let well enough alone, and we take things pretty much as they come; but we meddle with nobody, and, after all, we don't do any especial harm."

"We don't do anything whatever in especial, Rudolph. That would be precisely the theme of my story of the real Lichfield if I were ever bold enough to write it. There seems to be a sort of blight upon Lichfield. Oh, yes! it would be unfair, perhaps, to contrast it with the bigger Southern cities, like Richmond and Atlanta and New Orleans; but even the inhabitants of smaller Southern towns are beginning to buy excursion tickets, and thereby ascertain that the twentieth century has really begun. Yes, it is only in Lichfield I can detect the raw stuff of a genuine tragedy; for, depend upon it, Rudolph, the most pathetic tragedy in life is to get nothing in particular out of it."

"But, for my part, I don't see what you are driving at," the colonel stoutly said.

And Charteris only laughed. "And I hardly expected you to do so, Rudolph—or not yet, at least."

PART V
SOUVENIR

"I am contented by remembrances—
Dreams of dead passions, wraiths of vanished times,
Fragments of vows, and by-ends of old rhymes—
Flotsam and jetsam tumbling in the seas
Whereon, long since, put forth our argosies
Which, bent on traffic in the Isles of Love,
Lie foundered somewhere in some firth thereof,
Encradled by eternal silences."

"Thus, having come to naked bankruptcy,
Let us part friends, as thrifty tradesmen do
When common ventures fail, for it may be
These battered oaths and rhymes may yet ring true
To some fair woman's hearing, so that she
Will listen and think of love, and I of you."

—F. Ashcroft Wheeler. *Revisions*

I

When the *Reliance*, the *Constitution* and the *Columbia* were holding trial races off Newport to decide which one of these yachts should defend the *America's* cup; when the tone of the Japanese press as to Russia's actions in Manchuria was beginning to grow ominous; when the Jews of America were drafting a petition to the Czar; and when it was rumored that the health of Pope Leo XIII was commencing to fail:—at this remote time, the Musgraves gave their first house-party.

And at this period Colonel Musgrave noted and admired the apparent unconcern with which John Charteris and Clarice Pendomer encountered at Matocton. And at this period Colonel Musgrave noted with approval the intimacy which was, obviously, flourishing between the little novelist and Patricia.

Also Colonel Musgrave had presently good reason to lament a contretemps, over which he was sulking when Mrs. Pendomer rustled to her seat at the breakfast-table, with a shortness of breath that was partly due to the stairs, and in part attributable to her youthful dress, which fitted a trifle too perfectly.

"Waffles?" said Mrs. Pendomer. "At my age and weight the first is an experiment and the fifth an amiable indiscretion of which I am invariably guilty. Sugar, please." She yawned, and reached a generously-proportioned arm toward the sugar-bowl. "Yes, that will do, Pilkins."

Colonel Musgrave—since the remainder of his house-party had already breakfasted—raised his fine eyes toward the chandelier, and sighed, as Pilkins demurely closed the dining-room door.

Leander Pilkins—butler for a long while now to the Musgraves of Matocton—would here, if space permitted, be the subject of an encomium. Leander Pilkins was in Lichfield considered to be, upon the whole, the handsomest man whom Lichfield had produced; for this quadroon's skin was like old ivory, and his profile would have done credit to an emperor. His terrapin is still spoken of in Lichfield as people in less favored localities speak of the Golden Age, and his mayonnaise (boasts Lichfield) would have compelled an Olympian to plead for a second helping. For the rest, his deportment in all functions of butlership is best described as super-Chesterfieldian; and, indeed, he was generally known to be a byblow of Captain Beverley Musgrave's, who in his day was Lichfield's arbiter as touched the social graces. And so, no more of Pilkins.

Mrs. Pendomer partook of chops. "Is this remorse," she queried, "or a convivially induced requirement for bromides? At this unearthly hour of the morning it is very often difficult to disentangle the two."

"It is neither," said Colonel Musgrave, and almost snappishly.

Followed an interval of silence. "Really," said Mrs. Pendomer, and as with sympathy, "one would think you had at last been confronted with one of your thirty-seven pasts—or is it thirty-eight, Rudolph?"

Colonel Musgrave frowned disapprovingly at her frivolity; he swallowed his coffee, and buttered a superfluous potato. "H'm!" said he; "then you know?"

"I know," sighed she, "that a sleeping past frequently suffers from insomnia."

"And in that case," said he, darkly, "it is not the only sufferer."

Mrs. Pendomer considered the attractions of a third waffle—a mellow blending of autumnal yellows, fringed with a crisp and irresistible brown, that, for the moment, put to flight all dreams and visions of slenderness.

"And Patricia?" she queried, with a mental hiatus.

Colonel Musgrave flushed.

"Patricia," he conceded, with mingled dignity and sadness, "is, after all, still in her twenties—"

"Yes," said Mrs. Pendomer, with a dryness which might mean anything or nothing; "she *was* only twenty-one when she married you."

"I mean," he explained, with obvious patience, "that at her age she—not unnaturally—takes an immature view of things. Her unspoiled purity," he added, meditatively, "and innocence and general unsophistication are, of course, adorable, but I can admit to thinking that for a journey through life they impress me as excess baggage."

"Patricia," said Mrs. Pendomer, soothingly, "has ideals. And ideals, like a hare-lip or a mission in life, should be pitied rather than condemned, when our friends possess them; especially," she continued, buttering her waffle, "as so many women have them sandwiched between their last attack of measles and their first imported complexion. No one of the three is lasting, Rudolph."

"H'm!" said he.

There was another silence. The colonel desperately felt that matters were not advancing.

"H'm!" said she, with something of interrogation in her voice.

"See here, Clarice, I have known you—"

"You have not!" cried she, very earnestly; "not by five years!"

"Well, say for some time. You are a sensible woman—"

"A man," Mrs. Pendomer lamented, parenthetically, "never suspects a woman of discretion, until she begins to lose her waist."

"—and I am sure that I can rely upon your womanly tact, and finer instincts,—and that sort of thing, you know—to help me out of a deuce of a mess."

Mrs. Pendomer ate on, in an exceedingly noncommittal fashion, as he paused, inquiringly.

"She has been reading some letters," said he, at length; "some letters that I wrote a long time ago."

"In the case of so young a girl," observed Mrs. Pendomer, with perfect comprehension, "I should have undoubtedly recommended a judicious supervision of her reading-matter."

"She was looking through an old escritoire," he explained; "Jack Charteris had suggested that some of my father's letters—during the War, you know—might be of value—"

He paused, for Mrs. Pendomer appeared on the verge of a question.

But she only said, "So it was Mr. Charteris who suggested Patricia's searching the desk. Ah, yes! And then—?"

"And it was years ago—and just the usual sort of thing, though it may have seemed from the letters—Why, I hadn't given the girl a thought," he cried, in virtuous indignation, "until Patricia found the letters—and read them!"

"Naturally," she assented—"yes,—just as I read George's."

The smile with which she accompanied this remark, suggested that both Mr. Pendomer's correspondence and home life were at times of an interesting nature.

"I had destroyed the envelopes when she returned them," continued Colonel Musgrave, with morose confusion of persons. "Patricia doesn't even know who the girl was—her name, somehow, was not mentioned."

"'Woman of my heart'—'Dearest girl in all the world,'" quoted Mrs. Pendomer, reminiscently, "and suchlike tender phrases, scattered in with a pepper-cruet, after the rough copy was made in pencil, and dated just 'Wednesday,' or 'Thursday,' of course. Ah, you were always very careful, Rudolph," she sighed; "and now that makes it all the worse, because—as far as all the evidence goes—these letters may have been returned yesterday."

"Why—!" Colonel Musgrave pulled up short, hardly seeing his way clear through the indignant periods on which he had entered. "I declined," said he, somewhat lamely, "to discuss the matter with her, in her present excited and perfectly unreasonable condition."

Mrs. Pendomer's penciled eyebrows rose, and her lips—which were quite as red as there was any necessity for their being—twitched.

"Hysterics?" she asked.

"Worse!" groaned Colonel Musgrave; "patient resignation under unmerited affliction!"

He had picked up a teaspoon, and he carefully balanced it upon his forefinger.

"There were certain phrases in these letters which were, somehow, repeated in certain letters I wrote to Patricia the summer we were engaged, and—not to put too fine a point upon it—she doesn't like it."

Mrs. Pendomer smiled, as though she considered this not improbable; and he continued, with growing embarrassment and indignation:

"She says there must have been others"—Mrs. Pendomer's smile grew reminiscent—"any number of others; that she is only an incident in my life. Er—as you have mentioned, Patricia has certain notions—Northern idiocies about the awfulness of a young fellow's sowing his wild oats, which you and I know perfectly well he is going to do, anyhow, if he is worth his salt. But she doesn't know it, poor little girl. So she won't listen to reason, and she won't come downstairs—which," lamented Rudolph Musgrave, plaintively, "is particularly awkward in a house-party."

He drummed his fingers, for a moment, on the table.

"It is," he summed up, "a combination of Ibsen and hysterics, and of—er, rather declamatory observations concerning there being one law for the man and another for the woman, and Patricia's realization of the mistake we both made—and all that sort of nonsense, you know, exactly as if, I give you my word, she were one of those women who want to vote." The colonel, patently, considered that feminine outrageousness could go no farther. "And she is taking menthol and green tea and mustard plasters and I don't know what all, in bed, prior to—to—"

"Taking leave?" Mrs. Pendomer suggested.

"Er—that was mentioned, I believe," said Colonel Musgrave. "But of course she was only talking."

Mrs. Pendomer looked about her; and, without, the clean-shaven lawns and trim box-hedges were very beautiful in the morning sunlight; within, the same sunlight sparkled over the heavy breakfast service, and gleamed in the high walnut panels of the breakfast-room. She viewed the comfortable appointments about her a little wistfully, for Mrs. Pendomer's purse was not over-full.

"Of course," said she, as in meditation, "there was the money."

"Yes," said Rudolph Musgrave, slowly; "there was the money."

He sprang to his feet, and drew himself erect. Here was a moment he must give its full dramatic value.

"Oh, no, Clarice, my marriage may have been an eminently sensible one, but I love my wife. Oh, believe me, I love her very tenderly, poor little Patricia! I have weathered some forty-seven birthdays; and I have done much as other men do, and all that—there have been flirtations and suchlike, and—er—some women have been kinder to me than I deserved. But I love her; and there has not been a moment since she came into my life I haven't loved her, and been—" he waved his hands now impotently, almost theatrically—"sickened at the thought of the others."

Mrs. Pendomer's foot tapped the floor whilst he spoke. When he had made an ending, she inclined her head toward him.

"Thank you!" said Mrs. Pendomer.

Colonel Musgrave bit his lip; and he flushed.

"That," said he, hastily, "was different."

But the difference, whatever may have been its nature, was seemingly a matter of unimportance to Mrs. Pendomer, who was in meditation. She rested her ample chin on a much-bejeweled hand for a moment; and, when Mrs. Pendomer raised her face, her voice was free from affectation.

"You will probably never understand that this particular July day is a crucial point in your life. You will probably remember it, if you remember it at all, simply as that morning when Patricia found some girl-or-another's old letters, and behaved rather unreasonably about them. It was the merest trifle, you will think. . . John Charteris understands women better than you do, Rudolph."

"I need not pretend at this late day to be as clever as Jack," the colonel said, in some bewilderment. "But why not more succinctly state that the Escurial is not a dromedary, although there are many flies in France? For what on earth has Jack to do with crucial points and July mornings?"

"Why, I suppose, I only made bold to introduce his name for the sake of an illustration, Rudolph. For the last person in the world to realize, precisely, why any woman did anything is invariably the woman who did it. . . Yet there comes in every married woman's existence that time when she realizes, suddenly, that her husband has a past which might be taken as, in itself, a complete and rounded life—as a life which had run the gamut of all ordinary human passions, and had become familiar with all ordinary human passions a dishearteningly long while before she ever came into that life. A woman never realizes that of her lover, somehow. But to know that your husband, the father of your child, has lived for other women a life in which you had no part, and never can have part!—she realizes that, at one time or another, and—and it sickens her." Mrs. Pendomer smiled as she echoed his phrase, but her eyes were not mirthful.

"Ah, she hungers for those dead years, Rudolph, and, though you devote your whole remaining life to her, nothing can ever make up for them; and she always hates those shadowy women who have stolen them from her. A woman never, at heart, forgives the other women who have loved her husband, even though she cease to care for him herself. For she remembers—ah, you men forget so easily, Rudolph! God had not invented memory when he created Adam; it was kept for the woman."

Then ensued a pause, during which Rudolph Musgrave smiled down upon her, irresolutely; for he abhorred "a scene," as his vernacular phrased it, and to him Clarice's present manner bordered upon both the scenic and the incomprehensible.

"Ah!—you women!" he temporized.

There was a glance from eyes whose luster time and irregular living had conspired to dim.

"Ah!—you men!" Mrs. Pendomer retorted. "And there we have the tragedy of life in a nutshell!"

Silence lasted for a while. The colonel was finding this matutinal talk discomfortably opulent in pauses.

"Rudolph, and has it never occurred to you that in marrying Patricia you swindled her?"

And naturally his eyebrows lifted.

"Because a woman wants love."

"Well, well! and don't I love Patricia?"

"I dare say that you think you do. Only you have played at loving so long you are really unable to love anybody as a girl has every right to be loved in her twenties. Yes, Rudolph, you are being rather subtly punished for the good times you have had. And, after all, the saddest punishment is something that happens in us, not something which happens to us."

"I wish you wouldn't laugh, Clarice—"

"I wish I didn't have to. For I would get far more comfort out of crying, and I don't dare to, because of my complexion. It comes in a round pasteboard box nowadays, you know, Rudolph, with French mendacities all over the top—and my eyebrows come in a fat crayon, and the healthful glow of my lips comes in a little porcelain tub."

Mrs. Pendomer was playing with a teaspoon now, and a smile hovered about the aforementioned lips.

"And yet, do you remember, Rudolph," said she, "that evening at Assequin, when I wore a blue gown, and they were playing *Fleurs d'Amour*, and—you said—?"

"Yes"—there was an effective little catch in his voice—"you were a wonderful girl, Clarice—'my sunshine girl,' I used to call you. And blue was always your color; it went with your eyes so exactly. And those big sleeves they wore then—those tell-tale, crushable sleeves!—they suited your slender youthfulness so perfectly! Ah, I remember it as though it were yesterday!"

Mrs. Pendomer majestically rose to her feet.

"It was pink! And it was at the Whitebrier you said—what you said! And—and you don't deserve anything but what you are getting," she concluded, grimly.

"I—it was so long ago," Rudolph Musgrave apologized, with mingled discomfort and vagueness.

"Yes," she conceded, rather sadly; "it was so long—oh, very long ago! For we were young then, and we believed in things, and—and Jack Charteris had not taken a fancy to me—" She sighed and drummed her fingers on the table. "But women have always helped and shielded you, haven't they, Rudolph? And now I am going to help you too, for you have shown me the way. You don't deserve it in the least, but I'll do it."

II

Thus it shortly came about that Mrs. Pendomer mounted, in meditative mood, to Mrs. Musgrave's rooms; and that Mrs. Pendomer, recovering her breath, entered, without knocking, into a gloom where cologne and menthol and the odor of warm rubber contended for mastery. For Patricia had decided that she was very ill indeed, and was sobbing softly in bed.

Very calmly, Mrs. Pendomer opened a window, letting in a flood of fresh air and sunshine; very calmly, she drew a chair—a substantial arm-chair—to the bedside, and, very calmly, she began:

"My dear, Rudolph has told me of this ridiculous affair, and—oh, you equally ridiculous girl!"

She removed, with deft fingers, a damp and clinging bandage from about Patricia's head, and patted the back of Patricia's hand, placidly. Patricia was by this time sitting erect in bed, and her coppery hair was thick about her face, which was colorless; and, altogether, she was very rigid and very indignant and very pretty, and very, very young.

"How dare he tell you—or anybody else!" she cried.

"We are such old friends, remember," Mrs. Pendomer pleaded, and rearranged the pillows, soothingly, about her hostess; "and I want to talk to you quietly and sensibly."

Patricia sank back among the pillows, and inhaled the fresh air, which, in spite of herself, she found agreeable. "I—somehow, I don't feel very sensible," she murmured, half sulky and half shame-faced.

Mrs. Pendomer hesitated for a moment, and then plunged into the heart of things. "You are a woman, dear," she said, gently, "though heaven knows it must have been only yesterday you were playing about the nursery—and one of the facts we women must face, eventually, is that man is a polygamous animal. It is unfortunate, perhaps, but it is true. Civilization may veneer the fact, but nothing will ever override it, not even in these new horseless carriages. A man may give his wife the best that is in him—his love, his trust, his life's work—but it is only the best there is left. We give our hearts; men dole out theirs, as people feed bread to birds, with a crumb for everyone. His wife has the remnant. And the best we women can do is to remember we are credibly informed that half a loaf is preferable to no bread at all."

Her face sobered, and she added, pensively: "We might contrive a better universe, we sister women, but this is not permitted us. So we must take it as it is."

Patricia stirred, as talking died away. "I don't believe it," said she; and she added, with emphasis: "And, anyhow, I hate that nasty trollop!"

"Ah, but you do believe it." Mrs. Pendomer's voice was insistent. "You knew it years before you went into long frocks. That knowledge is, I suppose, a legacy from our mothers."

Patricia frowned, petulantly, and then burst into choking sobs. "Oh!" she cried, "it's damnable! Some other woman has had what I can never have. And I wanted it so!—that first love that means everything—the love he gave her when I was only a messy little girl, with pig-tails and too many hands and feet! Oh, that—that hell-cat! She's had everything!"

There was an interval, during which Mrs. Pendomer smiled crookedly, and Patricia continued to sob, although at lengthening intervals. Then, Mrs. Pendomer lifted the packet of letters lying on the bed, and cleared her throat.

"H'm!" said she; "so this is what caused all the trouble? You don't mind?"

And, considering silence as equivalent to acquiescence, she drew out a letter at hazard, and read aloud:

"'Just a line, woman of all the world, to tell you. . . but what have I to tell you, after all? Only the old, old message, so often told that it seems scarcely worth while to bother the postman about it. Just three words that innumerable dead lips have whispered, while life was yet good and old people were unreasonable and skies were blue—three words that our unborn children's children will whisper to one another when we too have gone to help the grasses in their growing or to nourish the victorious, swaying hosts of some field of daffodils. Just three words—that is my message to you, my lady. . . Ah, it is weary waiting for a sight of your dear face through these long days that are so much alike and all so empty and colorless! My heart grows hungry as I think of your great, green eyes and of the mouth that is like a little wound. I want you so, O, dearest girl in all the world! I want you. . . Ah, time travels very slowly that brings you back to me, and, meanwhile, I can but dream of you and send you impotent scrawls that only vex me with their futility. For my desire of you—'

"The remainder," said Mrs. Pendomer, clearing her throat once more, "appears to consist of insanity and heretical sentiments, in about equal proportions, all written at the top of a boy's breaking voice. It isn't Colonel Musgrave's voice—quite—is it?"

During the reading, Patricia, leaning on one elbow, had regarded her companion with wide eyes and flushed cheeks. "Now, you see!" she cried indignantly; "he loved her! He was simply crazy about her."

"Why, yes." Mrs. Pendomer replaced the letter, carefully, almost caressingly, among its companions. "My dear, it was years ago. I think time has by this wreaked a vengeance far more bitter than you could ever plan on the woman who, after all, never thought to wrong you. For the bitterest of all bitter things to a woman—to some women, at least—is to grow old."

She sighed, and her well-manicured fingers fretted for a moment with the counterpane.

"Ah, who will write the tragedy of us women who were 'famous Southern beauties' once? We were queens of men while our youth lasted, and diarists still prattle charmingly concerning us. But nothing was expected of us save to be beautiful and to condescend to be made much of, and that is our tragedy. For very few things, my dear, are more pitiable than the middle-age of the pitiful butterfly woman, whose mind cannot—cannot, because of its very nature—reach to anything higher! Middle-age strips her of everything—the admiration, the flattery, the shallow merriment—all the little things that her little mind longs for—and other women take her place, in spite of her futile, pitiful efforts to remain young. And the world goes on as before, and there is a whispering in the moonlit garden, and young people steal off for wholly superfluous glasses of water, and the men give her duty dances, and she is old—ah, so old!—under the rouge and inane smiles and dainty fripperies that caricature her lost youth! No, my dear, you needn't envy this woman! Pity her, my dear!" pleaded Clarice Pendomer, and with a note of earnestness in her voice.

"Such a woman," said Patricia, with distinctness, "deserves no pity."

"Well," Mrs. Pendomer conceded, drily, "she doesn't get it. Probably, because she always grows fat, from sheer lack of will-power to resist sloth and gluttony—the only agreeable vices left her; and by no stretch of the imagination can a fat woman be converted into either a pleasing or heroic figure."

Mrs. Pendomer paused for a breathing-space, and smiled, though not very pleasantly.

"It is, doubtless," said she, "a sight for gods—and quite certainly for men—to laugh at, this silly woman striving to regain a vanished frugality of waist. Yes, I suppose it is amusing—but it is also pitiful. And it is more pitiful still if she has ever loved a man in the unreasoning way these shallow women sometimes do. Men age so slowly; the men a girl first knows are young long after she has reached middle-age—yes, they go on dancing cotillions and talking nonsense in the garden, long after she has taken to common-sense shoes. And the man is still young—and he cares for some other woman, who is young and has all that she has lost—and it seems so unfair!" said Mrs. Pendomer.

Patricia regarded her for a moment. The purple eyes were alert, their glance was hard. "You seem to know all about this woman," Patricia began, in a level voice. "I have heard, of course, what everyone in Lichfield whispers about you and Rudolph. I have even teased Rudolph about it, but until today I had believed it was a lie."

"It is often a mistake to indulge in uncommon opinions," said Mrs. Pendomer. "You get more fun and interest out of it, I don't deny, but the bill, my dear, is unconscionable."

"So! you confess it!"

"My dear, and who am I to stand aside like a coward and see you make a mountain of this boy-and-girl affair—an affair which Rudolph and I had practically forgotten—oh, years ago!—until today? Why—why, you *can't* be jealous of me!" Mrs. Pendomer concluded, half-mockingly.

Patricia regarded her with deliberation.

In the windy sunlight, Mrs. Pendomer was a well-preserved woman, but, unmistakably, preserved; moreover, there was a great deal of her, and her nose was in need of a judicious application of powder, of which there was a superfluity behind her ears. Was this the siren Patricia had dreaded? Patricia clearly perceived that, whatever had been her husband's relations with this woman, he had been manifestly entrapped into the imbroglio—a victim to Mrs. Pendomer's inordinate love of attention, which was, indeed, tolerably notorious; and Patricia's anger against Rudolph Musgrave gave way to a rather contemptuous pity and a half-maternal remorse for not having taken better care of him.

"No," answered Mrs. Pendomer, to her unspoken thought; "no woman could be seriously jealous of me. Yes, I dare say, I am *passée* and vain and frivolous and—harmless. But," she added, meditatively, "you hate me, just the same."

"My dear Mrs. Pendomer—" Patricia began, with cool courtesy; then hesitated. "Yes," she conceded; "I dare say, it is unreasonable—but I do hate you like the very old Nick."

"Why, then," spoke Mrs. Pendomer, with cheerfulness, "everything is as it should be." She rose and smiled. "I am sorry to say I must be leaving Matocton today; the Ullwethers are very pressing, and I really don't know how to get out of paying them a visit—"

"So sorry to lose you," cooed Patricia; "but, of course, you know best. I believe some very good people are visiting the Ullwethers nowadays?" She extended the letters, blandly. "May I restore your property?" she queried, with utmost gentleness.

"Thanks!" Clarice Pendomer took them, and kissed her hostess, not without tenderness, on the brow. "My dear, be kind to Rudolph. He—he is rather an attractive man, you know,—and other women are kind to him. We of Lichfield have always said that he and Jack Charteris were the most dangerous men that even Lichfield has ever produced—"

"Why, do people really find Mr. Charteris particularly attractive?" Patricia demanded, so quickly and so innocently that Mrs. Pendomer could not deny herself the glance of a charlatan who applauds his fellow's legerdemain.

And Patricia colored.

"Oh, well—! You know how Lichfield gossips," said Mrs. Pendomer.

III

Colonel Musgrave had smoked a preposterous number of unsatisfying cigarettes on the big front porch of Matocton whilst Mrs. Pendomer was absent on her mission; and on her return, flushed and triumphant, he rose in eloquent silence.

"I've done it, Rudolph," said Mrs. Pendomer.

"Done what?" he queried, blankly.

"Restored what my incomprehensible lawyers call the *status quo*; achieved peace with honor; carried off the spoils of war; and—in short—arranged everything," answered Mrs. Pendomer, and sank into a rustic chair, which creaked admonishingly. "And all," she added, bringing a fan into play, "without a single falsehood. *I* am not to blame if Patricia has jumped at the conclusion that these letters were written to me."

"My word!" said Rudolph Musgrave, "your methods of restoring domestic peace to a distracted household are, to say the least, original!" He seated himself, and lighted another cigarette.

"Oh, well, Patricia is not deaf, you know, and she has lived in Lichfield quite a while." Mrs. Pendomer said abruptly, "I have half a mind to tell you some of the things I know about Aline Van Orden."

"Please don't," said Colonel Musgrave, "for I would inevitably beard you on my own porch and smite you to the door-mat. And I am hardly young enough for such adventures."

"And poor Aline is dead! And the rest of us are middle-aged now, Rudolph, and we go in to dinner with the veterans who call us 'Madam,' and we are prominent in charitable enterprises. . . But there was a time when we were not exactly hideous in appearance, and men did many mad things for our sakes, and we never lose the memory of that time. Pleasant memories are among the many privileges of women. Yes," added Mrs. Pendomer, meditatively, "we derive much the same pleasure from them a cripple does from rearranging the athletic medals he once won, or a starving man from thinking of the many excellent dinners he has eaten; but we can't and we wouldn't part with them, nevertheless."

Rudolph Musgrave, however, had not honored her with much attention, and was puzzling over the more or less incomprehensible situation; and, perceiving this, she ran on, after a little:

"Oh, it worked—it worked beautifully! You see, she would always have been very jealous of that other woman; but with me it is different.

She has always known that scandalous story about you and me. And she has always known me as I am—a frivolous and—say, corpulent, for it is a more dignified word—and generally unattractive chaperon; and she can't think of me as ever having been anything else. Young people never really believe in their elders' youth, Rudolph; at heart, they think we came into the world with crow's-feet and pepper-and-salt hair, all complete. So, she is only sorry for you now—rather as a mother would be for a naughty child; as for me, she isn't jealous—but," sighed Mrs. Pendomer, "she isn't over-fond of me."

Colonel Musgrave rose to his feet. "It isn't fair," said he; "the letters were distinctly compromising. It isn't fair you should shoulder the blame for a woman who was nothing to you. It isn't fair you should be placed in such a false position."

"What matter?" pleaded Mrs. Pendomer. "The letters are mine to burn, if I choose. I have read one of them, by the way, and it is almost word for word a letter you wrote me a good twenty years ago. And you re-hashed it for Patricia's benefit too, it seems! You ought to get a mimeograph. Oh, very well! It doesn't matter now, for Patricia will say nothing—or not at least to you," she added.

"Still—" he began.

"Ah, Rudolph, if I want to do a foolish thing, why won't you let me? What else is a woman for? They are always doing foolish things. I have known a woman to throw a man over, because she had seen him without a collar; and I have known another actually to marry a man, because she happened to be in love with him. I have known a woman to go on wearing pink organdie after she has passed forty, and I have known a woman to go on caring for a man who, she knew, wasn't worth caring for, long after he had forgotten. We are not brave and sensible, like you men. So why not let me be foolish, if I want to be?"

"If," said Colonel Musgrave in some perplexity, "I understand one word of this farrago, I will be—qualified in various ways."

"But you don't have to understand," she pleaded.

"You mean—?" he asked.

"I mean that I was always fond of Aline, anyhow."

"Nonsense!" And he was conscious, with vexation, that he had undeniably flushed.

"I mean, then, I am a woman, and *I* understand. Everything is as near what it should be as is possible while Patricia is seeing so much of—we will call it the artistic temperament." Mrs. Pendomer shrugged. "But if I went on in that line you would believe I was jealous. And heaven knows I am not the least bit so—with the unavoidable qualification that, being a woman, I can't help rising superior to common-sense."

He said, "You mean Jack Charteris—? But what on earth has he to do with these letters?"

"I don't mean any proper names at all. I simply mean you are not to undo my work. It would only signify trouble and dissatisfaction and giving up all this"—she waved her hand lightly toward the lawns of Matocton,—"and it would mean our giving you up, for, you know, you haven't any money of your own, Rudolph. Ah, Rudolph, we can't give you up! We need you to lead our Lichfield germans, and to tell us naughty little stories, and keep us amused. So *please* be sensible, Rudolph."

"Permit me to point out I firmly believe that silence is the perfectest herald of joy," observed Colonel Musgrave. "Only I do *not* understand why you should have dragged John Charteris's name into this ludicrous affair—"

"You really do not understand—?"

But Colonel Musgrave's handsome face declared very plainly that he did not.

"Well," Mrs. Pendomer reflected, "I dare say it is best, upon the whole, you shouldn't. And now you must excuse me, for I am leaving for the Ullwethers' today, and I shan't ever be invited to Matocton again, and I must tell my maid to pack up. She is a little fool and it will break her heart to be leaving Pilkins. All human beings are tediously alike. But, allowing ample time for her to dispose of my best lingerie and of her unavoidable lamentations, I ought to make the six-forty-five. I have noticed that one usually does—somehow," said Mrs. Pendomer, and seemed to smack of allegories.

And yet it may have been because she knew—as who knew better?—something of that mischief's nature which was now afoot.

IV

The colonel burned the malefic letters that afternoon. Indeed, the episode set him to ransacking the desk in which Patricia had found them—a desk which, as you have heard, was heaped with the miscellaneous correspondence of the colonel's father dating back a half-century and more. Much curious matter the colonel discovered there, for "Wild Will" Musgrave's had been a full-blooded career. And over one packet of letters, in particular, the colonel sat for a long while with an unwontedly troubled face.

PART VI

BYWAYS

"Cry Kismet! *and take heart. Eros is gone,*
Nor may we follow to that loftier air
Olympians breathe. Take heart, and enter where
A lighter Love, vine-crowned, laughs i' the sun,
Oblivious of tangled webs ill-spun
By ancient wearied weavers, for it may be
His guidance leads to lovers of such as we
And hearts so credulous as to be won.

"Cry Kismet! *Put away vain memories*
Of all old sorrows and of all old joys,
And learn that life is never quite amiss
So long as unreflective girls and boys
Remember that young lips were meant to kiss,
And hold that laughter is a seemly noise."

—Paul Vanderhoffen. *Egeria Answers*

I

Patricia sat in the great maple-grove that stands behind Matocton, and pondered over a note from her husband, who was in Lichfield superintending the appearance of the July number of the *Lichfield Historical Association's Quarterly Magazine*. Mr. Charteris lay at her feet, glancing rapidly over a lengthy letter, which was from his wife, in Richmond.

The morning mail was just in, and Patricia had despatched Charteris for her letters, on the plea that the woods were too beautiful to leave, and that Matocton, in the unsettled state which marks the end of the week in a house-party, was intolerable.

She, undoubtedly, was partial to the grove, having spent the last ten mornings there. Mr. Charteris had overrated her modest literary abilities so far as to ask her advice in certain details of his new book, which was to appear in the autumn, and they had found a vernal solitude, besides being extremely picturesque, to be conducive to the forming of really matured opinions. Moreover, she was assured that none of the members of the house-party would misunderstand her motives; people were so much less censorious in the country; there was something in the pastoral purity of Nature, seen face to face, which brought out one's noblest instincts, and put an end to all horrid gossip and scandal-mongering.

Didn't Mrs. Barry-Smith think so? And what was her real opinion of that rumor about the Hardresses, and was the woman as bad as people said she was? Thus had Patricia spoken in the privacy of her chamber, at that hour when ladies do up their hair for the night, and discourse of mysteries. It is at this time they are said to babble out their hearts to one another; and so, beyond doubt, this must have been the real state of the case.

As Patricia admitted, she had given up bridge and taken to literature only during the past year. She might more honestly have said within the last two weeks. In any event, she now conversed of authors with a fitful persistence like that of an ill-regulated machine. Her comments were delightfully frank and original, as she had an unusually good memory. Of two books she was apt to prefer the one with the wider margin, and she was becoming sufficiently familiar with a number of poets to quote them inaccurately.

We have all seen John Charteris's portraits, and most of us have read his books—or at least, the volume entitled *In Old Lichfield*, which caused the *Lichfield Courier-Herald* to apostrophize its author as a "Child of Genius! whose ardent soul has sounded the mysteries of life, whose inner vision sweeps over ever widening fields of thought, and whose chiseled phrases continue patriotically to perpetuate the beauty of Lichfield's past." But for present purposes it is sufficient to say that this jewelsmith of words was slight and dark and hook-nosed, and that his hair was thin, and that he was not ill-favored. It may be of interest to his admirers—a growing cult—to add that his reason for wearing a mustache in a period of clean-shaven faces was that, without it, his mouth was not pleasant to look upon.

"Heigho!" Patricia said, at length, with a little laugh; "it is very strange that both of our encumbrances should arrive on the same day!"

"It is unfortunate," Mr. Charteris admitted, lazily; "but the blessed state of matrimony is liable to these mishaps. Let us be thankful that my wife's whim to visit her aunt has given us, at least, two perfect, golden weeks. Husbands are like bad pennies; and wives resemble the cat whose adventures have been commemorated by one of our really popular poets. They always come back."

Patricia communed with herself, and to Charteris seemed, as she sat in the chequered sunlight, far more desirable than a married woman has any right to be.

"I wish—" she began, slowly. "Oh, but, you know, it was positively criminal negligence not to have included a dozen fairies among my sponsors."

"I too have desiderated this sensible precaution," said Charteris, and laughed his utter comprehension. "But, after all," he said, and snapped his fingers gaily, "we still have twenty-four hours, Patricia! Let us forget the crudities of life, and say foolish things to each other. For I am pastorally inclined this morning, Patricia; I wish to lie at your feet and pipe amorous ditties upon an oaten reed. Have you such an article about you, Patricia?"

He drew a key-ring from his pocket, and pondered over it.

"Or would you prefer that I whistle into the opening of this door-key, to the effect that we must gather our rose-buds while we may, for Time is still a-flying, fa-la, and that a drear old age, not to mention our spouses, will soon descend upon us, fa-la-di-leero? A door-key is not Arcadian, Patricia, but it makes a very creditable noise."

"Don't be foolish, *mon ami*!" she protested, with an indulgent smile. "I am unhappy."

"Unhappy that I have chanced to fall in love with you, Patricia? It is an accident which might befall any really intelligent person."

She shrugged her shoulders, ruefully.

"I have done wrong to let you talk to me as you have done of late. I—oh, Jack, I am afraid!"

Mr. Charteris meditated. Somewhere in a neighboring thicket a bird trilled out his song—a contented, half-hushed song that called his mate to witness how infinitely blest above all other birds was he. Mr. Charteris heard him to the end, and languidly made as to applaud; then Mr. Charteris raised his eyebrows.

"Of your husband, Patricia?" he queried.

"I—Rudolph doesn't bother about me nowadays sufficiently to—notice anything."

Mr. Charteris smiled. "Of my wife, Patricia?"

"Good gracious, no! I have not the least doubt you will explain matters satisfactorily to your wife, for I have always heard that practise makes perfect."

Mr. Charteris laughed—a low and very musical laugh.

"Of me, then, Patricia?"

"I—I think it is rather of myself I am afraid. Oh, I hate you when you smile like that! You have evil eyes, Jack! Stop it! Quit hounding me with your illicit fascinations." The hand she had raised in threatening fashion fell back into her lap, and she shrugged her shoulders once more. "My nerves are somewhat upset by the approaching prospect of connubial felicity, I suppose. Really, though, *mon ami*, your conceit is appalling."

Charteris gave vent to a chuckle, and raised the door-key to his lips.

"When you are quite through your histrionic efforts," he suggested, apologetically, "I will proceed with my amorous pipings. Really, Patricia, one might fancy you the heroine of a society drama, working up the sympathies of the audience before taking to evil ways. Surely, you are not about to leave your dear, good, patient husband, Patricia? Heroines only do that on dark and stormy nights, and in an opera toilette; wearing her best gown seems always to affect a heroine in that way."

Mr. Charteris, at this point, dropped the key-ring, and drew nearer to her; his voice sank to a pleading cadence.

"We are in Arcadia, Patricia; virtue and vice are contraband in this charming country, and must be left at the frontier. Let us be adorably foolish and happy, my lady, and forget for a little the evil days that approach. Can you not fancy this to be Arcadia, Patricia?—it requires the merest trifle of imagination. Listen very carefully, and you will hear the hoofs of fauns rustling among the fallen leaves; they are watching us, Patricia, from behind every tree-bole. They think you a dryad—the queen of all the dryads, with the most glorious eyes and hair and the most tempting lips in all the forest. After a little, shaggy, big-thewed ventripotent Pan will grow jealous, and ravish you away from me, as he stole Syrinx from her lover. You are very beautiful, Patricia; you are quite incredibly beautiful. I adore you, Patricia. Would you mind if I held your hand? It is a foolish thing to do, but it is preëminently Arcadian."

She heard him with downcast eyes; and her cheeks flushed a pink color that was agreeable to contemplation.

"Do—do you really care for me, Jack?" she asked, softly; then cried, "No, no, you needn't answer—because, of course, you worship me madly, unboundedly, distractedly. They all do, but you do it more convincingly. You have been taking lessons at night-school, I dare say, at all sorts of murky institutions. And, Jack, really, cross my heart, I always stopped the others when they talked this way. I tried to stop you, too. You know I did?"

She raised her lashes, a trifle uncertainly, and withdrew her hand from his, a trifle slowly. "It is wrong—all horribly wrong. I wonder at myself, I can't understand how in the world I can be such a fool about you. I must not be alone with you again. I must tell my husband—everything," she concluded, and manifestly not meaning a word of what she said.

"By all means," assented Mr. Charteris, readily. "Let's tell my wife, too. It will make things so very interesting."

"Rudolph would be terribly unhappy," she reflected.

"He would probably never smile again," said Mr. Charteris. "And my wife—oh, it would upset Anne, quite frightfully! It is our altruistic, nay, our bounden duty to save them from such misery."

"I—I don't know what to do!" she wailed.

"The obvious course," said he, after reflection, "is to shake off the bonds of matrimony, without further delay. So let's elope, Patricia."

Patricia, who was really unhappy, took refuge in flippancy, and laughed.

“I make it a rule,” said she, “never to elope on Fridays. Besides, now I think of it, there is, Rudolph—Ah, Rudolph doesn’t care a button’s worth about me, I know. The funny part is that he doesn’t know it. He has simply assumed he is devoted to me, because all respectable people are devoted to their wives. I can assure you, *mon ami*, he would be a veritable Othello, if there were any scandal, and would infinitely prefer the bolster to the divorce-court. He would have us followed and torn apart by wild policemen.”

Mr. Charteris meditated for a moment.

“Rudolph, as you are perfectly aware, would simply deplore the terribly lax modern notions in regard to marriage and talk to newspaper reporters about this much—” he measured it between thumb and forefinger—“concerning the beauty and chivalry of the South. He would do nothing more. I question if Rudolph Musgrave would ever in any circumstances be capable of decisive action.”

“Ah, don’t make fun of Rudolph!” she cried, quickly. “Rudolph can’t help it if he is conscientious and in consequence rather depressing to live with. And for all that he so often plays the jackass-fool about women, like Grandma Pendomer, he is a man, Jack—a well-meaning, clean and dunderheaded man! You aren’t; you are puny and frivolous, and you sneer too much, and you are making a fool of me, and—and that’s why I like you, I suppose. Oh, I wish I were good! I have always tried to be good, and there doesn’t seem to be a hatpin in the world that makes a halo sit comfortably. Now, Jack, you know I’ve tried to be good! I’ve never let you kiss me, and I’ve never let you hold my hand—until today—and—and—”

Patricia paused, and laughed.

“But we were talking of Rudolph,” she said, with a touch of weariness. “Rudolph has all the virtues that a woman most admires until she attempts to live in the same house with them.”

“I thank you,” said Mr. Charteris, “for the high opinion you entertain of my moral character.” He bestowed a reproachful sigh upon her, and continued: “At any rate, Rudolph Musgrave has been an unusually lucky man—the luckiest that I know of.”

Patricia had risen as if to go. She turned her big purple eyes on him for a moment.

“You—you think so?” she queried, hesitatingly.

Afterward she spread out her hands in a helpless gesture, and laughed for no apparent reason, and sat down again.

"Why?" said Patricia.

It took Charteris fully an hour to point out all the reasons.

Patricia told him very frankly that she considered him to be talking nonsense, but she seemed quite willing to listen.

II

Sunset was approaching on the following afternoon when Rudolph Musgrave, fresh from Lichfield,—whither, as has been recorded, the bringing out of the July number of the *Lichfield Historical Associations Quarterly Magazine* had called him,—came out on the front porch at Matocton. He had arrived on the afternoon train, about an hour previously, in time to superintend little Roger's customary evening transactions with an astounding quantity of bread and milk; and, Roger abed, his father, having dressed at once for supper, found himself ready for that meal somewhat in advance of the rest of the house-party.

Indeed, only one of them was visible at this moment—a woman, who was reading on a rustic bench some distance from the house, and whose back was turned to him. The poise of her head, however, was not unfamiliar; also, it is not everyone who has hair that is like a nimbus of thrice-polished gold.

Colonel Musgrave threw back his shoulders, and drew a deep breath. Subsequently, with a fine air of unconcern, he inspected the view from the porch, which was, in fact, quite worthy of his attention. Interesting things have happened at Matocton—many events that have been preserved in the local mythology, not always to the credit of the old Musgraves, and a few which have slipped into a modest niche in history. It was, perhaps, on these that Colonel Musgrave pondered so intently.

Once the farthingaled and red-heeled gentry came in sluggish barges to Matocton, and the broad river on which the estate faces was thick with bellying sails; since the days of railroads, one approaches the mansion through the maple-grove in the rear, and enters ignominiously by the back-door.

The house stands on a considerable elevation. The main portion, with its hipped roof and mullioned windows, is very old, but the two wings that stretch to the east and west are comparatively modern, and date back little over a century. Time has mellowed them into harmony with the major part of the house, and the kindly Virginia creeper has done its utmost to conceal the fact that they are constructed of plebeian bricks which were baked in this country; but Matocton was Matocton long before these wings were built, and a mere affair of yesterday, such as the Revolution, antedates them. They were not standing when Tarleton paid his famous visit to Matocton.

In the main hall, you may still see the stairs up which he rode on horseback, and the slashes which his saber hacked upon the handrail.

To the front of the mansion lies a close-shaven lawn, dotted with sundry oaks and maples; and thence, the formal gardens descend in six broad terraces. There is when summer reigns no lovelier spot than this bright medley of squares and stars and triangles and circles—all Euclid in flowerage—which glow with multitudinous colors where the sun strikes. You will find no new flowers at Matocton, though. Here are verbenas, poppies, lavender and marigolds, sweet-william, hollyhocks and columbine, phlox, and larkspur, and meadowsweet, and heart's-ease, just as they were when Thomasine Musgrave, Matocton's first châtelaine, was wont to tend them; and of all floral parvenus the gardens are innocent. Box-hedges mark the walkways.

The seventh terrace was, until lately, uncultivated, the trees having been cleared away to afford pasturage. It is now closely planted with beeches, none of great size, and extends to a tangled thicket of fieldpines and cedar and sassafras and blackberry bushes, which again masks a drop of some ten feet to the river.

The beach here is narrow; at high tide, it is rarely more than fifteen feet in breadth, and is in many places completely submerged. Past this, the river lapses into the horizon line without a break, save on an extraordinarily clear day when Bigelow's Island may be seen as a dim smudge upon the west.

All these things, Rudolph Musgrave regarded with curiously deep interest for one who had seen them so many times before. Then, with a shrug of the shoulders, he sauntered forward across the lawn. He had planned several appropriate speeches, but, when it came to the point of giving them utterance, he merely held out his hand in an awkward fashion, and said:

"Anne!"

She looked up from her reading.

She did this with two red-brown eyes that had no apparent limits to their depth. Her hand was soft; it seemed quite lost in the broad palm of a man's hand.

"Dear Rudolph," she said, as simply as though they had parted yesterday, "it's awfully good to see you again."

Colonel Musgrave cleared his throat, and sat down beside her.

A moment later Colonel Musgrave cleared his throat once more.

Then Mrs. Charteris laughed. It was a pleasant laugh—a clear, rippling carol of clean mirth that sparkled in her eyes, and dimpled in her wholesome cheeks.

"So! do you find it very, very awkward?"

"Awkward!" he cried. Their glances met in a flash of comprehension which seemed to purge the air. Musgrave was not in the least self-conscious now. He laughed, and lifted an admonitory forefinger.

"Oh, good Cynara," he said, "I am not what I was. And so I cannot do it, my dear—I really cannot possibly live up to the requirements of being a Buried Past. In a proper story-book or play, I would have to come back from New Zealand or the Transvaal, all covered with glory and epaulets, and have found you in the last throes of consumption: instead, you have fattened, Anne, which a Buried Past never does, and which shows a sad lack of appreciation for my feelings. And I—ah, my dear, I must confess that my hair is growing gray, and that my life has not been entirely empty without you, and that I ate and enjoyed two mutton-chops at luncheon, though I knew I should see you today. I am afraid we are neither of us up to heroics, Anne. So let's be sensible and comfy, my dear."

"You brute!" she cried—not looking irreparably angry, yet not without a real touch of vexation; "don't you know that every woman cherishes the picture of her former lovers sitting alone in the twilight, and growing lackadaisical over undying memories and faded letters? And you—you approach me, after I don't dare to think how many years, as calmly as if I were an old schoolmate of your mother's, and attempt to talk to me about mutton-chops! You ought to be ashamed of yourself, Rudolph Musgrave. You might, at least, have started a little at seeing me, and have clasped your hand to your heart, and have said, 'You, you!' or something of the sort. I had every right to expect it."

Mrs. Charteris pouted, and then trifled for a moment with the pages of her book.

"And—and I want to tell you that I am sorry for the way I spoke to you—that night," she swiftly said. Anne did not look at him. "Women don't understand things that are perfectly simple to men, I suppose—I mean—that is, Jack said—"

"That you ought to apologize? It was very like him"—and Colonel Musgrave smiled to think how like John Charteris it was. "Jack is quite wonderful," he observed.

She looked up, saying impulsively, "Rudolph, you don't know how happy he makes me."

"Heartless woman, and would you tempt me to end the tragedy of my life with a Shakesperian fifth act of poisonings and assassination? I spurn you, temptress. For, after all, it was an unpleasantly long while ago we went mad for each other," Musgrave announced, and he smiled. "I fancy that the boy and girl we knew of are as dead now as Nebuchadnezzar. 'Marian's married, and I sit here alive and merry at'—well, not at forty year, unluckily—"

"If you continue in that heartless strain, I shall go into the house," Mrs. Charteris protested.

Her indignation was exaggerated, but it was not altogether feigned; women cannot quite pardon a rejected suitor who marries and is content. They wish him all imaginable happiness and prosperity, of course; and they are honestly interested in his welfare; but it seems unexpectedly callous in him. And besides his wife is so perfectly commonplace.

Mrs. Charteris, therefore, added, with emphasis: "I am really disgracefully happy."

"Glad to hear it," said Musgrave, placidly. "So am I."

"Oh, Rudolph, Rudolph, you are hopeless!" she sighed. "And you used to make such a nice lover!"

Mrs. Charteris looked out over the river, which was like melting gold, and for a moment was silent.

"I was frightfully in love with you, Rudolph," she said, as half in wonder. "After—after that horrible time when my parents forced us to behave rationally, I wept—oh, I must have wept deluges! I firmly intended to pine away to an early grave. And that second time I liked you too, but then—there was Jack, you see."

"H'm!" said Colonel Musgrave; "yes, I see."

"I want you to continue to be friends with Jack," she went on, and her face lighted up, and her voice grew tender. "He has the artistic temperament, and naturally that makes him sensitive, and a trifle irritable at times. It takes so little to upset him, you see, for he feels so acutely what he calls the discords of life. I think most men are jealous of his talents; so they call him selfish and finicky and conceited. He isn't really, you know. Only, he can't help feeling a little superior to the majority of men, and his artistic temperament leads him to magnify the lesser mishaps of life—such as the steak being overdone, or missing a train. Oh, really, a thing like that worries him as much as the loss of a fortune, or a death in the family, would upset anyone else. Jack says there are no such things as trifles in a harmonious and well-proportioned life, and I suppose that's true to men of genius. Of course, I am rather a Philistine, and I grate on him at times—that is, I used to, but he says I have improved wonderfully. And so we are ridiculously happy, Jack and I."

Musgrave cast about vainly for an appropriate speech. Then he compromised with his conscience, and said: "Your husband is a very clever man."

"Isn't he?" She had flushed for pleasure at hearing him praised. Oh, yes, Anne loved Jack Charteris! There was no questioning that; it was written in her face, was vibrant in her voice as she spoke of him.

"Now, really, Rudolph, aren't his books wonderful? I don't appreciate them, of course, for I'm not clever, but I know you do. I don't see why men think him selfish. I know better. You have to live with Jack to really appreciate him. And every day I discover some new side of his character that makes him dearer to me. He's so clever—and so noble. Why, I remember—Well, before Jack made his first hit with *Astaroth's Lackey*, he lived with his sister. They hadn't any money, and, of course, Jack couldn't be expected to take a clerkship or anything like that, because business details make his head ache, poor boy. So, his sister taught school, and he lived with her. They were very happy—his sister simply adores him, and I am positively jealous of her sometimes—but, unfortunately, the bank in which she kept her money failed one day. I remember it was just before he asked me to marry him, and told me, in his dear, laughing manner, that he hadn't a penny in the world, and that we would have to live on bread and cheese and kisses. Of course, I had a plenty for us both, though, so we weren't really in danger of being reduced to that. Well, I wanted to make his sister an allowance. But Jack pointed out, with considerable reason, that one person could live very comfortably on an income that had formerly supported two. He said it wasn't right I should be burdened with the support of his family. Jack was so sensitive, you see, lest people might think he was making a mercenary marriage, and that his sister was profiting by it. Now, I call that one of the noblest things I ever heard of, for he is devotedly attached to his sister, and, naturally, it is a great grief to him to see her compelled to work for a living. His last book was dedicated to her, and the dedication is one of the most tender and pathetic things I ever read."

Musgrave was hardly conscious of what she was saying. She was not particularly intelligent, this handsome, cheery woman, but her voice, and the richness and sweetness of it, and the vitality of her laugh, contented his soul.

Anne was different; the knowledge came again to him quite simply that Anne was different, and in the nature of things must always be a little different from all other people—even Patricia Musgrave. He had no desire to tell Anne Charteris of this, no idea that it would affect in any way the tenor of his life. He merely accepted the fact that she was, after all, Anne Willoughby, and that her dear presence seemed, somehow, to strengthen and cheer and comfort and content beyond the reach of expression.

Yet Musgrave recognized her lack of cleverness, and liked and admired her none the less. A vision of Patricia arose—a vision of a dainty, shallow, Dresden-china face with a surprising quantity of vivid hair about it. Patricia was beautiful; and Patricia was clever, in her pinchbeck way. But Rudolph Musgrave doubted very much if her mocking eyes now ever softened into that brooding, sacred tenderness he had seen in Anne's eyes; and he likewise questioned if a hurried, happy thrill ran through Patricia's voice when Patricia spoke of her husband.

"You have unquestionably married an unusual man," Musgrave said. "I—by Jove, you know, I fancy my wife finds him almost as attractive as you do."

"Ah, Rudolph, I can't fancy anyone whom—whom you loved caring for anyone else. Don't I remember, sir, how irresistible you can be when you choose?"

Anne laughed, and raised plump hands to heaven.

"Really, though, women pursue him to a perfectly indecent extent. I have to watch over him carefully; not that I distrust him, of course, for—dear Jack!—he is so devoted to me, and cares so little for other women, that Joseph would seem in comparison only a depraved *roué*. But the *women*—why, Rudolph, there was an Italian countess at Rome—the impudent minx!—who actually made me believe—However, Jack explained all that, after I had made both a spectacle and a nuisance of myself, and he had behaved so nobly in the entire affair that for days afterwards I was positively limp with repentance. Then in Paris that flighty Mrs. Hardress—but he explained that, too. Some women are shameless, Rudolph," Mrs. Charteris concluded, and sighed her pity for them.

"Utterly so," Musgrave assented, gravely.

He was feeling a thought uncomfortable. To him the place had grown portentous. The sun was low, and the long shadows of the trees were black on the dim lawn. People were assembling for supper, and passing to and fro under low-hanging branches; and the gaily-colored gowns of the women glimmered through a faint blue haze like that with which Boucher and Watteau and Fragonard loved to veil, and thereby to make wistful, somehow, the antics of those fine parroquet-like manikins who figure in their *fêtes galantes.*

Inside the house, someone was playing an unpleasant sort of air on the piano—an air which was quite needlessly creepy and haunting and insistent. It all seemed like a grim bit out of a play. The tenderness and pride that shone in Anne's eyes as she boasted of her happiness troubled Rudolph Musgrave. He had a perfectly unreasonable desire to carry her away, by force, if necessary, and to protect her from clever people, and to buy things for her.

"So, I am an old, old married woman now, and—and I think in some ways I suit Jack better than a more brilliant person might. I am glad your wife has taken a fancy to him. And I want you to profit by her example. Jack says she is one of the most attractive women he ever met. He asked me today why I didn't do my hair like hers. She must make you very happy, Rudolph?"

"My wife," Colonel Musgrave said, "is in my partial opinion, a very clever and very beautiful woman."

"Yes; cleverness and beauty are sufficient to make any man happy, I suppose," Anne hazarded. "Jack says, though—*Are* cleverness and beauty the main things in life, Rudolph?"

"Undoubtedly," he protested.

"Now, that," she said, judicially, "shows the difference in men. Jack says a man loves a woman, not for her beauty or any other quality she possesses, but just because she is the woman he loves and can't help loving."

"Ah! I dare say that is the usual reason. Yes," said Colonel Musgrave,—"because she is the woman he loves and cannot help loving!"

Anne clapped her hands. "Ah, so I have penetrated your indifference at last, sir!"

Impulsively, she laid her hand upon his arm, and spoke with earnestness. "Dear Rudolph, I am so glad you've found the woman you can really love. Jack says there is only one possible woman in the world for each man, and that only in a month of Sundays does he find her."

"Yes." said Musgrave. He had risen, and was looking down in friendly fashion into her honest, lovely eyes. "Yes, there is only one possible woman. And—yes, I think I found her, Anne, some years ago."

III

Thus it befell that all passed smoothly with Rudolph Musgrave and Anne Charteris, with whom he was not in the least in love any longer (he reflected), although in the nature of things she must always seem to him a little different from all other people.

And it befell, too, that the following noon—this day being a Sunday, warm, clear, and somnolent—Anne Charteris and Rudolph Musgrave sat upon the lawn before Matocton, and little Roger Musgrave was with them. In fact, these two had been high-handedly press-ganged by this small despot to serve against an enemy then harassing his majesty's equanimity and by him, revilingly, designated as Nothing-to-do.

And so Anne made for Roger—as she had learned to do for her dead son—in addition to a respectable navy of paper boats, a vast number of "boxes" and "Nantucket sinks" and "picture frames" and "footballs." She had used up the greater part of a magazine before the imp grew tired of her novel accomplishments.

For as he invidiously observed, "I can make them for myself now, most as good as you, only I always tear the bottom of the boat when you pull it out, and my sinks are kind of wobbly. And besides, I've made up a story just like your husband gets money for doing. And if I had a quarter I would buy that green and yellow snake in the toy-store window and wiggle it at people and scare them into fits."

"Sonnikins," said Colonel Musgrave, "suppose you tell us the story, and then we will see if it is really worth a quarter, and try to save you from this unblushing mendicancy."

"Well, God bless Father and Mother and little cousins—Oh, no, that's what I say at night." Roger's voice now altered, assuming shrill singsong cadences. His pensive gravity would have appeared excessive if manifested by the Great Sphinx. "What I meant to say was that once upon a time when the Battle of Gettysburg was going on and houses were being robbed and burned, and my dear grandfather was being shot through the heart, a certain house, where the richest man in town lived, was having feast and merriment, never dreaming of any harm, or thinking of their little child Rachel, who was on the front porch watching the battle and screaming with joy at every man that fell dead. One dark-faced man was struck with a bullet and was hurt. He saw the child laughing at him and his heart was full of revenge. So that night, when all had gone to bed, the old dark-faced man went softly in the house and got the little girl and set the house on fire. And he carried her out in the mountains, and is that worth a quarter?"

"Good heavens, no!" said Anne. "How dare you leave us in such harrowing suspense?"

"Well, a whole lot more happened, because all the while Rachel was asleep. When she woke up, she did not know where under the sun she was. So she walked along for about an hour and came to a little village, and after a few minutes she came to a large rock, and guess who she met? She met her father, and when he saw her he hugged her so hard that when he got through she did not have any breath left in her. And they walked along, and after a while they came to the wood, and it was now about six o'clock, and it was very dark, and just then nine robbers jumped out from behind the trees, and they took a pistol and shot Rachel's father, and the child fainted. Her papa was dead, so she dug a hole and buried him, and went right back home. And of course that was all, and if I had that snake, I wouldn't try to scare you with it, father, anyhow."

So Colonel Musgrave gave his son a well-earned coin, as the colonel considered, and it having been decreed, "Now, father, *you* tell a story," obediently read aloud from a fat red-covered book. The tale was of the colonel's selecting, and it dealt with a shepherdess and a chimney-sweep.

"And so," the colonel perorated, "the little china people remained together, and were thankful for the rivet in grandfather's neck, and continued to love each other until they were broken to pieces—And the tale is a parable, my son. You will find that out some day. I wish you didn't have to."

"But is that all, father?"

"You will find it rather more than enough, sonnikins, when you begin to interpret. Yes, that is all. Only you are to remember always that they climbed to the very top of the chimney, where they could see the stars, before they decided to go back and live upon the parlor table under the brand-new looking-glass. For the stars are disconcertingly unconcerned when you have climbed to them, and so altogether unimpressed by your achievement that it is the nature of all china people to slink home again, precisely as your Rachel did—and as Mrs. Charteris will assure you."

"I?" said Anne. "Now, honestly, Rudolph, I was thinking you ought not to let him sit upon the grass, because he really has a cold. And if I were you, I would give him a good dose of castor-oil tonight. Some people give it in lemon-juice, I know, but I found with my boy that peppermint is rather less disagreeable. And you could easily send somebody over to the store at the station—"

Anne broke off short. "Was I being inadequate again? I am sorry, but with children you never know what a cold may lead to, and I really do not believe it good for him to sit in this damp grass."

"Sonnikins," said Rudolph Musgrave, "you had better climb up into my lap, before you and I are Podsnapped from the universe by the only embodiment of common-sense just now within our reach."

He patted the boy's head and latterly resumed: "I am afraid of you, Anne. Whenever I am imagining vain things or stitching romantic possibilities, like embroideries, about the fabric of my past, I always find the real you in my path, as undeniable as a gas-bill. I don't believe you ever dare to think, because there is no telling what it might lead to. You are simply unassailably armored by the courage of other people's convictions."

Her candid eyes met his over the boy's bright head. "And what in the world are you talking about?"

"I am lamenting. I am rending the air and beating my breast on account of your obstinate preference for being always in the right. I do wish you would endeavor to impersonate a human being a trifle more convincingly—"

But the great gong, booming out for luncheon, interrupted him at this point, and Colonel Musgrave was never permitted to finish his complaint against Anne's unimaginativeness.

IV

On that same Sunday morning, while Anne Charteris and Rudolph Musgrave contended with little Roger's boredom on the lawn before Matocton, Patricia and Charteris met by accident on the seventh terrace of the gardens. Patricia had mentioned casually at the breakfast-table that she intended to spend the forenoon on this terrace unsabbatically making notes for a paper on "The Symbolism of Dante," which she was to read before the Lichfield Woman's Club in October; but Mr. Charteris had not overheard her.

He was seated on the front porch, working out a somewhat difficult point in his new book, when it had first occurred to him that this particular terrace would be an inspiring and appropriate place in which to think the matter over, undisturbed, he said. And it was impossible he should have known that anyone was there, as the seventh terrace happens to be the only one that, being planted with beech-trees, is completely screened from observation. From the house, you cannot see anything that happens there.

It was a curious accident, though. It really seemed, now that Patricia had put an ending to their meetings in the maple-grove, Fate was conspiring to bring them together.

However, as Mr. Charteris pointed out, there could be no possible objection to this conspiracy, since they had decided that their friendship was to be of a purely platonic nature. It was a severe trial to him, he confessed, to be forced to put aside certain dreams he had had of the future—mad dreams, perhaps, but such as had seemed very dear and very plausible to his impractical artistic temperament.

Still, it heartened him to hope that their friendship—since it was to be no more—might prove a survival, or rather a veritable renaissance, of the beautiful old Greek spirit in such matters. And, though the blind chance that mismanaged the world had chained them to uncongenial, though certainly well-meaning, persons, this was no logical reason why he and Patricia should be deprived of the pleasures of intellectual intercourse. Their souls were too closely akin.

For Mr. Charteris admitted that his soul was Grecian to the core, and out of place and puzzled and very lonely in a sordid, bustling world; and he assured Patricia—she did not object if he called her Patricia?—that her own soul possessed all the beauty and purity and calm of an

Aphrodite sculptured by Phidias. It was such a soul as Horace might have loved, as Theocritus might have hymned in glad Greek song. Patricia flushed, and dissented somewhat.

"Frankly, *mon ami*," she said, "you are far too attractive for your company to be quite safe. You are such an adept in the nameless little attentions that women love—so profuse with lesser sugar-plums of speech and action—that after two weeks one's husband is really necessary as an antidote. Sugar-plums are good, but, like all palatable things, unwholesome. So I shall prescribe Rudolph's company for myself, to ward off an attack of moral indigestion. I am very glad he has come back—really glad," she added, conscientiously. "Poor old Rudolph! what between his interminable antiquities and those demented sections of the alphabet—What are those things, *mon ami*, that are always going up and down in Wall Street?"

"Elevators?" Mr. Charteris suggested.

"Oh, you jay-bird! I mean those N.P. 's and N.Y.C.'s and those other letters that are always having flurries and panics and passed dividends. They keep him incredibly busy."

And she sighed, tolerantly. Patricia had come within the last two weeks to believe that she was neglected, if not positively ill-treated, by her husband; and she had no earthly objection to Mr. Charteris thinking likewise. Her face expressed patient resignation now, as they walked under the close-matted foliage of the beech-trees, which made a pleasant, sun-flecked gloom about them.

Patricia removed her hat—the morning really was rather close—and paused where a sunbeam fell upon her copper-colored hair, and glorified her wistful countenance. She sighed once more, and added a finishing touch to the portrait of a *femme incomprise*.

"Pray, don't think, *mon ami*," she said very earnestly, "that I am blaming Rudolph! I suppose no wife can ever hope to have any part in her husband's inner life."

"Not in her own husband's, of course," said Charteris, cryptically.

"No, for while a woman gives her heart all at once, men crumble theirs away, as one feeds bread to birds—a crumb to this woman, a crumb to that—and such a little crumb, sometimes! And his wife gets what is left over."

"Pray, where did you read that?" said Charteris.

"I didn't read it anywhere. It was simply a thought that came to me," Patricia lied, gently. "But don't let's try to be clever. Cleverness is always a tax, but before luncheon it is an extortion. Personally, it makes me feel as if I had attended a welsh-rabbit supper the night before. Your wife must be very patient."

"My wife," cried Charteris, in turn resolved to screen an unappreciative mate, "is the most dear and most kind-hearted among the Philistines. And yet, at times, I grant you—"

"Oh, but, of course!" Patricia said impatiently. "I don't for a moment question that your wife is an angel."

"And why?" His eyebrows lifted, and he smiled.

"Why, wasn't it an angel," Patricia queried, all impishness now, "who kept the first man and woman out of paradise?"

"If—if I thought you meant that—!" he cried; and then he shrugged his shoulders. "My wife's virtues merit a better husband than Fate has accorded her. Anne is the best woman I have ever known."

Patricia was not unnaturally irritated. After all, one does not take the trouble to meet a man accidentally in a plantation of young beech-trees in order to hear him discourse of his wife's good qualities; and besides, Mr. Charteris was speaking in a disagreeably solemn manner, rather as if he fancied himself in a cathedral.

Therefore Patricia cast down her eyes again, and said:

"Men of genius are so rarely understood by their wives."

"We will waive the question of genius." Mr. Charteris laughed heartily, but he had flushed with pleasure.

"I suppose," he continued, pacing up and down with cat-like fervor, "that matrimony is always more or less of a compromise—like two convicts chained together trying to catch each other's gait. After a while, they succeed to a certain extent; the chain is still heavy, of course, but it does not gall them as poignantly as it used to do. And I fear the artistic temperament is not suited to marriage; its capacity for suffering is too great."

Mr. Charteris caught his breath in shuddering fashion, and he paused before Patricia. After a moment he grasped her by both wrists.

"We are chained fast enough, my lady," he cried, bitterly, "and our sentence is for life! There are green fields yonder, but our allotted place is here in the prison-yard. There is laughter yonder in the fields, and the scent of wild flowers floats in to us at times when we are weary, and the whispering trees sway their branches over the prison-wall, and their fruit is good to look on, and they hang within reach—ah, we might reach them very easily! But this is forbidden fruit, my lady; and it is not included in our wholesome prison-fare. And so don't think of it! We have been happy, you and I, for a little. We might—don't think of it! Don't dare think of it! Go back and help your husband drag his chain; it galls him as sorely as it does you. It galls us all. It is the heaviest chain was ever forged; but we do not dare shake it off!"

"I—oh, Jack, Jack, don't you dare to talk to me like that! We must be brave. We must be sensible." Patricia, regardless of her skirts, sat down upon the ground, and produced a pocket-handkerchief. "I—oh, what do you mean by making me so unhappy?" she demanded, indignantly.

"Ah, Patricia," he murmured, as he knelt beside her, "how can you hope to have a man ever talk to you in a sane fashion? You shouldn't have such eyes, Patricia! They are purple and fathomless like the ocean, and when a man looks into them too long his sanity grows weak, and sinks and drowns in their cool depths, and the man must babble out his foolish heart to you. Oh, but indeed, you shouldn't have such eyes, Patricia! They are dangerous, and to ask anybody to believe in their splendor is an insult to his intelligence, and besides, they are much too bright to wear in the morning. They are bad form, Patricia."

"We must be sensible," she babbled. "Your wife is here; my husband is here. And we—we aren't children or madmen, Jack dear. So we really must be sensible, I suppose. Oh, Jack," she cried, upon a sudden; "this isn't honorable!"

"Why, no! Poor little Anne!"

Mr. Charteris's eyes grew tender for a moment, because his wife, in a fashion, was dear to him. Then he laughed, very musically.

"And how can a man remember honor, Patricia, when the choice lies between honor and you? You shouldn't have such hair, Patricia! It is a net spun out of the raw stuff of fire and blood and of portentous sunsets; and its tendrils have curled around what little honor I ever boasted, and they hold it fast, Patricia. It is dishonorable to love you, but I cannot think of that when I am with you and hear you speak. And when I am not with you, just to remember that dear voice is enough to set my pulses beating faster. Oh, Patricia, you shouldn't have such a voice!"

Charteris broke off in speech. "'Scuse me for interruptin'," the old mulattress Virginia was saying, "but Mis' Pilkins sen' me say lunch raydy, Miss Patrisy."

Virginia seemed to notice nothing out-of-the-way. Having delivered her message, she went away quietly, her pleasant yellow face as imperturbable as an idol's. But Patricia shivered.

"She frightens me, *mon ami*. Yes, that old woman always gives me gooseflesh, and I don't know why—because she is as deaf as a post—and I simply can't get rid of her. She is a sort of symbol—she, and how many others, I wonder! . . . Oh, well, let's hurry."

So Mr. Charteris was never permitted to finish his complaint against Patricia's voice.

It was absolutely imperative they should be on time for luncheon; for, as Patricia pointed out, the majority of people are censorious and lose no opportunity for saying nasty things. They are even capable of sneering at a purely platonic friendship which is attempting to preserve the beautiful old Greek spirit.

She was chattering either of her plans for the autumn, or of Dante and the discovery of his missing cantos, or else of how abominably Bob Townsend had treated Rosalind Jemmett, and they had almost reached the upper terrace—little Roger, indeed, his red head blazing in the sunlight, was already sidling by shy instalments toward them—when Patricia moaned inconsequently and for no ascertainable cause fainted.

It was the first time for four years she had been guilty of such an indiscretion, she was shortly afterward explaining to various members of the Musgraves' house-party. It was the heat, no doubt. But since everybody insisted upon it, she would very willingly toast them in another bumper of aromatic spirits of ammonia.

"Just look at that, Rudolph! you've spilt it all over your coat sleeve. I do wish you would try to be a little less clumsy. Oh, well, I'm spruce as a new penny now. So let's all go to luncheon."

V

Patricia had not been in perfect health for a long while. It seemed to her, in retrospect, that ever since the agonies of little Roger's birth she had been the victim of what she described as "a sort of all-overishness." Then, too, as has been previously recorded, Patricia had been operated upon by surgeons, and more than once. . .

"Good Lord!" as she herself declared, "it has reached the point that when I see a turkey coming to the dinner-table to be carved I can't help treating it as an ingénue."

Yet for the last four years she had never fainted, until this. It disquieted her. Then, too, awoke faint pricking memories of certain symptoms. . . which she had not talked about. . .

Now they alarmed her; and in consequence she took the next morning's train to Lichfield.

VI

Mrs. Ashmeade, who has been previously quoted, now comes into the story. She is only an episode. Still, her intervention led to peculiar results—results, curiously enough, in which she was not in the least concerned. She simply comes into the story for a moment, and then goes out of it; but her part is an important one.

She is like the watchman who announces the coming of Agamemnon; Clytemnestra sharpens her ax at the news, and the fatal bath is prepared for the *anax andron*. The tragedy moves on; the house of Atreus falls, and the wrath of implacable gods bellows across the heavens; meanwhile, the watchman has gone home to have tea with his family, and we hear no more of him. There are any number of morals to this.

Mrs. Ashmeade comes into the story on the day Patricia went to Lichfield, and some weeks after John Charteris's arrival at Matocton. Since then, affairs had progressed in a not unnatural sequence. Mr. Charteris, as we have seen, attributed it to Fate; and, assuredly, there must be a special providence of some kind that presides over country houses—a freakish and whimsical providence, which hugely rejoices in confounding one's sense of time and direction.

Through its agency, people unaccountably lose their way in the simplest walks, and turn up late and embarrassed for luncheon. At the end of the evening, it brings any number of couples blinking out of the dark, with no idea the clock was striking more than half-past nine.

And it delights in sending one into the garden—in search of roses or dahlias or upas-trees or something of the sort, of course—and thereby causing one to encounter the most unlikely people, and really, quite the last person one would have thought of meeting, as all frequenters of house-party junketings will assure you. And thus is this special house-party providence responsible for a great number of marriages, and, it may be, for a large percentage of the divorce cases; for, if you desire very heartily to see anything of another member of a house-party, this lax-minded and easy-going providence will somehow always bring the event about in a specious manner, and without any apparent thought of the consequences.

And the Musgraves' house-party was no exception.

Mrs. Ashmeade, for reasons of her own, took daily note of this. The others were largely engrossed by their own affairs; they did not seriously concern themselves about the doings of their fellow-guests. And, besides, if John Charteris manifestly sought the company of Patricia Musgrave, her husband did not appear to be exorbitantly dissatisfied or angry or even lonely; and, be this as it might, the fact remained that Celia Reindan was at this time more than a little interested in Teddy Anstruther; and Felix Kennaston was undeniably very attentive to Kathleen Saumarez; and Tom Gelwix was quite certainly devoting the major part of his existence to sitting upon the beach with Rosalind Jemmett.

For, in Lichfield at all events, everyone's house has at least a pane or so of glass in it; and, if indiscriminate stone-throwing were ever to become the fashion, there is really no telling what damage might ensue. And so had Mrs. Ashmeade been a younger woman—had time and an adoring husband not rendered her as immune to an insanity *à deux* as any of us may hope to be upon this side of saintship or senility—why, Mrs. Ashmeade would most probably have remained passive, and Mrs. Ashmeade would never have come into this story at all.

As it was, she approached Rudolph Musgrave with a fixed purpose this morning as he smoked an after-breakfast cigarette on the front porch of Matocton. And,

"Rudolph," said Mrs. Ashmeade, "are you blind?"

"You mean—?" he asked, and he broke off, for he had really no conception of what she meant.

And Mrs. Ashmeade said, "I mean Patricia and Charteris. Did you think I was by any chance referring to the man in the moon and the Queen of Sheba?"

If ever amazement showed in a man's eyes, it shone now in Rudolph Musgrave's. After a little, the pupils widened in a sort of terror. So this was what Clarice Pendomer had been hinting at.

"Nonsense!" he cried. "Why—why, it is utter, preposterous, Bedlamite nonsense!" He caught his breath in wonder at the notion of such a jest, remembering a little packet of letters hidden in his desk. "It—oh, no, Fate hasn't quite so fine a sense of humor as that. The thing is incredible!" Musgrave laughed, and flushed. "I mean—"

"I don't think you need tell me what you mean," said Mrs. Ashmeade. She sat down in a large rocking-chair, and fanned herself, for the day was warm. "Of course, it is officious and presumptuous and disagreeable of me to meddle. I don't mind your thinking that. But Rudolph, don't make the mistake of thinking that Fate ever misses a chance of humiliating us by showing how poor are our imaginations. The gipsy never does. She is a posturing mountebank, who thrives by astounding humanity."

Mrs. Ashmeade paused, and her eyes were full of memories, and very wise.

"I am only a looker-on at the tragic farce that is being played here," she continued, after a little, "but lookers-on, you know, see most of the game. They are not playing fairly with you, Rudolph. When people set about an infringement of the Decalogue they owe it to their self-respect to treat with Heaven as a formidable antagonist. To mark the cards is not enough. They are not playing fairly, my dear, and you ought to know it."

He walked up and down the porch once or twice, with his hands behind him; then he stopped before Mrs. Ashmeade, and smiled down at her. Without, many locusts shrilled monotonously.

"No, I do not think you are officious or meddling or anything of the sort, I think you are one of the best and kindest-hearted women in the world. But—bless your motherly soul, Polly! the thing is utterly preposterous. Of course, Patricia is young, and likes attention, and it pleases her to have men admire her. That, Polly, is perfectly natural. Why, you wouldn't expect her to sit around under the trees, and read poetry with her own husband, would you? We have been married far too long for that, Patricia and I. She thinks me rather prosy and stupid at times, poor girl, because—well, because, in point of fact, I am. But, at the bottom of her heart—Oh, it's preposterous! We are the best friends in the world, I tell you! It is simply that she and Jack have a great deal in common—"

"You don't understand John Charteris. I do," said Mrs. Ashmeade, placidly. "Charteris is simply a baby with a vocabulary. His moral standpoint is entirely that of infancy. It would be ludicrous to describe him as selfish, because he is selfishness incarnate. I sometimes believe it is the only characteristic the man possesses. He reaches out his hand and takes whatever he wants, just as a baby would, quite simply, and as a matter of course. He wants your wife now, and he is reaching out his hand to take her. He probably isn't conscious of doing anything especially wrong; he is always so plausible in whatever he does that he ends by deceiving himself, I suppose. For he is always plausible. It is worse than useless to argue any matter with him, because he invariably ends by making you feel as if you had been caught stealing a hat. The only argument that would get the better of John Charteris is knocking him down, just as spanking is the only argument which ever gets the better of a baby. Yes, he is very like a baby—thoroughly selfish and thoroughly dependent on other people; only, he is a clever baby who exaggerates his own helplessness in order to appeal to women. He has a taste for women. And women naturally like him, for he impresses them as an irresponsible child astray in an artful and designing world. They want to protect him. Even I do, at times. It is really maternal, you know; we would infinitely prefer for him to be soft and little, so that we could pick him up, and cuddle him. But as it is, he is dangerous. He believes whatever he tells himself, you see."

Her voice died away, and Mrs. Ashmeade fanned herself in the fashion addicted by perturbed women who, nevertheless, mean to have their say out—slowly and impersonally, and quite as if she was fanning someone else through motives of charity.

"I don't question," Musgrave said, at length, "that Jack is the highly estimable character you describe. But—oh, it is all nonsense, Polly!" he cried, with petulance, and with a tinge—if but the merest nuance—of conviction lacking in his voice.

The fan continued its majestic sweep from the shade into the sunlight, and back again into the shadow. Without, many locusts shrilled monotonously.

"Rudolph, I know what you meant by saying that Fate hadn't such a fine sense of humor."

"My dear madam, it was simply thrown out, in the heat of conversation—as an axiom—"

For a moment the fan paused; then went on as before. It was never charged against Pauline Ashmeade, whatever her shortcomings, that she was given to unnecessary verbiage.

Colonel Musgrave was striding up and down, divided between a disposition to swear at the universe at large and a desire to laugh at it. Somehow, it did not occur to him to doubt what she had told him. He comprehended now that, chafing under his indebtedness in the affair of Mrs. Pendomer, Charteris would most naturally retaliate by making love to his benefactor's wife, because the colonel also knew John Charteris. And for the rest, it was useless to struggle against a Fate that planned such preposterous and elaborate jokes; one might more rationally depend on Fate to work out some both ludicrous and horrible solution, he reflected, remembering a little packet of letters hidden in his desk.

Nevertheless, he paused after a while, and laughed, with a tolerable affectation of mirth.

"I say—I—and what in heaven's name, Polly, prompted you to bring me this choice specimen of a mare's-nest?"

"Because I am fond of you, I suppose. Isn't one always privileged to be disagreeable to one's friends? We have been friends a long while, you know."

Mrs. Ashmeade was looking out over the river now, but she seemed to see a great way, a very great way, beyond its glaring waters, and to be rather uncertain as to whether what she beheld there was of a humorous or pathetic nature.

"Rudolph, do you remember that evening—the first summer that I knew you—at Fortress Monroe, when we sat upon the pier so frightfully late, and the moon rose out of the bay, and made a great, solid-looking, silver path that led straight over the rim of the world, and you talked to me about—about what, now?"

"Oh, yes, yes!—I remember perfectly! One of the most beautiful evenings I ever saw. I remember it quite distinctly. I talked—I—and what, in the Lord's name, did I talk about, Polly?"

"Ah, men forget! A woman never forgets when she is really friends with a man. I know now you were telling me about Anne Charteris, for you have been in love with her all your life, Rudolph, in your own particular half-hearted and dawdling fashion. Perhaps that is why you have had so many affairs. You plainly found the run of women so unimportant that it put every woman on her pride to prove she was different. Yes, I remember. But that night I thought you were trying to make love to me, and I was disappointed in you, and—yes, rather pleased. Women are all vain and perfectly inconsistent. But then, girl-children always take after their fathers."

Mrs. Ashmeade rose from her chair. Her fan shut with a snap.

"You were a dear boy, Rudolph, when I first knew you—and what I liked was that you never made love to me. Of all the boys I have known and helped to form, you were the only sensible one—the only one who never presumed. That was rather clever of you, Rudolph. It would have been ridiculous, for even arithmetically I am older than you.

"Wouldn't it have been ridiculous, Rudolph?" she demanded, suddenly.

"Not in the least," Musgrave protested, in courteous wise. "You—why, Polly, you were a wonderfully handsome woman. Any boy—"

"Oh, yes!—I was. I'm not now, am I, Rudolph?" Mrs. Ashmeade threw back her head and laughed naturally. "Ah, dear boy that was, it is unfair, isn't it, for an old woman to seize upon you in this fashion, and insist on your making love to her? But I will let you off. You don't have to do it."

She caught her skirts in her left hand, preparatory to going, and her right hand rested lightly on his arm. She spoke in a rather peculiar voice.

"Yes," she said, "the boy was a very, very dear boy, and I want the man to be equally brave and—sensible."

Musgrave stared after her. "I wonder—I wonder—? Oh, no, that couldn't be," he said, and wearily.

"There must be some preposterous situations that don't come about."

And afterward he strolled across the lawn, where the locusts were shrilling, as if in a stubborn prediction of something which was inevitable, and he meditated upon a great number of things. There were a host of fleecy little clouds in the sky. He looked up at them, interrogatively.

And then he smiled and shook his head.

"Yet I don't know," said he; "for I am coming to the conclusion that the world is run on an extremely humorous basis."

And oddly enough, it was at the same moment that Patricia—in Lichfield—reached the same conclusion.

PART VII

YOKED

"We are as time moulds us, lacking wherewithal
To shape out nobler fortunes or contend
Against all-patient Fates, who may not mend
The allotted pattern of things temporal
Or alter it a jot or e'er let fall
A single stitch thereof, until at last
The web and its drear weavers be overcast
And predetermined darkness swallow all.

"They have ordained for us a time to sing,
A time to love, a time wherein to tire
Of all spent songs and kisses; caroling
Such elegies as buried dreams require,
Love now departs, and leaves us shivering
Beside the embers of a burned-out fire."

—Paul Vanderhoffen. *Egeria Answers*

I

The doctor's waiting-room smelt strongly of antiseptics. That was Patricia's predominating thought as she wandered aimlessly about the apartment. She fingered its dusty furniture. She remembered afterward the steel-engraving of Jefferson Davis and his Cabinet, with General Lee explaining some evidently important matter to those attentive and unhumanly stiff politicians; and she remembered, too, how in depicting one statesman, who unavoidably sat with his back to the spectator, the artist had exceeded anatomical possibilities in order to obtain a recognizable full-faced portrait. Yet at the time this picture had not roused her conscious attention.

She went presently to the long table austerely decorated with two rows of magazines, each partly covered by its neighbor, just as shingles are placed. The arrangement irritated her unreasonably. She wanted to disarrange these dog-eared pamphlets, to throw them on the floor, to destroy them. She wondered how many other miserable people had tried to read these hateful books while they waited in this abominable room.

She started when the door of the consultation-room opened. The doctor was patting the silk glove of a harassed-looking woman in black as he escorted her to the outer door, and was assuring her that everything was going very well indeed, and that she was not to worry, and so on.

And presently he spoke with Patricia, for a long while, quite levelly, of matters which it is not suitable to record. Discreet man that he was, Wendell Pemberton could not entirely conceal his wonder that Patricia should have remained so long in ignorance of her condition. He spoke concerning malformation and functional weaknesses and, although obscurely because of the bugbear of professional courtesy, voiced his opinion that Patricia had not received the most adroit medical treatment at the time of little Roger's birth.

She was dividedly conscious of a desire to laugh and of the notion that she must remain outwardly serious, because though this horrible Pemberton man was talking abject nonsense, she would presently be having him as a dinner-guest.

But what if he were not talking nonsense? The possibility, considered, roused a sensation of falling through infinity.

"Yes, yes," Patricia civilly assented. "These young doctors have taken this out of me, and that out of me, as you might take the works out of a watch. And it has done no good; and they were mistaken in their first diagnoses, because what they took for true osteomalacia was only—— Would you mind telling me again? Oh, yes; I had only a pseudo-osteomalacic rhachitic pelvis, to begin with. To think of anybody's being mistaken about a simple little trouble like that! And I suppose I was just born with it, like my mother and all those other luckless women with Musgrave blood in them?"

"Fehling and Schliephake at least consider this variety of pelvic anomaly to be congenital in the majority of cases. But, without going into the question of heredity at all, I think it only, fair to tell you, Mrs. Musgrave—" And Pemberton went on talking.

Neither of the two showed any emotion.

The doctor went on talking. Patricia did not listen. The man was talking, she comprehended, but to her his words seemed blurred and indistinguishable. "Like a talking-machine when it isn't wound up enough," she decided.

Subconsciously Patricia was thinking, "You have two big beads of perspiration on your nose, and if I were to allude to the fact you would very probably die of embarrassment."

Aloud Patricia said: "You mean, then, that, to cap it all, a functional disorder of my heart has become organic, so that I would inevitably die under another operation? or even at a sudden shock? And that particular operation is now the solitary chance of saving my life! The dilemma is neat, isn't it? How God must laugh at the jokes He contrives," said Patricia. "I wish that I could laugh. And I will. I don't care whether you think me a reprobate or not, Dr. Pemberton, I want a good stiff drink of whiskey—the Musgrave size."

He gave it to her.

II

Patricia had as yet an hour to spend in Lichfield before her train left. She passed it in the garden of her own home, where she had first seen Rudolph Musgrave and he had fought with Pevensey. All that seemed very long ago.

The dahlia leaves, she noticed, were edged with yellow. She must look to it that the place was more frequently watered; and that the bulbs were dug up in September. Next year she meant to set the dahlias thinly, like a hedge. . .

"Oh, yes, I meant to. Only I won't be alive next year," she recollected.

She went about the garden to see if Ned had weeded out the wild-pea vines—a pest which had invaded the trim place lately. Only a few of the intruders remained, burnt-out and withered as they are annually by the mid-summer sun. There would be no more fight until next April.

"Oh, and I have prayed to You, I have always tried to do what You wanted, and I never asked You to let me be born locked up in a good-for-nothing Musgrave body! And You won't even let me see a wild-pea vine again! That isn't much to ask, I think. But You won't let me do it. You really do have rather funny notions about Your jokes."

She began to laugh.

"Oh, very well!" Patricia said aloud. "It is none of my affair that You elect to run Your world on an extremely humorous basis."

She was at Matocton in good time for luncheon.

III

Colonel Musgrave had a brief interview with his wife after luncheon. He began with quiet remonstrance, and ended with an unheard extenuation of his presumption. Patricia's speech on this occasion was of an unfettered and heady nature.

"You ought to be ashamed of yourself," she said, when she had finally paused for breath, and had wiped away her tears, and had powdered her nose, viciously, "to bully a weak and defenseless woman in this way. I dare say everybody in the house has heard us—brawling and squabbling just like a hod-carrier and his wife. What's that? You haven't said a word for fifteen minutes? Oh, la, la, la! well, I don't care. Anyhow, I have, and I am perfectly sure they heard me, and I am sure I don't care in the least, and it's all your fault, anyway. Oh, but you have an abominable nature, Rudolph—a mean and cruel and suspicious nature. Your bald-headed little Charteris is nothing whatever to me; and I would have been quite willing to give him up if you had spoken to me in a decent manner about it. You only *said*—? I don't care what you said; and besides, if you did speak to me in a decent manner, it simply shows that your thoughts were so horrid and vulgar that even you weren't so abandoned as to dare to put them into words. Very well, then, I won't be seen so much with him in future. I realize you are quite capable of beating me if I don't give way to your absurd prejudices. Yes, you are, Rudolph; you're just the sort of man to take pleasure in beating a woman. After the exhibition of temper you've given this afternoon, I believe you are capable of anything. Hand me that parasol! Don't keep on talking to me; for I don't wish to hear anything you have to say. You're simply driving me to my grave with your continual nagging and abuse and fault-finding. I'm sure I wish I were dead as much as you do. Is my hat on straight? How do you expect me to see into that mirror if you stand directly in front of it? There! not content with robbing me of every pleasure in life, I verily believe you were going to let me go downstairs with my hat cocked over one ear. And don't you snort and look at me like that. I'm not going to meet Mr. Charteris. I'm going driving with Felix Kennaston; he asked me at luncheon. I suppose you'll object to him next; you object to all my friends. Very well! Now you've made me utterly miserable for the entire afternoon, and I'm sure I hope you are satisfied."

There was a rustle of skirts, and the door slammed.

IV

Colonel Musgrave went to his own room, where he spent an interval in meditation. He opened his desk and took out a small packet of papers, some of which he read listlessly. How curiously life re-echoed itself! he reflected, for here, again, were castby love-letters potent to breed mischief; and his talk with Polly Ashmeade had been peculiarly reminiscent of his more ancient talk with Clarice Pendomer. Everything that happened seemed to have happened before.

But presently he shook his head, sighing. Chance had put into his hands a weapon, and a formidable weapon, it seemed to him, but the colonel did not care to use it. He preferred to strike with some less grimy cudgel.

Then he rang for one of the servants, questioned him, and was informed that Mr. Charteris had gone down to the beach just after luncheon. A moment later, Colonel Musgrave was walking through the gardens in this direction.

As he came to the thicket which screens the beach, he called Charteris's name loudly, in order to ascertain his whereabouts. And the novelist's voice answered—yet not at once, but after a brief silence. It chanced that, at this moment, Musgrave had come to a thin place in the thicket, and could plainly see Mr. Charteris; he was concealing some white object in the hollow of a log that lay by the river. A little later, Musgrave came out upon the beach, and found Charteris seated upon the same log, an open book upon his knees, and looking back over his shoulder wonderingly.

"Oh," said John Charteris, "so it was you, Rudolph? I could not imagine who it was that called."

"Yes—I wanted a word with you, Jack."

Now, there are five little red-and-white bath-houses upon the beach at Matocton; the nearest of them was some thirty feet from Mr. Charteris. It might have been either imagination or the prevalent breeze, but Musgrave certainly thought he heard a door closing. Moreover, as he walked around the end of the log, he glanced downward as in a casual manner, and perceived a protrusion which bore an undeniable resemblance to the handle of a parasol. Musgrave whistled, though, at the bottom of his heart, he was not surprised; and then, he sat down upon the log, and for a moment was silent.

"A beautiful evening," said Mr. Charteris.

Musgrave lighted a cigarette.

"Jack, I have something rather difficult to say to you—yes, it is deuced difficult, and the sooner it is over the better. I—why, confound it all, man! I want you to stop making love to my wife."

Mr. Charteris's eyebrows rose. "Really, Colonel Musgrave—" he began, coolly.

"Now, you are about to make a scene, you know," said Musgrave, raising his hand in protest, "and we are not here for that. We are not going to tear any passions to tatters; we are not going to rant; we are simply going to have a quiet and sensible talk. We don't happen to be characters in a romance; for you aren't Lancelot, you know, and I am not up to the part of Arthur by a great deal. I am not angry, I am not jealous, nor do I put the matter on any high moral grounds. I simply say it won't do—no, hang it, it won't do!"

"I dare not question you are an authority in such matters," said John Charteris, sweetly—"since among many others, Clarice Pendomer is near enough to be an obtainable witness."

Colonel Musgrave grimaced. "But what a gesture!" he thought, half-enviously. Jack Charteris, quite certainly, meant to make the most of the immunity Musgrave had purchased for him. None the less, Musgrave had now his cue. Patricia must be listening.

And so what Colonel Musgrave said was: "Put it that a burnt child dreads the fire—is that a reason he should not warn his friends against it?"

"At least," said Charteris at length, "you are commendably frank. I appreciate that, Rudolph. I honestly appreciate the fact you have come to me, not as the husband of that fiction in which kitchen-maids delight, breathing fire and speaking balderdash, but as one sensible man to another. Let us be frank, then; let us play with the cards upon the table. You have charged me with loving your wife; and I answer you frankly—I do. She does me the honor to return this affection. What, then, Rudolph?"

Musgrave blew out a puff of smoke. "I don't especially mind," he said, slowly. "According to tradition, of course, I ought to spring at your throat with a smothered curse. But, as a matter of fact, I don't see why I should be irritated. No, in common reason," he added, upon consideration, "I am only rather sorry for you both."

Mr. Charteris sprang to his feet, and walked up and down the beach. "Ah, you hide your feelings well," he cried, and his laughter was a trifle unconvincing and a bit angry. "But it is unavailing with me. I know! I know the sick and impotent hatred of me that is seething in your heart; and I feel for you the pity you pretend to entertain toward me. Yes, I pity you. But what would you have? Frankly, while in many ways an estimable man, you are no fit mate for Patricia. She has the sensitive, artistic temperament, poor girl; and only we who are cursed with it can tell you what its possession implies. And you—since frankness is the order of the day, you know—well, you impress me as being a trifle inadequate. It is not your fault, perhaps, but the fact remains that you have never amounted to anything personally. You have simply traded upon the accident of being born a Musgrave of Matocton. In consequence you were enabled to marry Patricia's money, just as the Musgraves of Matocton always marry some woman who is able to support them. Ah, but it was her money you married, and not Patricia! Any community of interest between you was impossible, and is radically impossible. Your marriage was a hideous mistake, just as mine was. For you are starving her soul, Rudolph, just as Anne has starved mine. And now, at last, when Patricia and I have seen our single chance of happiness, we cannot—no! we cannot and we will not—defer to any outworn tradition or to fear of Mrs. Grundy's narrow-minded prattle!"

Charteris swept aside the dogmas of the world with an indignant gesture of somewhat conscious nobility; and he turned to his companion in an attitude of defiance.

Musgrave was smiling. He smoked and seemed to enjoy his cigarette.

The day was approaching sunset. The sun, a glowing ball of copper, hung low in the west over a rampart of purple clouds, whose heights were smeared with red. A slight, almost imperceptible, mist rose from the river, and, where the horizon should have been, a dubious cloudland prevailed. Far to the west were orange-colored quiverings upon the stream's surface, but, nearer, the river dimpled with silver-tipped waves; and, at their feet, the water grew transparent, and splashed over the sleek, brown sand, and sucked back, leaving a curved line of bubbles which, one by one, winked, gaped and burst. There was a drowsy peacefulness in the air; behind them, among the beeches, were many stealthy wood-sounds; and, at long intervals, a sleepy, peevish twittering went about the nested trees.

In Colonel Musgrave's face, the primal peace was mirrored.

"May I ask," said he at length, "what you propose doing?"

Mr. Charteris answered promptly. "I, of course, propose," said he, "to ask Patricia to share the remainder of my life."

"A euphemism, as I take it, for an elopement. I hardly thought you intended going so far."

"Rudolph!" cried Charteris, drawing himself to his full height—and he was not to blame for the fact that it was but five-feet-six—"I am, I hope, an honorable man! I cannot eat your salt and steal your honor. So I loot openly, or not at all."

The colonel shrugged his shoulders.

"I presuppose you have counted the cost—and estimated the necessary breakage?"

"True love," the novelist declared, in a hushed, sweet voice, "is above such considerations."

"I think," said Musgrave slowly, "that any love worthy of the name will always appraise the cost—to the woman. It is of Patricia I am thinking."

"She loves me," Charteris murmured. He glanced up and laughed. "Upon my soul, you know, I cannot help thinking the situation a bit farcical—you and I talking over matters in this fashion. But I honestly believe the one chance of happiness for any of us hinges on Patricia and me chucking the whole affair, and bolting."

"No! it won't do—no, hang it, Jack, it will not do!" Musgrave glanced toward the bath-house, and he lifted his voice. "I am not considering you in the least—and under the circumstances, you could hardly expect me to. It is of Patricia I am thinking. I haven't made her altogether happy. Our marriage was a mating of incongruities—and possibly you are justified in calling it a mistake. Yet, day in and day out, I think we get along as well together as do most couples; and it is wasting time to cry over spilt milk. Instead, it rests with us, the two men who love her, to decide what is best for Patricia. It is she and only she we must consider."

"Ah, you are right!" said Charteris, and his eyes grew tender. "She must have what she most desires; and all must be sacrificed to that." He turned and spoke as simply as a child. "Of course, you know, I shall be giving up a great deal for love of her, but—I am willing."

Musgrave looked at him for a moment. "H'm doubtless," he assented. "Why, then, we won't consider the others. We will not consider your wife, who—who worships you. We won't consider the boy. I, for my part, think it is a mother's duty to leave an unsullied name to her child, but, probably, my ideas are bourgeois. We won't consider Patricia's relatives, who, perhaps, will find it rather unpleasant. In short, we must consider no one save Patricia."

"Of course, one cannot make an omelet without breaking a few eggs."

"No; the question is whether it is absolutely necessary to make the omelet. I say no."

"And I," quoth Charteris smiling gently, "say yes."

"For Patricia," Musgrave went on, as in meditation, but speaking very clearly, "it means giving up—everything. It means giving up her friends and the life to which she is accustomed; it means being ashamed to face those who were formerly her friends. We, the world, our world of Lichfield, I mean—are lax enough as to the divorce question, heaven knows, but we can't pardon immorality when coupled with poverty. And you would be poor, you know. Your books are tremendously clever, Jack, but—as I happen to know—the proceeds from them would not support two people in luxury; and Patricia has nothing. That is a sordid detail, of course, but it is worth considering. Patricia would never be happy in a three-pair back."

Mr. Charteris was frankly surprised. "Patricia has—nothing?"

"Bless your soul, of course not! Her father left the greater part of his money to our boy, you know. Most of it is still held in trust for our boy, who is named after him. Not a penny of it belongs to Patricia, and even I cannot touch anything but a certain amount of interest."

Mr. Charteris looked at the colonel with eyes that were sad and hurt and wistful. "I am perfectly aware of your reason for telling me this," he said, candidly. "I know I have always been thought a mercenary man since my marriage. At that time I fancied myself too much in love with Anne to permit any sordid considerations of fortune to stand in the way of our union. Poor Anne! she little knows what sacrifices I have made for her! She, too, would be dreadfully unhappy if I permitted her to realize that our marriage was a mistake."

"God help her—yes!" groaned Musgrave.

"And as concerns Patricia, you are entirely right. It would be hideously unfair to condemn her to a life of comparative poverty. My books sell better than you think, Rudolph, but still an author cannot hope to attain affluence so long as he is handicapped by any reverence for the English language. Yes, I was about to do Patricia a great wrong. I rejoice that you have pointed out my selfishness. For I have been abominably selfish. I confess it."

"I think so," assented Musgrave, calmly. "But, then, my opinion is, naturally, rather prejudiced."

"Yes, I can understand what Patricia must mean to you"—Mr. Charteris sighed, and passed his hand over his forehead in a graceful fashion,—"and I, also, love her far too dearly to imperil her happiness. I think that heaven never made a woman more worthy to be loved. And I had hoped—ah, well, after all, we cannot utterly defy society! Its prejudices, however unfounded, must be respected. What would you have? This dunderheaded giantess of a Mrs. Grundy condemns me to be miserable, and I am powerless. The utmost I can do is to refrain from whining over the unavoidable. And, Rudolph, you have my word of honor that henceforth I shall bear in mind more constantly my duty toward one of my best and oldest friends. I have not dealt with you quite honestly. I confess it, and I ask your pardon." Mr. Charteris held out his hand to seal the compact.

"Word of honor?" queried Colonel Musgrave, with an odd quizzing sort of fondness for the little novelist, as the colonel took the proffered hand. "Why, then, that is settled, and I am glad of it. I told you, you know, it wouldn't do. See you at supper, I suppose?"

And Rudolph Musgrave glanced at the bath-house, turned on his heel, and presently plunged into the beech plantation, whistling cheerfully. The effect of the melody was somewhat impaired by the apparent necessity of breaking off, at intervals, in order to smile.

The comedy had been admirably enacted, he considered, on both sides; and he did not object to Jack Charteris's retiring with all the honors of war.

V

The colonel had not gone far, however, before he paused, thrust both hands into his trousers' pockets, and stared down at the ground for a matter of five minutes.

Musgrave shook his head. "After all," said he, "I can't trust them. Patricia is too erratic and too used to having her own way. Jack will try to break off with her now, of course; but Jack, where women are concerned, is as weak as water. It is not a nice thing to do, but—well! one must fight fire with fire."

Thereupon, he retraced his steps. When he had come to the thin spot in the thicket, Rudolph Musgrave left the path, and entered the shrubbery. There he composedly sat down in the shadow of a small cedar. The sight of his wife upon the beach in converse with Mr. Charteris did not appear to surprise Colonel Musgrave.

Patricia was speaking quickly. She held a bedraggled parasol in one hand. Her husband noted, with a faint thrill of wonder, that, at times, and in a rather unwholesome, elfish way, Patricia was actually beautiful. Her big eyes glowed; they flashed with changing lights as deep waters glitter in the sun; her copper-colored hair seemed luminous, and her cheeks flushed, arbutus-like. The soft, white stuff that gowned her had the look of foam; against the gray sky she seemed a freakish spirit in the act of vanishing. For sky and water were all one lambent gray by this. In the west was a thin smear of orange; but, for the rest, the world was of a uniform and gleaming gray. She and Charteris stood in the heart of a great pearl.

"Ah, believe me," she was saying, "Rudolph isn't an ophthalmic bat. But God keep us all respectable! is Rudolph's notion of a sensible morning-prayer. So he just preferred to see nothing and bleat out edifying axioms. That is one of his favorite tricks. No, it was a comedy for my benefit, I tell you. He will allow a deal for the artistic temperament, no doubt, but he doesn't suppose you fetch along a white-lace parasol when you go to watch a sunset—especially a parasol he gave me last month."

"Indeed," protested Mr. Charteris, "he saw nothing. I was too quick for him."

She shrugged her shoulders. "I saw him looking at it. Accordingly, I paid no attention to what he said. But you—ah, Jack, you were splendid! I suppose we shall have to elope at once now, though?"

Charteris gave her no immediate answer. "I am not quite sure, Patricia, that your husband is not—to a certain extent—in the right. Believe me, he did not know you were about. He approached me in a perfectly sensible manner, and exhibited commendable self-restraint; he has played a difficult part to admiration. I could not have done it better myself. And it is not for us who have been endowed with gifts denied to Rudolph, to reproach him for lacking the finer perceptions and sensibilities of life. Yet, I must admit that, for the time, I was a little hurt by his evident belief that we would allow our feeling for each other—which is rather beyond his comprehension, isn't it, dear?—to be coerced by mercenary considerations."

"Oh, Rudolph is just a jackass-fool, anyway." She was not particularly interested in the subject.

"He can't help that, you know," Charteris reminded her, gently; then, he asked, after a little: "I suppose it is all true?"

"That what is true?"

"About your having no money of your own?" He laughed, but she could see how deeply he had been pained by Musgrave's suspicions. "I ask, because, as your husband has discovered, I am utterly sordid, my lady, and care only for your wealth."

"Ah, how can you expect a man like that to understand—you? Why, Jack, how ridiculous in you to be hurt by what the brute thinks! You're as solemn as an owl, my dear. Yes, it's true enough. My father was not very well pleased with us—and that horrid will—Ah, Jack, Jack, how grotesque, how characteristic it was, his thinking such things would influence you—you, of all men, who scarcely know what money is!"

"It was even more grotesque I should have been pained by his thinking it," Charteris said, sadly. "But what would you have? I am so abominably in love with you that it seemed a sort of desecration when the man lugged your name into a discussion of money-matters. It really did. And then, besides—ah, my lady, you know that I would glory in the thought that I had given up all for you. You know, I think, that I would willingly work my fingers to the bone just that I might possess you always. So I had dreamed of love in a cottage—an idyl of blissful poverty, where Cupid contents himself with crusts and kisses, and mocks at the proverbial wolf on the doorstep. And I give you my word that until today I had not suspected how blindly selfish I have been! For poor old prosaic Rudolph is in the right, after all. Your delicate, tender beauty must not be dragged down to face the unlovely realities and petty deprivations and squalid makeshifts of such an existence as ours would be. True, I would glory in them—ah, luxury and riches mean little to me, my dear, and I can conceive of no greater happiness than to starve with you. But true love knows how to sacrifice itself. Your husband was right; it would not be fair to you, Patricia."

"You—you are going to leave me?"

"Yes; and I pray that I may be strong enough to relinquish you forever, because your welfare is more dear to me than my own happiness. No, I do not pretend that this is easy to do. But when my misery is earned by serving you I prize my misery." Charteris tried to smile. "What would you have? I love you," he said, simply.

"Ah, my dear!" she cried.

Musgrave's heart was sick within him as he heard the same notes in her voice that echoed in Anne's voice when she spoke of her husband. This was a new Patricia; her speech was low and gentle now, and her eyes held a light Rudolph Musgrave had not seen there for a long while.

"Ah, my dear, you are the noblest man I have ever known; I wish we women could be like men. But, oh, Jack, Jack, don't be quixotic! I can't give you up, my dear—that would never be for my good. Think how unhappy I have been all these years; think how Rudolph is starving my soul! I want to be free, Jack; I want to live my own life,—for at least a month or so—"

Patricia shivered here. "But none of us is sure of living for a month. You've shown me a glimpse of what life might be; don't let me sink back into the old, humdrum existence from a foolish sense of honor! I tell you, I should go mad! I mean to have my fling while I can get it. And I mean to have it with you, Jack—just you! I don't fear poverty. You could write some more wonderful books. I could work, too, Jack dear. I—I could teach music—or take in washing—or something, anyway. Lots of women support themselves, you know. Oh, Jack, we would be so happy! Don't be honorable and brave and disagreeable, Jack dear!"

For a moment Charteris was silent. The nostrils of his beak-like nose widened a little, and a curious look came into his face. He discovered something in the sand that interested him.

"After all," he demanded, slowly, "is it necessary—to go away—to be happy?"

"I don't understand." Her hand lifted from his arm; then quick remorse smote her, and it fluttered back, confidingly.

Charteris rose to his feet. "It is, doubtless, a very spectacular and very stirring performance to cast your cap over the wind-mill in the face of the world; but, after all, is it not a bit foolish, Patricia? Lots of people manage these things—more quietly."

"Oh, Jack!" Patricia's face turned red, then white, and stiffened in a sort of sick terror. She was a frightened Columbine in stone. "I thought you cared for me—really, not—that way."

Patricia rose and spoke with composure. "I think I'll go back to the house, Mr. Charteris. It's a bit chilly here. You needn't bother to come."

Then Mr. Charteris laughed—a choking, sobbing laugh. He raised his hands impotently toward heaven. "And to think," he cried, "to think that a man may love a woman with his whole heart—with all that is best and noblest in him—and she understand him so little!"

"I do not think I have misunderstood you," Patricia said, in a crisp voice. "Your proposition was very explicit. I—am sorry. I thought I had found one thing in the world which I would regret to leave—"

"And you really believed that I could sully the great love I bear you by stooping to—that! You really believed that I would sacrifice to you my home life, my honor, my prospects—all that a man can give—without testing the quality of your love! You did not know that I spoke to try you—you actually did not know! Eh, but yours is a light nature, Patricia! I do not reproach you, for you are only as your narrow Philistine life has made you. Yet I had hoped better things of you, Patricia. But you, who pretend to care for me, have leaped at your first opportunity to pain me—and, if it be any comfort to you, I confess you have pained me beyond words." And he sank down on the log, and buried his face in his hands.

She came to him—it was pitiable to see how she came to him, laughing and sobbing all in one breath—and knelt humbly by his side, and raised a grieved, shamed, penitent face to his.

"Forgive me!" she wailed; "oh, forgive me!"

"You have pained me beyond words, Patricia," he repeated. He was not angry—only sorrowful and very much hurt.

"Ah, Jack! dear Jack, forgive me!"

Mr. Charteris sighed. "But, of course, I forgive you, Patricia," he said. "I cannot help it, though, that I am foolishly sensitive where you are concerned. And I had hoped you knew as much."

She was happy now. "Dear boy," she murmured, "don't you see it's just these constant proofs of the greatness and the wonderfulness of your love—Really, though, Jack, wasn't it too horrid of me to misunderstand you so? Are you quite sure you're forgiven me entirely—without any nasty little reservations?"

Mr. Charteris was quite sure. His face was still sad, but it was benevolent.

"Don't you see," she went on, "that it's just these things that make me care for you so much, and feel sure as eggs is eggs we will be happy? Ah, Jack, we will be so utterly happy that I am almost afraid to think of it!" Patricia wiped away the last tear, and laughed, and added, in a matter-of-fact fashion: "There's a train at six-five in the morning; we can leave by that, before anyone is up."

Charteris started. "Your husband loves you," he said, in gentle reproof. "And quite candidly, you know, Rudolph is worth ten of me."

"Bah, I tell you, that was a comedy for my benefit," she protested, and began to laugh. Patricia was unutterably happy now, because she, and not John Charteris, had been in the wrong. "Poor Rudolph!—he has such a smug horror of the divorce-court that he would even go so far as to pretend to be in love with his own wife in order to keep out of it. Really, Jack, both our better-halves are horribly commonplace and they will be much better off without us."

"You forget that Rudolph has my word of honor," said Mr. Charteris, in indignation.

And that instant, with one of his baffling changes of mood, he began to laugh. "Really, though, Patricia, you are very pretty. You are April embodied in sweet flesh; your soul is just a wisp of April cloud, and your life an April day, half sun that only seems to warm, and half tempest that only plays at ferocity; but you are very pretty. That is why I am thinking, light-headedly, it would be a fine and past doubt an agreeable exploit to give up everything for such a woman, and am complacently comparing myself to Antony at Actium. I am thinking it would be an interesting episode in one's *Life and Letters*. You see, my dear, I honestly believe the world revolves around John Charteris—although of course I would never admit that to you if I thought for a moment you would take me seriously."

Then presently, sighing, he was grave again. "But, no! Rudolph has my word of honor," Mr. Charteris repeated, and with unconcealed regret.

"Ah, does that matter?" she cried. "Does anything matter, except that we love each other? I tell you I have given the best part of my life to that man, but I mean to make the most of what is left. He has had my youth, my love—there was a time, you know, when I actually fancied I cared for him—and he has only made me unhappy. I hate him, I loathe him, I detest him, I despise him! I never intend to speak to him again—oh, yes, I shall have to at supper, I suppose, but that doesn't count. And I tell you I mean to be happy in the only way that's possible. Everyone has a right to do that. A woman has an especial right to take her share of happiness in any way she can, because her hour of it is so short. Sometimes—sometimes the woman knows how short it is and it almost frightens her. . . But at best, a woman can be really happy through love alone, Jack dear, and it's only when we are young and good to look at that men care for us; after that, there is nothing left but to take to either religion or hand-embroidery, so what does it matter, after all? Yes, they all grow tired after a while. Jack, I am only a vain and frivolous person of superlative charm, but I love you very much, my dear, and I solemnly swear to commit suicide the moment my first wrinkle arrives. You shall never grow tired of me, my dear."

She laughed to think how true this was.

She hurried on: "Jack, kneel down at once, and swear that you are perfectly sore with loving me, as that ridiculous person says in Dickens, and whose name I never could remember. Oh, I forgot—Dickens caricatures nature, doesn't he, and isn't read by really cultured people? You will have to educate me up to your level, Jack, and I warn you in advance you will not have time to do it. Yes, I am quite aware that I am talking nonsense, and am on the verge of hysterics, thank you, but I rather like it. It is because I am going to have you all to myself for whatever future there is, and the thought makes me quite drunk. Will you kindly ring for the patrol-wagon, Jack? Jack, are you quite sure you love me? Are you perfectly certain you never loved any one else half so much? No, don't answer me, for I intend to do all the talking for both of us for the future! I shall tyrannize over you frightfully, and you will like it. All I ask in return is that you will be a good boy—by which I mean a naughty boy—and do solemnly swear, promise and affirm that you will meet me at the side-door at half-past five in the morning, with a portmanteau and the intention of never going back to your wife. You swear it? Thank you so much! Now, I think I would like to cry for a few minutes, and, after that, we will go back to the house, before supper is over and my eyes are perfectly crimson."

In fact, Mr. Charteris had consented. Patricia was irresistible as she pleaded and mocked and scolded and coaxed and laughed and cried, all in one bewildering breath. Her plan was simple; it was to slip out of Matocton at dawn, and walk to the near-by station. There they would take the train, and snap their fingers at convention. The scheme sounded preposterous in outline, but she demonstrated its practicability in performance. And Mr. Charteris consented.

Rudolph Musgrave sat in the shadow of the cedar with fierce and confused emotions whirling in his soul. He certainly had never thought of this contingency.

PART VIII
HARVEST

"Time was I coveted the woes they rued
Whose love commemorates them,—I that meant
To get like grace of love then!—and intent
To win as they had done love's plenitude,
Rapture and havoc, vauntingly I sued
That love like theirs might make a toy of me,
At will caressed, at will (if publicly)
Demolished, as Love found or found not good.

"Today I am no longer overbrave.
I have a fever,—I that always knew
This hour was certain!—and am too weak to rave,
Too tired to seek (as later I must do)
Tried remedies—time, manhood and the grave—
To drug, abate and banish love of you."

—Allen Rossiter. *A Fragment*

I

When Patricia and Charteris had left the beach, Colonel Musgrave parted the underbrush and stepped down upon the sand He must have air—air and an open place wherein to fight this out.

Night had risen about him in bland emptiness. There were no stars overhead, but a patient, wearied, ancient moon pushed through the clouds. The trees and the river conferred with one another doubtfully.

He paced up and down the beach. . .

Musgrave laughed in the darkness. His heart was racing, racing in him, and his thoughts were blown foam. He raised his hat and bowed fantastically in the darkness, because the colonel loved his gesture.

"Signor Lucifer, I present my compliments. You have discoursed with me very plausibly. I honor your cunning, signor, but if you are indeed a gentleman, as I have always heard, you will now withdraw and permit me to regard the matter from a standpoint other than my own. For the others are weak, signor; as you have doubtless discovered, good women and bad men are the weakest of their sex. I am the strongest among them, for all that I am no Hercules; and the outcome of this matter must rest with me."

So he sat presently upon the log, where Charteris had sat when Musgrave came to this beach at sunset. Very long ago that seemed now. For now the colonel was tired—physically outworn, it seemed to him, as if after prolonged exertion—and now the moon looked down upon him, passionless, cold, inexorable, and seemed to await the colonel's decision.

And it was woefully hard to come to any decision. For, as you know by this, it was the colonel's besetting infirmity to shrink from making changes; instinctively he balked—under shelter of whatever grandiloquent excuse—against commission of any action which would alter his relations with accustomed circumstances or persons. To guide events was never his forte, as he forlornly knew; and here he was condemned perforce to play that uncongenial rôle, with slender chances of reward.

Yet always Anne's face floated in the darkness. Always Anne's voice whispered through the lisping of the beeches, through the murmur of the water. . .

He sat thus for a long while.

II

Musgrave was, not unnaturally, late for supper. It is not to be supposed that at this meal the colonel faltered in his duties as a host, for, to the contrary, he narrated several anecdotes in his neatest style. It was with him a point of honor always to be in company the social triumph of his generation. He observed with idle interest that Charteris and Patricia avoided each other in a rather marked manner. Both seemed a trifle more serious than they were wont to be.

After supper, Tom Gelwix brought forth a mandolin, and most of the house-party sang songs, sentimental and otherwise, upon the front porch of Matocton. Anne had disappeared somewhere. Musgrave subsequently discovered her in one of the drawing-rooms, puzzling over a number of papers which her maid had evidently just brought to her.

Mrs. Charteris looked up with a puckered brow. "Rudolph," said she, "haven't you an account at the Occidental Bank?"

"Hardly an account, dear lady,—merely a deposit large enough to entitle me to receive monthly notices that I have overdrawn it."

"Why, then, of course, you have a cheque-book. Horrible things, aren't they?—such a nuisance remembering to fill out those little stubs. Of course, I forgot to bring mine with me—I always do; and equally, of course, a vexatious debt turns up and finds me without an Occidental Bank cheque to my name."

Musgrave was amused. "That," said he, "is easily remedied. I will get you one; though even if—Ah, well, what is the good of trying to teach you adorable women anything about business! You shall have your indispensable blank form in three minutes."

He returned in rather less than that time, with the cheque. Anne was alone now. She was gowned in some dull, soft, yellow stuff, and sat by a small, marble-topped table, twiddling a fountain-pen.

"You mustn't sneer at my business methods, Rudolph," she said, pouting a little as she filled out the cheque. "It isn't polite, sir, in the first place, and, in the second, I am really very methodical. Of course, I am always losing my cheque-book, and drawing cheques and forgetting to enter them, and I usually put down the same deposit two or three times—all women do that; but, otherwise, I am really very careful. I manage all the accounts; I can't expect Jack to do that, you know." Mrs. Charteris signed her name with a flourish, and nodded at the colonel wisely. "Dear infant, but he is quite too horribly unpractical. Do you know this bill has been due—oh, for months—and he forgot it entirely until this evening. Fortunately, he can settle it tomorrow; those disagreeable publishers of his have telegraphed for him to come to New York at once, you know. Otherwise—dear, dear! but marrying a genius is absolutely ruinous to one's credit, isn't it, Rudolph? The tradespeople will refuse to trust us soon."

Involuntarily, Musgrave had seen the cheque. It was for a considerable amount, and it was made out to John Charteris.

"Beyond doubt," said Musgrave, in his soul, "Jack is colossal! He is actually drawing on his wife for the necessary expenses for running away with another woman!"

The colonel sat down abruptly before the great, open fireplace, and stared hard at the pine-boughs which were heaped up in it.

"A penny," said she, at length.

He glanced up with a smile. "My dear madam, it would be robbery! For a penny, you may read of the subject of my thoughts in any of the yellow journals, only far more vividly set forth, and obtain a variety of more or less savory additions, to boot. I was thinking of the Lethbury case, and wondering how we could have been so long deceived by the man."

"Ah, poor Mrs. Lethbury!" Anne sighed, "I am very sorry for her, Rudolph; she was a good woman, and was always interested in charitable work."

"Do you know," said Colonel Musgrave, with deliberation, "it is she I cannot understand. To discover that he had been systematically hoodwinking her for some ten years; that, after making away with as much of her fortune as he was able to lay hands on, he has betrayed business trust after business trust in order to—to maintain another establishment; that he has never cared for her, and has made her his dupe time after time, in order to obtain money for his gambling debts and other even less reputable obligations—she must realize all these things now, you know, and one would have thought no woman's love could possibly survive such a test. Yet, she is standing by him through thick and thin. Yes, I confess, Amelia Lethbury puzzles me. I don't understand her mental attitude."

Musgrave was looking at Anne very intently as he ended.

"Why, but of course," said Anne, "she realizes that it was all the fault of that—that other woman; and, besides, the—the entanglement has been going on only a little over eight years—not ten, Rudolph."

She was entirely in earnest; Colonel Musgrave could see it plainly.

"I admit I hadn't looked on it in that light," said he, at length, and was silent for a moment Then, "Upon my soul, Anne," he cried, "I believe you think the woman is only doing the natural thing, only doing the thing one has a right to expect of her, in sticking to that blackguard after she has found him out!"

Mrs. Charteris raised her eyebrows; she was really surprised. "Naturally, she must stand by her husband when he is in trouble; why, if his own wife didn't, who would, Rudolph? It is just now that he needs her most. It would be abominable to desert him now."

Anne paused and thought. "Depend upon it, she knows a better side of his nature than we can see; she knows him, possibly, to have been misled, or to have acted thoughtlessly; because otherwise, she would not stand by him so firmly." Having reached this satisfactory conclusion, Anne began to laugh—at Musgrave's lack of penetration, probably. "So, you see, Rudolph, in either case, her conduct is perfectly natural."

"And this," he cried, "this is how women reason!"

"Am I very stupid? Jack says I am a bit illogical at times. But, Rudolph, you mustn't expect a woman to judge the man she loves; if you call on her to do that, she doesn't reason about it; she just goes on loving him, and thinking how horrid you are. Women love men as they do children; they punish them sometimes, but only in deference to public opinion. A woman will always find an excuse for the man she loves. If he deserts her, she is miserable until she succeeds in demonstrating to herself it was entirely her own fault; after that, she is properly repentant, but far less unhappy; and, anyhow, she goes on loving him just the same."

The colonel pondered over this. "Women are different," he said.

"I don't know. I think that, if all women could be thrown with good men, they would all be good. Women want to be good; but there comes a time to each one of them when she wants to make a certain man happy, and wants that more than anything else in the world; and then, of course, if he wants—very much—for her to be bad, she will be bad. A bad woman is always to be explained by a bad man."

Anne nodded, very wisely; then, she began to laugh, but this time at herself. "I am talking quite like a book," she said. "Really, I had no idea I was so clever. But I have thought of this before, Rudolph, and been sorry for those poor women who—who haven't found the right sort of man to care for."

"Yes." Musgrave's face was alert. "You have been luckier than most, Anne," he said.

"Lucky!" she cried, and that queer little thrill of happiness woke again in her rich voice. "Ah, you don't know how lucky I have been, Rudolph! I have never cared for any one except—well, yes, you, a great while ago—and Jack. And you are both good men. Ah, Rudolph, it was very dear and sweet and foolish, the way we loved each other, but you don't mind—very, very much—do you, if I think Jack is the best man in the world, and by far the best man in the world for me? He is so good to me; he is so good and kind and considerate to me, and, even after all these years of matrimony, he is always the lover. A woman appreciates that, Rudolph; she wants her husband to be always her lover, just as Jack is, and never to give in when she coaxes—because she only coaxes when she knows she is in the wrong—and never, never, to let her see him shaving himself. If a husband observes these simple rules, Rudolph, his wife will be a happy woman; and Jack does. In consequence, every day I live I grow fonder of him, and appreciate him more and more; he grows upon me just as a taste for strong drink might. Without him—without him—" Anne's voice died away; then she faced Musgrave, indignantly. "Oh, Rudolph!" she cried, "how horrid of you, how mean of you, to come here and suggest the possibility of Jack's dying or running away from me, or doing anything dreadful like that!"

Colonel Musgrave was smiling, "I?" said he, equably. "My dear madam! if you will reconsider,—"

"No," she conceded, after deliberation, "it wasn't exactly your fault. I got started on the subject of Jack, and imagined all sorts of horrible and impossible things. But there is a sort of a something in the air tonight; probably a storm is coming down the river. So I feel very morbid and very foolish, Rudolph; but, then, I am in love, you see. Isn't it funny, after all these years?" Anne asked with a smile;—"and so you are not to be angry, Rudolph."

"My dear," he said, "I assure you, the emotion you raise in me is very far from resembling that of anger." Musgrave rose and laughed. "I fear, you know, we will create a scandal if we sit here any longer. Let's see what the others are doing."

III

That night, after his guests had retired, Colonel Musgrave smoked a cigarette on the front porch of Matocton. The moon, now in the zenith, was bright and chill. After a while, Musgrave raised his face toward it, and laughed.

"Isn't it—isn't it funny?" he demanded, echoing Anne's query ruefully.

"Eh, well! perhaps I still retained some lingering hope; in a season of discomfort, most of us look vaguely for a miracle. And, at times, it comes, but, more often, not; life isn't always a pantomime, with a fairy god-mother waiting to break through the darkness in a burst of glory and reunite the severed lovers, and transform their enemies into pantaloons. In this case, it is certain that the fairy will not come. I am condemned to be my own god in the machine."

Having demonstrated this to himself, Musgrave went into the house and drugged his mind correcting proofsheets—for the *Lichfield Historical Association's Quarterly Magazine*—and brought down to the year 1805 his "List of Wills Recorded in Brummell County."

IV

The night was well advanced when Charteris stepped noiselessly into the room. The colonel was then sedately writing amid a host of motionless mute watchers, for at Matocton most of the portraits hang in the East Drawing-room.

Thus, above the great marble mantel,—carved with thyrsi, and supported by proud deep-bosomed caryatides,—you will find burly Sebastian Musgrave, "the Speaker," an all-overbearing man even on canvas. "Paint me among dukes and earls with my hat on, to show I am in all things a Republican, and the finest diamond in the Colony shall be yours," he had directed the painter, and this was done. Then there is frail Wilhelmina Musgrave—that famed beauty whose two-hundred-year-old story all Lichfield knows, and no genealogist has ever cared to detail—eternally weaving flowers about her shepherd hat. There, too, is Evelyn Ramsay, before whose roguish loveliness, as you may remember, the colonel had snapped his fingers in those roseate days when he so joyously considered his profound unworthiness to be Patricia's husband. There is also the colonial governor of Albemarle—a Van Dyck this—two Knellers, and Lely's portrait of Thomas Musgrave, "the poet," with serious blue eyes and flaxen hair. The painting of Captain George Musgrave, who distinguished himself at the siege of Cartagena, is admittedly an inferior piece of work, but it has vigor, none the less; and below it hangs the sword which was presented to him by the Lord High Admiral.

So quietly did Charteris come that the colonel was not aware of his entrance until the novelist had coughed gently. He was in a dressing-gown, and looked unusually wizened.

"I saw your light," he said. "I don't seem to be able to sleep, somehow. It is so infernally hot and still. I suppose there is going to be a thunderstorm. I hate thunderstorms. They frighten me." The little man was speaking like a peevish child.

"Oh, well—! it will at least clear the air," said Rudolph Musgrave. "Sit down and have a smoke, won't you?"

"No, thanks." Charteris had gone to the bookshelves and was gently pushing and pulling at the books so as to arrange their backs in a mathematically straight line. "I thought I would borrow something to read—Why, this is the Tennyson you had at college, isn't it? Yes, I remember it perfectly."

These two had roomed together through their college days.

"Yes; it is the old Tennyson. And yonder is the identical Swinburne you used to spout from, too. Lord, Jack, it seems a century since I used to listen by the hour to *The Triumph of Time and Dolores!*"

"Ah, but you didn't really care for them—not even then." Charteris reached up, his back still turned, and moved a candlestick the fraction of an inch. "There is something so disgustingly wholesome about you, Rudolph. And it appears to be ineradicable. I can't imagine how I ever came to be fond of you."

The colonel was twirling his pen, his eyes intent upon it. "And yet—we *were* fond of each other, weren't we, Jack?"

"Why, I positively adored you. You were such a strong and healthy animal. Upon my word, I don't believe I ever missed a single football game you played in. In fact, I almost learned to understand the game on your account. You see—it was so good to watch you raging about with touzled hair, like the only original bull of Bashan, and the others tumbling like ninepins. It used to make me quite inordinately proud."

The colonel smoked. "But, Lord! how proud *I* was when you got medals!"

"Yes—I remember."

"Even if I did bully you sometimes. Remember how I used to twist your arm to make you write my Latin exercises, Jack?"

"I liked to have you do that," Charteris said, simply. "It hurt a great deal, but I liked it."

He had come up behind the colonel, who was still seated. "Yes, that was a long while ago," said Charteris. "It is rather terrible—isn't it?—to reflect precisely how long ago it was. Why, I shall be bald in a year or two from now. But you have kept almost all your beautiful hair, Rudolph."

Charteris touched the colonel's head, stroking his hair ever so lightly once or twice. It was in effect a caress.

The colonel was aware of the odor of myrrh which always accompanied Charteris and felt that the little man was trembling.

"Isn't there—anything you want to tell me, Jack?" the colonel said. He sat quite still.

There was the tiniest pause. The caressing finger-tips lifted from Musgrave's head, but presently gave it one more brief and half-timid touch.

"Why, only *au revoir*, I believe. I am leaving at a rather ungodly hour tomorrow and won't see you, but I hope to return within the week."

"I hope so, Jack."

"And, after all, it is too late to be reading. I shall go back to bed and take more trional. And then, I dare say, I shall sleep. So good-by, Rudolph."

"Good-night, Jack."

"Oh, yes—! I meant good-night, of course."

The colonel sighed; then he spoke abruptly:

"No, just a moment, Jack. I didn't ask you to come here tonight; but since you have come, by chance, I am going to follow the promptings of that chance, and strike a blow for righteousness with soiled weapons. Jack, do you remember suggesting that my father's correspondence during the War might be of value, and that his desk ought to be overhauled?"

"Why, yes, of course. Mrs. Musgrave was telling me she began the task," said Charteris, and smiled a little.

"Unluckily; yes—but—well! in any event, it suggested to me that old letters are dangerous. I really had no idea what that desk contained. My father had preserved great stacks of letters. I have been going through them. They were most of them from women—letters which should never have been written in the first place, and which he certainly had no right to keep."

"What! and is 'Wild Will's' love-correspondence still extant? I fancy it made interesting reading, Rudolph."

"There were some letters which in a measure concern you, Jack." The colonel handed him a small packet of letters. "If you will read the top one it will explain. I will just go on with my writing."

He wrote steadily for a moment or two. . . Then Charteris laughed musically.

"I have always known there was a love-affair between my mother and 'Wild Will.' But I never suspected until tonight that I had the honor to be your half-brother, Rudolph—one of 'Wild Will's' innumerable bastards." Charteris was pallid, and though he seemed perfectly composed, his eyes glittered as with gusty brilliancies. "I understand now why my reputed father always made such a difference between my sister and myself. I never liked old Alvin Charteris, you know. It is a distinct relief to be informed I have no share in his blood, although of course the knowledge comes a trifle suddenly."

"Perhaps I should have kept that knowledge to myself. I know it would have been kinder. I had meant to be kind. I loathe myself for dabbling in this mess. But, in view of all things, it seemed necessary to let you know I am your own brother in the flesh, and that Patricia is your brother's wife."

"I see," said Charteris. "According to your standards that would make a great difference. I don't know, speaking frankly, that it makes much difference with me." He turned again to the bookshelves, so that Musgrave could no longer see his face. Charteris ran his fingers caressingly over the backs of a row of volumes. "I loved my mother, Rudolph. I never loved anyone else. That makes a difference." Then he said, "We Musgraves—how patly I catalogue myself already!—we Musgraves have a deal to answer for, Rudolph."

"And doesn't that make it all the more our duty to live clean and honest lives? to make the debt no greater than it is?" Both men were oddly quiet.

"Eh, I am not so sure." John Charteris waved airily toward Sebastian Musgrave's counterfeit, then toward the other portraits. "It was they who compounded our inheritances, Rudolph—all that we were to have in this world of wit and strength and desire and endurance. We know their histories. They were proud, brave and thriftless, a greedy and lecherous race, who squeezed life dry as one does an orange, and left us the dregs. I think that it is droll, but I am not sure it places us under any obligation. In fact, I rather think God owes us an apology, Rudolph."

He spoke with quaint wistfulness. The colonel sat regarding him in silence, with shocked, disapproving eyes. Then Charteris cocked his head to one side and grinned like a hobgoblin.

"What wouldn't you give," he demanded, "to know what I am really thinking of at this very moment while I talk so calmly? Well, you will never know. And for the rest, you are at liberty to use your all-important documents as you may elect. I am John Charteris; whatever man begot my body, he is rotten bones today, and it is as such I value him. I was never anybody's son—or friend or brother or lover,—but just a pen that someone far bigger and far nobler than John Charteris writes with occasionally. Whereas you—but, oh, you are funny, Rudolph!" And then, "Good-night, dear brother," Charteris added, sweetly, as he left the room.

And Rudolph Musgrave could not quite believe in the actuality of what had just happened. In common with most of us, he got his general notions concerning the laws of life from reading fiction; and here was the material for a Renaissance tragedy wasted so far as any dénouement went. Destiny, once more, was hardly rising to the possibilities of the situation. The weapon chance had forged had failed Rudolph Musgrave utterly; and, indeed, he wondered now how he could ever have esteemed it formidable. Jack was his half-brother. In noveldom or in a melodrama this discovery would have transformed their mutual dealings; but as a workaday world's fact, Musgrave would not honestly say that it had in any way affected his feelings toward Jack, and it appeared to have left Charteris equally unaltered.

"I am not sure, though. We can only guess where Jack is concerned. He goes his own way always, tricky and furtive and lonelier than any other human being I have ever known. It is loneliness that looks out of his eyes, really, even when he is mocking and sneering," the colonel meditated.

Then he sighed and went back to the tabulation of his lists of wills.

V

The day was growing strong in the maple-grove behind Matocton. As yet, the climbing sun fired only the topmost branches, and flooded them with a tempered radiance through which birds plunged and shrilled vague rumors to one another. Beneath, a green twilight lingered—twilight which held a gem-like glow, chill and lucent and steady as that of an emerald. Vagrant little puffs of wind bustled among the leaves, with a thin pretense of purpose, and then lapsed, and merged in the large, ambiguous whispering which went stealthily about the grove.

Rudolph Musgrave sat on a stone beside the road that winds through the woods toward the railway station, and smoked, nervously. He was disheartened of the business of living, and, absurdly enough, as it seemed to him, he was hungry.

"It has to be done quietly and without the remotest chance of Anne's ever hearing of it, and without the remotest chance of its ever having to be done again. I have about fifteen minutes in which to convince Patricia both of her own folly and of the fact that Jack is an unmitigated cad, and to get him off the place quietly, so that Anne will suspect nothing. And I never knew any reasonable argument to appeal to Patricia, and Jack will be a cornered rat! Yes, it is a large contract, and I would give a great deal—a very great deal—to know how I am going to fulfil it."

At this moment his wife and Mr. Charteris, carrying two portmanteaux, came around a bend in the road not twenty feet from Musgrave. They were both rather cross. In the clean and more prosaic light of morning an elopement seemed almost silly; moreover, Patricia had had no breakfast, and Charteris had been much annoyed by his wife, who had breakfasted with him, and had insisted on driving to the station with him. It was a trivial-seeming fact, but, perhaps, not unworthy of notice, that Patricia was carrying her own portmanteau, as well as an umbrella.

The three faced one another in the cool twilight. The woods stirred lazily about them. The birds were singing on a wager now.

"Ah," said Colonel Musgrave, "so you have come at last. I have been expecting you for some time."

Patricia dropped her portmanteau, sullenly. Mr. Charteris placed his with care to the side of the road, and said, "Oh!" It was perhaps the only observation that occurred to him.

"Patricia," Musgrave began, very kindly and very gravely, "you are about to do a foolish thing. At the bottom of your heart, even now, you know you are about to do a foolish thing—a thing you will regret bitterly and unavailingly for the rest of time. You are turning your back on the world—our world—on the one possible world you could ever be happy in. You can't be happy in the half-world, Patricia; you aren't that sort. But you can never come back to us then, Patricia; it doesn't matter what the motive was, what the temptation was, or how great the repentance is—you cannot ever return. That is the law, Patricia; perhaps, it isn't always a just law. We didn't make it, you and I, but it is the law, and we must obey it. Our world merely says that, leaving it once, you cannot ever return: such is the only punishment it awards you, for it knows, this wise old world of ours, that such is the bitterest punishment which could ever be devised for you. Our world has made you what you are; in every thought and ideal and emotion you possess, you are a product of our world. You couldn't live in the half-world, Patricia; you are a product of our world that can never take root in that alien soil. Come back to us before it is too late, Patricia!"

Musgrave shook himself all over, rather like a Newfoundland dog coming out of the water, and the grave note died from his voice. He smiled, and rubbed his hands together.

"And now," said he, "I will stop talking like a problem play, and we will say no more about it. Give me your portmanteau, my dear, and upon my word of honor, you will never hear a word further from me in the matter. Jack, here, can take the train, just as he intended. And—and you and I will go back to the house, and have a good, hot breakfast together. Eh, Patricia?"

She was thinking, unreasonably enough, how big and strong and clean her husband looked in the growing light. It was a pity Jack was so small. However, she faced Musgrave coldly, and thought how ludicrously wide of the mark were all these threats of ostracism. She shudderingly wished he would not talk of soil and taking root and hideous things like that, but otherwise the colonel left her unmoved. He was certainly good-looking, though.

Charteris was lighting a cigarette, with a queer, contented look. He knew the value of Patricia's stubbornness now; still, he appeared to be using an unnecessary number of matches.

"I should have thought you would have perceived the lack of dignity, as well as the utter uselessness, in making such a scene," Patricia said.

"We aren't suited for each other, Rudolph; and it is better—far better for both of us—to have done with the farce of pretending to be. I am sorry that you still care for me. I didn't know that. But, for the future, I intend to live my own life."

Patricia's voice faltered, and she stretched out her hands a little toward her husband in an odd gust of friendliness. He looked so kind; and he was not smiling in that way she never liked. "Surely that isn't so unpardonable a crime, Rudolph?" she asked, almost humbly.

"No, my dear," he answered, "it is not unpardonable—it is impossible. You can't lead your own life, Patricia; none of us can. Each life is bound up with many others, and every rash act of yours, every hasty word of yours, must affect to some extent the lives of those who are nearest and most dear to you. But, oh, it is not argument that I would be at! Patricia, there was a woman once—She was young, and wealthy, and—ah, well, I won't deceive you by exaggerating her personal attractions! I will serve up to you no praises of her sauced with lies. But fate and nature had combined to give her everything a woman can desire, and all this that woman freely gave to me—to me who hadn't youth or wealth or fame or anything! And I can't stand by, for that dear dead girl's sake, and watch your life go wrong, Patricia!"

"You are just like the rest of them, Olaf"—and when had she used that half-forgotten nickname last, he wondered. "You imagine you are in love with a girl because you happen to like the color of her eyes, or because there is a curve about her lips that appeals to you. That isn't love, Olaf, as we women understand it."

And wildly hideous and sad, it seemed to Colonel Musgrave—this dreary parody of their old love-talk. Only, he dimly knew that she had forgotten John Charteris existed, and that to her this moment seemed no less sardonic.

Charteris inhaled, lazily; yet, he did not like the trembling about Patricia's mouth. Her hands, too, opened and shut tight before she spoke.

"It is too late now," she said, dully. "I gave you all there was to give. You gave me just what Grandma Pendomer and all the others had left you able to give. That remnant isn't love, Olaf, as we women understand it. And, anyhow, it is too late now."

Yet Patricia was remembering a time when Rudolph's voice held always that grave, tender note in speaking to her; it seemed a great while ago. And he was big and manly, just like his voice, Rudolph was;

and he looked very kind. Desperately, Patricia began to count over the times her husband had offended her. Hadn't he talked to her in the most unwarrantable manner only yesterday afternoon?

"Too late!—oh, not a bit of it!" Musgrave cried. His voice sank persuasively. "Why, Patricia, you are only thinking the matter over for the first time. You have only begun to think of it. Why, there is the boy—our boy, Patricia! Surely, you hadn't thought of Roger?"

He had found the right chord at last. It quivered and thrilled under his touch; and the sense of mastery leaped in his blood. Of a sudden, he knew himself dominant. Her face was red, then white, and her eyes wavered before the blaze of his, that held her, compellingly.

"Now, honestly, just between you and me," the colonel said, confidentially, "was there ever a better and braver and quainter and handsomer boy in the world? Why, Patricia, surely, you wouldn't willingly—of your own accord—go away from him, and never see him again? Oh, you haven't thought, I tell you! Think, Patricia! Don't you remember that first day, when I came into your room at the hospital and he—ah, how wrinkled and red and old-looking he was then, wasn't he, little wife? Don't you remember how he was lying on your breast, and how I took you both in my arms, and held you close for a moment, and how for a long, long while there wasn't anything left of the whole wide world except just us three and God smiling down upon us? Don't you remember, Patricia? Don't you remember his first tooth—why, we were as proud of him, you and I, as if there had never been a tooth before in all the history of the world! Don't you remember the first day he walked? Why, he staggered a great distance—oh, nearly two yards!—and caught hold of my hand, and laughed and turned back—to you. You didn't run away from him then, Patricia. Are you going to do it now?"

She struggled under his look. She had an absurd desire to cry, just that he might console her. She knew he would. Why was it so hard to remember that she hated Rudolph! Of course, she hated him; she loved that other man yonder. His name was Jack. She turned toward Charteris, and the reassuring smile with which he greeted her, impressed Patricia as being singularly nasty. She hated both of them; she wanted—in that brief time which remained for having anything—only her boy, her soft, warm little Roger who had eyes like Rudolph's.

"I—I—it's too late, Rudolph," she stammered, parrot-like. "If you had only taken better care of me, Rudolph! If—No, it's too late, I tell you! You will be kind to Roger. I am only weak and frivolous and heartlesss. I am not fit to be his mother. I'm not fit, Rudolph! Rudolph, I tell you I'm not fit! Ah, let me go, my dear!—in mercy, let me go! For I haven't loved the boy as I ought to, and I am afraid to look you in the face, and you won't let me take my eyes away—you won't let me! Ah, Rudolph, let me go!"

"Not fit?" His voice thrilled with strength, and pulsed with tender cadences. "Ah, Patricia, I am not fit to be his father! But, between us—between us, mightn't we do much for him? Come back to us, Patricia—to me and the boy! We need you, my dear. Ah, I am only a stolid, unattractive fogy, I know; but you loved me once, and—I am the father of your child. My standards are out-of-date, perhaps, and in any event they are not your standards, and that difference has broken many ties between us; but I am the father of your child. You must—you *must* come back to me and the boy!" Musgrave caught her face between his hands, and lifted it toward his. "Patricia, don't make any mistake! There is nothing you care for so much as that boy. You can't give him up! If you had to walk over red-hot ploughshares to come to him, you would do it; if you could win him a moment's happiness by a lifetime of poverty and misery and degradation, you would do it. And so would I, little wife. That is the tie which still unites us; that is the tie which is too strong ever to break. Come back to us, Patricia—to me and the boy."

"I—Jack, Jack, take me away!" she wailed helplessly.

Charteris came forward with a smile. He was quite sure of Patricia now.

"Colonel Musgrave," he said, with a faint drawl, "if you have entirely finished your edifying and, I assure you, highly entertaining monologue, I will ask you to excuse us. I—oh, man, man!" Charteris cried, not unkindly, "don't you see it is the only possible outcome?"

Musgrave faced him. The glow of hard-earned victory was pulsing in the colonel's blood, but his eyes were chill stars. "Now, Jack," he said, equably, "I am going to talk to you. In fact, I am going to discharge an agreeable duty toward you."

Musgrave drew close to him. Charteris shrugged his shoulders; his smile, however, was not entirely satisfactory. It did not suggest enjoyment.

"I don't blame you for being what you are," Musgrave went on, curtly. "You were born so, doubtless. I don't blame a snake for being what it is. But, when I see a snake, I claim the right to set my foot on its head; when I see a man like you—well, this is the right I claim."

Thereupon Rudolph Musgrave struck his half-brother in the face with his open hand. The colonel was a strong man, physically, and, on this occasion, he made no effort to curb his strength.

"Now," Musgrave concluded, "you are going away from this place very quickly, and you are going alone. You will do this because I tell you to do so, and because you are afraid of me. Understand, also—if you will be so good—that the only reason I don't give you a thorough thrashing is that I don't think you are worth the trouble. I only want Patricia to perceive exactly what sort of man you are."

The blow staggered Charteris. He seemed to grow smaller. His clothes seemed to hang more loosely about him. His face was paper-white, and the red mark showed plainly upon it.

"There would be no earthly sense in my hitting you back," he said equably. "It would only necessitate my getting the thrashing which, I can assure you, we are equally anxious to avoid. Of course you are able to knock me down and so on, because you are nearly twice as big as I am. I fail to see that proves anything in particular. Come, Patricia!" And he turned to her, and reached out his hand.

She shrank from him. She drew away from him, without any vehemence, as if he had been some slimy, harmless reptile. A woman does not like to see fear in a man's eyes; and there was fear in Mr. Charteris's eyes, for all that he smiled. Patricia's heart sickened. She loathed him, and she was a little sorry for him.

"Oh, you cur, you cur!" she gasped, in a wondering whisper. Patricia went to her husband, and held out her hands. She was afraid of him. She was proud of him, the strong animal. "Take me away, Rudolph," she said, simply; "take me away from that—that coward. Take me away, my dear. You may beat me, too, if you like, Rudolph. I dare say I have deserved it. But I want you to deal brutally with me, to carry me away by force, just as you threatened to do the day we were married—at the Library, you remember, when the man was crying 'Fresh oranges!' and you smelt so deliciously of soap and leather and cigarette smoke."

Musgrave took both her hands in his. He smiled at Charteris.

The novelist returned the smile, intensifying its sweetness. "I fancy, Rudolph," he said, "that, after all, I shall have to take that train alone."

Mr. Charteris continued, with a grimace: "You have no notion, though, how annoying it is not to possess an iota of what is vulgarly considered manliness. But what am I to do? I was not born with the knack of enduring physical pain. Oh, yes, I am a coward, if you like to put it nakedly; but I was born so, willy-nilly. Personally, if I had been consulted in the matter, I would have preferred the usual portion of valor. However! the sanctity of the hearth has been most edifyingly preserved—and, after all, the woman is not worth squabbling about."

There was exceedingly little of the mountebank in him now; he kicked Patricia's portmanteau, frankly and viciously, as he stepped over it to lift his own. Holding this in one hand, John Charteris spoke, honestly:

"Rudolph, I had a trifle underrated your resources. For you are a brave man—we physical cowards, you know, admire that above all things—and a strong man and a clever man, in that you have adroitly played upon the purely brutal traits of women. Any she-animal clings to its young and looks for protection in its mate. Upon a higher ground I would have beaten you, but as an animal you are my superior. Still, a thing done has an end. You have won back your wife in open fight. I fancy, by the way, that you have rather laid up future trouble for yourself in doing so, but I honor the skill you have shown. Colonel Musgrave, it is to you that, as the vulgar phrase it, I take off my hat."

Thereupon, Mr. Charteris uncovered his head with perfect gravity, and turned on his heel, and went down the road, whistling melodiously.

Musgrave stared after him, for a while. The lust of victory died; the tumult and passion and fervor were gone from Musgrave's soul. He could very easily imagine the things Jack Charteris would say to Anne concerning him; and the colonel knew that she would believe them all. He had won the game; he had played it, heartily and skilfully and successfully; and his reward was that the old bickerings with Patricia should continue, and that Anne should be taught to loathe him. He foresaw it all very plainly as he stood, hand in hand with his wife.

But Anne would be happy. It was for that he had played.

VI

They came back to Matocton almost silently. The spell of the dawn was broken; it was honest, garish day now, and they were both hungry.

Patricia's spirits were rising, as a butterfly's might after a thunderstorm. Since she had only a few months to live, she would at least not waste them in squabbling. She would be conscientiously agreeable to everybody.

"Ah, Rudolph, Rudolph!" she cooed, "if I had only known all along that you loved me!"

"My dear," he protested, fondly, "it seemed such a matter of course." He was a little tired, perhaps; the portmanteau seemed very heavy.

"A woman likes to be told—a woman likes to be told every day. Otherwise, she forgets," Patricia murmured. Then her face grew tenderly reproachful. "Ah, Rudolph, Rudolph, see what your carelessness and neglect has nearly led to! It nearly led to my running away with a man like—like that! It would have been all your fault, Rudolph, if I had. You know it would have been, Rudolph."

And Patricia sighed once more, and then laughed and became magnanimous.

"Yes—yes, after all, you are the boy's father." She smiled up at him kindly and indulgently. "I forgive you, Rudolph," said Patricia.

He must have shown that pardon from Patricia just now was not unflavored with irony, for she continued, in another voice: "Who, after all, is the one human being you love? You know that it's the boy, and just the boy alone. I gave you that boy. You should remember that, I think—"

"I do remember it, Patricia—"

"I bore the child. I paid the price, not you," Patricia said, very quiet. "No, I don't mean the price all women have to pay—" She paused in their leisurely progress, and drew vague outlines in the roadway with the ferrule of her umbrella before she looked up into Rudolph Musgrave's face. She appraised it for a long while and quite as if her husband were a stranger.

"Yes, I could make you very sorry for me, if I wanted to." Her thoughts ran thus. "But what's the use? You could only become an interminable nuisance in trying to soothe my dying hours. You have just obstinately squatted around in Lichfield and devoted all your time to being beautiful and good and mooning around women for I don't know how many years. You make me tired, and I have half a mind to tell you so right now. And there really is no earthly sense in attempting to explain things to you. You have so got into the habit of being beautiful and good that you are capable of quoting Scripture after I have finished. Then I would assuredly box your jaws, because I don't yearn to be a poor stricken dear and weep on anybody's bosom. And I don't particularly care about your opinion of me, anyway."

Aloud she said: "Oh, well! let's go and get some breakfast."

VII

And thus the situation stayed. Patricia told him nothing. And Rudolph Musgrave, knowing that according to his lights he had behaved not unhandsomely, was the merest trifle patronizing and rather like a person speaking from a superior plane in his future dealings with Patricia. Moreover, he was engrossed at this time by his scholarly compilation of Lichfield Legislative Papers prior to 1800, which was printed the following February.

She told him nothing. She was a devoted mother for two days' space, and then candidly decided that Roger was developing into the most insufferable of little prigs.

"And, besides, if he had never been born I would quite probably have lived to keep my teeth in a glass of water at night. And I can't help thinking of that privilege being denied me whenever I look at him."

She told Rudolph Musgrave nothing. She was finding it mildly amusing to note how people came and went at Matocton, and to appraise these people disinterestedly, because she would never see them again.

Patricia was drawing her own conclusions as to Lichfield's aristocracy. These people—for the most part a preposterously handsome race—were the pleasantest of companions and their manners were perfection; but there was enough of old Roger Stapylton's blood in Patricia's veins to make her feel, however obscurely, that nobody is justified in living without even an attempt at any personal achievement. The younger men evinced a marked tendency to leave Lichfield, to make their homes elsewhere, she noted, and they very often attained prominence; there was Joe Parkinson, for instance, who had lunched at Oyster Bay only last Thursday, according to the *Lichfield Courier-Herald*. And, meanwhile, the men of her husband's generation clung to their old mansions, and were ornamental, certainly, and were, very certainly, profoundly self-satisfied; for they adhered to the customs of yesterday under the comfortable delusion that this was the only way to uphold yesterday's ideals. But what, in heaven's name, had any of these men of Rudolph Musgrave's circle ever done beyond enough perfunctory desk-work, say, to furnish him food and clothes?

"A hamlet of Hamlets," was Patricia's verdict as to Lichfield—"whose actual tragedy isn't that their fathers were badly treated, but that they themselves are constitutionally unable to do anything except talk about how badly their fathers were treated."

No, it was not altogether that these men were indolent. Rudolph and Rudolph's peers had been reared in the belief that when any manual labor became inevitable, you as a matter of course entrusted its execution to a negro; and, forced themselves to labor, they not unnaturally complied with an ever-present sense of unfair treatment, and, in consequence, performed the work inefficiently. Lichfield had no doubt preserved a comely manner of living; but it had produced in the last half-century nothing of real importance except John Charteris.

VIII

For Charteris was important. Patricia was rereading all the books that Charteris had published, and they engrossed her with an augmenting admiration.

But it is unnecessary to dilate upon the marvelous and winning pictures of life in Lichfield before the War between the States which Charteris has painted in his novels. "Even as the king of birds that with unwearied wing soars nearest to the sun, yet wears upon his breast the softest down,"—as we learn from no less eminent authority than that of the *Lichfield Courier-Herald*—"so Mr. Charteris is equally expert in depicting the derring-do and tenderness of those glorious days of chivalry, of fair women and brave men, of gentle breeding, of splendid culture and wholesome living."

Patricia was not a little puzzled by these books. The traditional Lichfield, she decided in the outcome, may very possibly have been just the trick-work of a charlatan's cleverness; but, even in that event, here were the tales of life in Lichfield—ardent, sumptuous and fragrant throughout with the fragrance of love and roses, of rhyme and of youth's lovely fallacies; and for the pot-pourri, if it deserved no higher name, all who believed that living ought to be a uniformly noble transaction could not fail to be grateful eternally.

Esthetic values apart—and, indeed, to all such values Patricia accorded a provisional respect—what most impressed her Stapyltonian mind was the fact that these books represented, in a perfectly tangible way, success. Patricia very heartily admired success when it was brevetted as such by the applause of others. And while to be a noted stylist, and even to be reasonably sure of annotated reissuement for the plaguing of unborn schoolchildren, was all well enough, in an unimportant, high-minded way, Patricia was far more vividly impressed by the blunt figures which told how many of John Charteris's books had been bought and paid for. She accepted these figures as his publishers gave them forth, implicitly; and she marveled over and took odd joy in these figures. They enabled her to admire Charteris's books without reservation.

By this time Mrs. Ashmeade had managed, in the most natural manner, to tell Patricia a deal concerning Charteris. No halo graced the portrait Mrs. Ashmeade painted. . . But, indeed, Patricia now viewed John Charteris, considered as a person, without any particular bias. She did not especially care—now—what the man had done or had omitted to do.

But the venerable incongruity of the writer and his work confronted her intriguingly. A Charteris writes *In Old Lichfield;* a Cockney drug-clerk writes *The Eve of St. Agnes;* a genteel printer evolves a Lovelace; and a cutpurse pens the *Ballad of Dead Ladies* in a brothel. It is manifestly impossible; and it happens.

So here, then, was a knave who held, somehow, the keys to a courtlier and nobler world. These tales made living seem a braver business, for all that they were written by a poltroon. Was it pure posturing? Patricia, at least, thought it was not. At worst, such dexterous maintenance of a pose was hardly despicable, she considered. And, anyhow, she preferred to believe that Charteris had by some miracle put the best of himself into these books, had somehow clarified the abhorrent mixture of ability and evil which was John Charteris; and the best in him she found, on this hypothesis, to be a deal more admirable than the best in Rudolph Musgrave.

"It *is* a part of Jack," she fiercely said. "It is, because I know it is. All this is part of him—as much a part of him as the cowardice and the trickery. So I don't really care if he is a liar and a coward. I ought to, I suppose. But at the bottom of my heart I admire him. He has made something; he has created these beautiful books, and they will be here when we are all dead. He doesn't leave the world just as he found it. That is the only real cowardice, I think—especially as I am going to do it—"

And later she said, belligerently: "If I had been a man I could have at least assassinated somebody who was prominent. I do wish Rudolph was not such a stick-in-the-mud. And I wish I liked Rudolph better. But on the whole I prefer the physical coward to the moral one. Rudolph simply bores me stiff with his benevolent airs. He just walks around the place forgiving me sixty times to the hour, and if he doesn't stop it I am going to slap him."

Thus Patricia.

IX

The world knows how Charteris was killed in Fairhaven by Jasper Hardress—the husband of "that flighty Mrs. Hardress" Anne had spoken of.

"And I hardly know," said Mrs. Ashmeade, "whether more to admire the justice or the sardonic humor of the performance. Here after hundreds of entanglements with women, John Charteris manages to be shot by a jealous maniac on account of a woman with whom—for a wonder—his relations were proven to be innocent. The man needed killing, but it is asking too much of human nature to put up with his being made a martyr of."

She cried a little, though. "It—it's because I remember him when he was turning out his first mustache," she explained, lucidly.

BUT WITH THE HORROR AND irony of John Charteris's assassination the biographer of Rudolph Musgrave has really nothing to do save in so far as this event influenced the life of Rudolph Musgrave.

It was on the day of Charteris's death—a fine, clear afternoon in late September—that Rudolph Musgrave went bass-fishing with some eight of his masculine guests. Luncheon was brought to them in a boat about two o'clock, along with the day's mail.

"I say—! But listen, everybody!" cried Alfred Chayter, whose mail included a morning paper—the *Lichfield Courier-Herald*, in fact.

He read aloud.

"I wish I could be with Anne," thought Colonel Musgrave. "It may be I could make things easier."

But Anne was in Lichfield now. . .

He had just finished dressing for supper when it occurred to him that since their return from the river he had not seen Patricia. He was afraid that Patricia, also, would be upset by this deplorable news.

As he crossed the hall Virginia came out of Patricia's rooms. The colonel raised his voice in speaking to her, for with age Virginia was growing very deaf.

"Yaas, suh," she said, "I'm doin' middlin' well, suh, thank yeh, suh. Jus' took the evenin' mail to Miss Patricy, like I always do, suh." She went away quietly, her pleasant yellow face as imperturbable as an idol's.

He went into Patricia's bedroom. Patricia had been taking an afternoon nap, and had not risen from the couch, where she lay with three or four unopened letters upon her breast. Two she had opened and dropped upon the floor. She seemed not to hear him when he spoke her name, and yet she was not asleep, because her eyes were partly unclosed.

There was no purple glint in them, as once there had been always. Her countenance, indeed, showed everywhere less brightly tinted than normally it should be. Her heavy copper-colored hair, alone undimmed, seemed, like some parasitic growth (he thought), to sustain its beauty by virtue of having drained Patricia's body of color and vitality.

There was a newspaper in her right hand, with flamboyant headlines, because to Lichfield the death of John Charteris was an event of importance.

Patricia seemed very young. You saw that she had suffered. You knew it was not fair to hurt a child like that.

But, indeed, Rudolph Musgrave hardly realized as yet that Patricia was dead. For Colonel Musgrave was thinking of that time when this same Patricia had first come to him, fire-new from the heart of an ancient sunset, and he had noted, for the first time, that her hair was like the reflection of a sunset in rippling waters, and that her mouth was an inconsiderable trifle, a scrap of sanguine curves, and that her eyes were purple glimpses of infinity.

"This same Patricia!" he said, aloud.

PART IX

RELICS

"You have chosen the love 'that lives sans murmurings,
Sans passion,' and incuriously endures
The gradual lapse of time. You have chosen as yours
A level life of little happenings;
And through the long autumnal evenings
Lord Love, no doubt, is of the company,
And hugs your ingleside contentedly,
Smiles at old griefs, and rustles needless wings.

"And yet I think that sometimes memories
Of divers trysts, of blood that urged like wine
On moonlit nights, and of that first long kiss
Whereby your lips were first made one with mine,
Awake and trouble you, and loving is
Once more important and perhaps divine."

—Allen Rossiter. *Two in October*

I

To those who knew John Charteris only through the medium of the printed page it must have appeared that the novelist was stayed in mid-career by an accident of unrelieved and singular brutality. And truly, thus extinguished by the unfounded jealousy of a madman, the force of Charteris's genius seemed, and seems today, as emphasized by that sinister caprice of chance which annihilated it.

But people in Lichfield, after the manner of each prophet's countrymen, had their own point of view. The artist always stood between these people and the artist's handiwork, in part obscuring it.

In any event, it was generally agreed in Lichfield that Anne Charteris's conduct after her husband's death was not all which could be desired. To begin with, she attended the funeral, in black, it was true, but wearing only the lightest of net veils pinned under her chin—"more as if she were going somewhere on the train, you know, than as if she were in genuine bereavement."

"Jack didn't approve of mourning. He said it was a heathen survival." That was the only explanation she offered.

It seemed inadequate to Lichfield. It was preferable, as good taste went, for a widow to be too overcome to attend her husband's funeral at all. And Mrs. Charteris had not wept once during the church ceremony, and had not even had hysterics during the interment at Cedarwood; and she had capped a scandalous morning's work by remaining with the undertaker and the bricklayers to supervise the closing of John Charteris's grave.

"Why, but of course. It is the last thing I will ever be allowed to do for him," she had said, in innocent surprise. "Why shouldn't I?"

Her air was such that you were both to talk to her about appearances.

"Because she isn't a bit like a widow," as Mrs. Ashmeade pointed out. "Anybody can condole with a widow, and devote two outer sheets to explaining that you realize nothing you can say will be of any comfort to her, and begin at the top of the inside page by telling her how much better off he is today—which I have always thought a double-edged assertion when advanced to a man's widow. But you cannot condole with a lantern whose light has been blown out. That is what Anne is."

Mrs. Ashmeade meditated and appeared dissatisfied. "And John Charteris of all people!"

Anne was presently about the Memorial Edition of her husband's collected writings. It was magnificently printed and when marketed achieved a flattering success. Robert Etheridge Townsend was commissioned to write the authorized *Life of John Charteris* and to arrange the two volumes of *Letters*.

Anne was considered an authority on literature and art in general, through virtue of reflected glory. And in the interviews she granted various journalists it was noticeable that she no longer referred to "Jack" or to "Mr. Charteris," but to "my husband." To have been his wife was her one claim on estimation. And, for the rest, it is inadequate to love the memory of a martyr. Worship is demanded; and so the wife became the priestess.

II

Into Colonel Musgrave's mental processes during this period it will not do to pry too closely. The man had his white nights and his battles, in part with real grief and regret, and in part with sundry emotions which he took on faith as the emotions he ought to have, and, therefore, manifestly, suffered under. . . "Patricia was my wife, Jack was my brother," ran his verdict in the outcome; and beyond that he did not care to go.

For death cowed his thoughts. In the colonel's explicit theology dead people were straightway conveyed to either one or the other of two places. He had very certainly never known anybody who in his opinion merited the torments of his orthodox Gehenna; so that in imagination he vaguely populated its blazing corridors with Nero and Judas and Caesar Borgia and Henry VIII, and Spanish Inquisitors and the aboriginal American Indians—excepting of course his ancestress Pocahontas—and with Benedict Arnold and all the "carpet-baggers" and suchlike other eminent practitioners of depravity. For no one whom Rudolph Musgrave had ever encountered in the flesh had been really and profoundly wicked, Rudolph Musgrave considered; and so, he always gravely estimated this-or-that acquaintance, after death, to be "better off, poor fellow"—as the colonel phrased it, with a tinge of self-contradiction—even if he actually refrained in fancy from endowing the deceased with aureate harps and crowns and footgear. In fine, death cowed the colonel's thoughts; beyond the grave they did not care to venture, and when confronted with that abyss they decorously balked.

Patricia and Jack were as a matter of course "better off," then—and, miraculously purged of faults, with all their defects somehow remedied, the colonel's wife and brother, with Agatha and the colonel's other interred relatives, were partaking of dignified joys in bright supernal iridescent realms, which the colonel resignedly looked forward to entering, on some comfortably remote day or another, and thus rejoining his transfigured kindred. . . Such was the colonel's charitable decision, in the forming whereof logic was in no way implicated. For religion, as the colonel would have told you sedately, was not a thing to be reasoned about. Attempting to do that, you became in Rudolph Musgrave's honest eyes regrettably flippant.

Meanwhile Cousin Lucy Fentnor was taking care of the colonel and little Roger. And Lichfield, long before the lettering on Patricia's tombstone had time to lose its first light dusty gray, had accredited Cousin Lucy Fentnor with illimitable willingness to become Mrs. Rudolph Musgrave, upon proper solicitation, although such tittle-tattle is neither here nor there; for at worst, a widowed, childless and impoverished second-cousin, discreetly advanced in her forties, was entitled to keep house for the colonel in his bereavement, as a jointly beneficial arrangement, without provoking scandal's tongue to more than a jocose innuendo or two when people met for "auction"—that new-fangled perplexing variant of bridge, just introduced, wherein you bid on the suits. . . And, besides, Cousin Lucy Fentnor (as befitted any one born an Allardyce) was to all accounts a notable housekeeper, famed alike for the perilous glassiness of her hardwood floors, her dexterous management of servants, her Honiton-braid fancy-work (familiar to every patron of Lichfield charity bazaars), and her unparalleled calves-foot jelly. Under Cousin Lucy Fentnor's systematized coddling little Roger grew like the proverbial ill weed, and the colonel likewise waxed perceptibly in girth.

Thus it was that accident and a woman's intervention seemed once more to combine in shielding Rudolph Musgrave from discomfort. And in consequence it was considered improbable that at this late day the colonel would do the proper thing by Clarice Pendomer, as, at the first tidings of Patricia's death, had been authentically rumored among the imaginative; and, in fact, Lichfield no longer considered that necessary. The claim of outraged morality against these two had been thrown out of court, through some unworded social statute of limitation, as far as Lichfield went. Of course it was interesting to note that the colonel called at Mrs. Pendomer's rather frequently nowadays; but, then, Clarice Pendomer had all sorts of callers now—though not many in skirts—and she played poker with men for money until unregenerate hours of the night, and was reputed with a wealth of corroborative detail to have even less discussable sources of income: so that, indeed, Clarice Pendomer was now rather precariously retained within the social pale through her initial precaution of having been born a Bellingham. . . But all such tittle-tattle, as has been said, is quite beside the mark, since with the decadence of Clarice Pendomer this chronicle has, in the outcome, as scant concern as with the marital aspirations of Cousin Lucy Fentnor.

And, moreover, the colonel—in colloquial phrase at least—went everywhere. After the six months of comparative seclusion which decency exacted of his widowerhood—and thereby afforded him ample leisure to complete and publish his *Lichfield Legislative Papers prior to 1800*—the colonel, be it repeated, went everywhere; and people found him no whit the worse company for his black gloves and the somber band stitched to his coatsleeve. So Lichfield again received him gladly, as the social triumph of his generation. Handsome and trim and affable, no imaginable tourist could possibly have divined—for everybody in Lichfield knew, of course—that Rudolph Musgrave had rounded his half-century; and he stayed, as ever, invaluable to Lichfield matrons alike against the entertainment of an "out-of-town" girl, the management of a cotillon, and the prevention of unpleasant pauses among incongruous dinner-companies.

But of Anne Charteris he saw very little nowadays. And, indeed, it was of her own choice that Anne lived apart from Lichfieldian junketings, contented with her dreams and her pride therein, and her remorseful tender memories of the things she might have done for Jack and had not done—lived upon exalted levels nowadays, to which the colonel's more urbane bereavement did not aspire.

III

Charteris" was engraved in large, raised letters upon the granite coping over which Anne stepped to enter the trim burial-plot wherein her dead lay.

The place today is one of the "points of interest" in Cedarwood. Tourists, passing through Lichfield, visit it as inevitably as they do the graves of the Presidents, the Southern generals and the many other famous people which the old cemetery contains; and the negro hackmen of Lichfield are already profuse in inaccurate information concerning its occupant. In a phrase, the post card which pictures "E 9436—Grave of John Charteris" is among the seven similar misinterpretations of localities most frequently demanded in Lichfieldian drugstores and news-stands.

Her victoria had paused a trifle farther up the hill, where two big sycamores overhung the roadway. She came into the place alone, walking quickly, for she was unwarrantably flustered by her late encounter. And when she found, of all people, Rudolph Musgrave standing by her husband's grave, as in a sort of puzzled and yet reverent meditation, she was, and somehow as half-guiltily, assuring herself there was no possible reason for the repugnance—nay, the rage,—which a mere glimpse of trudging, painted and flamboyant Clarice Pendomer had kindled. Yet it must be recorded that Anne had always detested Clarice.

Now Anne spoke, as the phrase runs, before she thought. "She came with you!"

And he answered, as from the depths of an uncalled-for comprehension which was distinctly irritating:

"Yes. And Harry, too, for that matter. Only our talk got somehow to be not quite the sort it would be salutary for him to take an interest in. So we told Harry to walk on slowly to the gate, and be sure not to do any number of things he would never have thought of if we hadn't suggested them. You know how people are with children—"

"Harry is—her boy?" Anne, being vexed, had almost added—"and yours?"

"Oh—! Say the *fons et origo* of the Pendomer divorce case, poor little chap. Yes, Harry is her boy."

Anne said, and again, as she perceived within the moment, a thought too expeditiously: "I wish you wouldn't bring them here, Colonel Musgrave."

Indeed, it seemed to her flat desecration that Musgrave should have brought his former mistress into this hallowed plot of ground. She did not mind—illogically, perhaps—his bringing the child.

"Eh—? Oh, yes," said Colonel Musgrave. He was sensibly nettled. "You wish 'Colonel Musgrave' wouldn't bring them here. But then, you see, we had been to Patricia's grave. And we remembered how Jack stood by us both when—when things bade fair to be even more unpleasant for Clarice and myself than they actually were. You shouldn't, I think, grudge even such moral reprobates the privilege of being properly appreciative of what he did for both of us. Besides, you always come on Saturdays, you know. We couldn't very well anticipate that you would be here this afternoon."

So he had been at pains to spy upon her! Anne phrased it thus in her soul, being irritated, and crisply answered:

"I am leaving Lichfield tomorrow. I had meant this to be my farewell to them until October."

Colonel Musgrave had glanced toward the little headstone, with its rather lengthy epitaph, which marked the resting-place of this woman's only child; and then to the tall shaft whereon was engraved just "John Charteris." The latter inscription was very characteristic of her view-point, he reflected; and yet reasonable, too; as one might mention a Hector or a Goethe, say, without being at pains to disclaim allusion to the minor sharers of either name.

"Yes," he said. "Well, I shall not intrude."

"No—wait," she dissented.

Her voice was altered now, for there had come into it a marvelous gentleness.

And Colonel Musgrave remained motionless. The whole world was motionless, ineffably expectant, as it seemed to him.

Sunset was at hand. On one side was the high wooden fence which showed the boundary of Cedarwood, and through its palings and above it, was visible the broad, shallow river, comfortably colored, for the most part, like *café au lait*, but flecked with many patches of foam and flat iron-colored rocks and innumerable islets, some no bigger than a billiard-table, but with even the tiniest boasting a tree or two. On the other—westward—was a mounting vista of close-shaven turf, and many copings, like magnified geometrical problems, and a host of stunted growing things—with the staid verdancy of evergreens predominant—and a multitude of candid shafts and slabs and crosses and dwarfed lambs and meditant angels.

Some of these thronged memorials were tinged with violet, and others were a-glitter like silver, just as the ordered trees shaded them or no from the low sun. The disposition of all worldly affairs, the man dimly knew, was very anciently prearranged by an illimitable and, upon the whole, a kindly wisdom.

She was considering the change in him. Anne was recollecting that Colonel Musgrave had somewhat pointedly avoided her since her widowhood. He seemed almost a stranger nowadays.

And she could not recognize in the man any resemblance to the boy whom she remembered—so long ago—excepting just his womanish mouth, which was as in the old time very full and red and sensitive. And, illogically enough, both this great change in him and this one feature that had never changed annoyed her equally.

She was also worried by his odd tone of flippancy. It jarred, it vaguely—for the phrase has no equivalent—"rubbed her the wrong way." Here at a martyr's tomb it was hideously out-of-place, and yet she did not see her way clear to rebuke. So she remained silent.

But Rudolph Musgrave was uncanny in some respects. For he said within the moment, "I am not a bit like John Charteris, am I?"

"No," she answered, quietly. It had been her actual thought.

Anne stayed a tiny while quite motionless. Her eyes saw nothing physical. It was the attitude, Colonel Musgrave reflected, of one who listens to a far-off music and, incommunicably, you knew that the music was of a martial sort. She was all in black, of course, very slim and pure and beautiful. The great cluster of red roses, loosely held, was like blood against the somber gown.

The widow of John Charteris, in fine, was a very different person from that Anne Willoughby whom Rudolph Musgrave had loved so long and long ago. This woman had tasted of tonic sorrows unknown to Rudolph Musgrave, and had got consolation too, somehow, in far half-credible uplands unvisited by him. But, he knew, she lived, and was so exquisite, mainly by virtue of that delusion which he, of all men, had preserved; Anne Charteris was of his creation, his masterpiece; and viewing her, he was aware of great reverence and joy.

Anne was happy. It was for that he had played.

But aloud, "I am envious," Rudolph Musgrave declared. "He is the single solitary man I ever knew whose widow was contented to be simply his relict for ever and ever, amen. For you will always be just the woman John Charteris loved, won't you? Yes, if you lived to be thirty-seven years older than Methuselah, and every genius and potentate in the world should come a-wooing in the meantime, it never would occur to you that you could possibly be anything, even to an insane person, except his relict. And he has been dead now all of three whole years! So I am envious, just as we ordinary mortals can't help being of you both; and—may I say it?—I am glad."

IV

They were standing thus when a boy of ten or eleven came unhurriedly into the "section." He assumed possession of Colonel Musgrave's hand as though the action were a matter of course.

"I got lost, Colonel Musgrave," the child composedly announced. "I walked ever so far, and the gate wasn't where we left it. And the roads kept turning and twisting so, it seemed I'd never get anywhere. I don't like being lost when it's getting dark and there's so many dead people 'round, do you?"

The colonel was moved to disapproval. "Young man, I suppose your poor deserted mother is looking for you everywhere, and has probably torn out every solitary strand of hair she possesses by this time."

"I reckon she is," the boy assented. The topic did not appear to be in his eyes of preëminent importance.

Then Anne Charteris said, "Harry," and her voice was such that Rudolph Musgrave wheeled with amazement in his face.

The boy had gone to her complaisantly, and she stood now with one hand on either of his shoulders, regarding him. Her lips were parted, but they did not move at all.

"You are Mrs. Pendomer's boy, aren't you?" said Anne Charteris, in a while. She had some difficulty in articulation.

"Yes'm," Harry assented, "and we come here 'most every Wednesday, and, please, ma'am, you're hurtin' me."

"I didn't mean to—dear," the woman added, painfully. "Don't interfere with me, Rudolph Musgrave! Your mother must be very fond of you, Harry. I had a little boy once. I was fond of him. He would have been eleven years old last February."

"Please, ma'am, I wasn't eleven till April, and I ain't tall for my age, but Tubby Parsons says—"

The woman gave an odd, unhuman sound. "Not until April!"

"Harry," said Colonel Musgrave then, "an enormous whale is coming down the river in precisely two minutes. Perhaps if you were to look through the palings of that fence you might see him. I don't suppose you would care to, though?"

And Harry strolled resignedly toward the fence. Harry Pendomer did not like this funny lady who had hurt, frightened eyes. He did not believe in the whale, of course, any more than he did in Santa Claus. But like most children, he patiently accepted the fact that grown people are unaccountable overlords appointed by some vast *bêtise*, whom, if only through prudential motives, it is preferable to humor.

V

Colonel Musgrave stood now upon the other side of John Charteris's grave—just in the spot that was reserved for her own occupancy some day.

"You are ill, Anne. You are not fit to be out. Go home."

"I had a little boy once," she said. "'But that's all past and gone, and good times and bad times and all times pass over.' There's an odd simple music in the sentence, isn't there? Yet I remember it chiefly because I used to read that book to him and he loved it. And it was my child that died. Why is this other child so like him?"

"Oh, then, that's it, is it?" said Rudolph Musgrave, as in relief. "Bless me, I suppose all these little shavers are pretty much alike. I can only tell Roger from the other boys by his red head. Humanity in the raw, you know. Still, it is no wonder it gave you a turn. You had much better go home, however, and not take any foolish risks, and put your feet in hot water, and rub cologne on your temples, and do all the other suitable things—"

"I remember now," she continued, without any apparent emotion, and as though he had not spoken. "When I came into the room you were saying that the child must be considered. You were both very angry, and I was alarmed—foolishly alarmed, perhaps. And my—and John Charteris said, 'Let him tell, then'—and you told me—"

"The truth, Anne."

"And he sat quietly by. Oh, if he'd had the grace, the common manliness—!" She shivered here. "But he never interrupted you. I—I was not looking at him. I was thinking how vile you were. And when you had ended, he said, 'My dear, I am sorry you should have been involved in this. But since you are, I think we can assure Rudolph that both of us will regard his confidence as sacred.' Then I remembered him, and thought how noble he was! And all those years that were so happy, hour by hour, he was letting you—meet his bills!" She seemed to wrench out the inadequate metaphor.

You could hear the far-off river, now, faint as the sound of boiling water.

After a few pacings Colonel Musgrave turned upon her. He spoke with a curious simplicity.

"There isn't any use in lying to you. You wouldn't believe. You would only go to someone else—some woman probably,—who would jump at the chance of telling you everything and a deal more. Yes, there are a great many 'they *do* say's' floating about. This was the only one that came near being—serious. The man was very clever.—Oh, he wasn't vulgarly lecherous. He was simply—Jack Charteris. He always irritated Lichfield, though, by not taking Lichfield very seriously. You would hear every by-end of retaliative and sniggered-over mythology, and in your present state of mind you would believe all of them. I happen to know that a great many of these stories are not true."

"A great many of these stories," Anne repeated, "aren't true! A great many aren't! That ought to be consoling, oughtn't it?" She spoke without a trace of bitterness.

"I express myself very badly. What I really mean, what I am aiming at, is that I wish you would let me answer any questions you might like to ask, because I will answer them truthfully. Very few people would. You see, you go about the world so like a gray-stone saint who has just stepped down from her niche for the fraction of a second," he added, as with venom, "that it is only human nature to dislike you."

Anne was not angry. It had come to her, quite as though she were considering some other woman, that what the man said was, in a fashion, true.

"There is sunlight and fresh air in the street," John Charteris had been wont to declare, "and there is a culvert at the corner. I think it is a mistake for us to emphasize the culvert."

So he had trained her to disbelieve in its existence. She saw this now. It did not matter. It seemed to her that nothing mattered any more.

"I've only one question, I think. Why did you do it?" She spoke with bright amazement in her eyes.

"Oh, my dear, my dear!" he seriocomically deplored. "Why, because it was such a noble thing to do. It was so like the estimable young man in a play, you know, who acknowledges the crime he never committed and takes a curtain-call immediately afterwards. In fine, I simply observed to myself, with the late Monsieur de Bergerac, 'But what a gesture!'" And he parodied an actor's motion in this rôle.

She stayed unsmiling and patiently awaiting veracity. Anne did not understand that Colonel Musgrave was telling the absolute truth. And so,

"You haven't *any* sense of humor," he lamented. "You used to have a deal, too, before you took to being conscientiously cheerful, and diffusing sweetness and light among your cowering associates. Well, it was because it helped him a little. Oh, I am being truthful now. I had some reason to dislike Jack Charteris, but odd as it is, I know today I never did. I ought to have, perhaps. But I didn't."

"My friend, you are being almost truthful. But I want the truth entire."

"It isn't polite to disbelieve people," he reproved her; "or at the very least, according to the best books on etiquette, you ought not to do it audibly. Would you mind if I smoked? I could be more veracious then. There is something in tobacco that makes frankness a matter of course. I thank you."

He produced an amber holder, fitted a cigarette into it, and presently inhaled twice. He said, with a curt voice:

"The reason, naturally, was you. You may remember certain things that happened just before John Charteris came and took you. Oh, that is precisely what he did! You are rather a narrow-minded woman now, in consequence—or in my humble opinion, at least—and deplorably superior. It pleased the man to have in his house—if you will overlook my venturing into metaphor,—one cool room very sparsely furnished where he could come when the mood seized him. He took the raw material from me, wherewith to build that room, because he wanted that room. I acquiesced, because I had not the skill wherewith to fight him."

Anne understood him now, as with a great drench of surprise. And fear was what she felt in chief when she saw for just this moment as though it had lightened, the man's face transfigured, and tender, and strange to her.

"I tried to buy your happiness, to—yes, just to keep you blind indefinitely. Had the price been heavier, I would have paid it the more gladly. Fate has played a sorry trick. *You* would never haye seen through him. My dear, I have wanted very often to shake you," he said.

And she knew, in a glorious terror, that she desired him to shake her, and as she had never desired anything else in life.

"Oh, well, I am just a common, ordinary, garden-sort of fool. The Musgraves always are, in one fashion or another," he sulkily concluded. And now the demigod was merely Rudolph Musgrave again, and she was not afraid any longer, but only inexpressibly fordone.

"Isn't that like a woman?" he presently demanded of the June heavens. "To drag something out of a man with inflexibility, monomania and moral grappling-irons, and *then* not like it! Oh, very well! I am disgusted by your sex's axiomatic variability. I shall take Harry to his fond mamma at once."

She did not say anything. A certain new discovery obsessed her like a piece of piercing music.

Then Rudolph Musgrave gave the tiniest of gestures downward. "And I have told you this, in chief, because we two remember him. He wanted you. He took you. You are his. You will always be. He gave you just a fragment of himself. That fragment was worth more than everything I had to offer."

Anne very carefully arranged her roses on the ivy-covered grave. "I do not know—meanwhile, I give these to our master. And my real widowhood begins today."

And as she rose he looked at her across the colorful mound, and smiled, half as with embarrassment. A lie, he thought, might ameliorate the situation, and he bravely hazarded a prodigious one. "Is it necessary to tell you that Jack loved you? And that the others never really counted?"

He rejoiced to see that Anne believed him. "No," she assented, "no, not with him. Oddly enough, I am proud of that, even now. But—don't you see?—I never loved him. I was just his priestess—the priestess of a stucco god! Otherwise, I would know it wasn't his fault, but altogether that of—the others."

He grimaced and gave a bantering flirt of his head. He said, with quizzing eyes:

"Would it do any good to quote Lombroso, and Maudsley, and Gall, and Krafft-Ebing, and Flechsig, and so on? and to tell you that the excessive use of one brain faculty must necessarily cause a lack of nutriment to all the other brain-cells? It would be rather up-to-date. There is a deal I could tell you also as to what poisonous blood he inherited; but to do this I have not the right." And then Rudolph Musgrave said in all sincerity: "'A wild, impetuous whirlwind of passion and faculty slumbered quiet there; such heavenly *melody* dwelling in the heart of it.'"

She had put aside alike the drolling and the palliative suggestion, like flimsy veils. "I think it wouldn't do any good whatever. When growing things are broken by the whirlwind, they don't, as a rule, discuss the theory of air-currents as a consolation. Men such as he was take what they desire. It isn't fair—to us others. But it's true, for all that—"

Their eyes met warily; and for no reason which they shared in common they smiled together.

"Poor little Lady of Shalott," said Rudolph Musgrave, "the mirror is cracked from side to side, isn't it? I am sorry. For life is not so easily disposed of. And there is only life to look at now, and life is a bewilderingly complex business, you will find, because the laws of it are so childishly simple—and implacable. And one of these laws seems to be that in our little planet, might makes right—"

He stayed to puff his cigarette.

"Oh, Rudolph dear, don't—don't be just a merry-Andrew!" she cried impulsively, before he had time to continue, which she perceived he meant to do, as if it did not matter.

And he took her full meaning, quite as he had been used in the old times to discourse upon a half-sentence. "I am afraid I am that, rather," he said, reflectively. "But then Clarice and I could hardly have weathered scandal except by making ourselves particularly agreeable to everybody. And somehow I got into the habit of making people laugh. It isn't very difficult. I am rather an adept at telling stories which just graze impropriety, for instance. You know, they call me the social triumph of my generation. And people are glad to see me because I am 'so awfully funny' and 'simply killing' and so on. And I suppose it tells in the long run—like the dyer's hand, you know."

"It does tell." Anne was thinking it would always tell. And that, too, would be John Charteris's handiwork.

Ensued a silence. Rudolph Musgrave was painstakingly intent upon his cigarette. A nestward-plunging bird called to his mate impatiently. Then Anne shook her head impatiently.

"Come, while I'm thinking, I will drive you back to Lichfield."

"Oh, no; that wouldn't do at all," he said, with absolute decision. "No, you see I have to return the boy. And I can't quite imagine your carriage waiting at the doors of 'that Mrs. Pendomer.'"

"Oh," Anne fleetingly thought, "*he* would have understood." But aloud she only said: "And do you think I hate her any longer? Yes, it is true I hated her until today, and now I'm just sincerely sorry for her. For she and I—and you and even the child yonder—and all that any of us is today—are just so many relics of John Charteris. Yet he has done with us—at last!"

She said this with an inhalation of the breath; but she did not look at him.

"Take care!" he said, with an unreasonable harshness. "For I forewarn you I am imagining vain things."

"I'm not afraid, somehow." But Anne did not look at him.

He saw as with a rending shock how like the widow of John Charteris was to Anne Willoughby; and unforgotten pulses, very strange and irrational and dear, perplexed him sorely. He debated, and flung aside the cigarette as an out-moded detail of his hobbling part.

"You say I did a noble thing for you. I tried to. But quixotism has its price. Today I am not quite the man who did that thing. John Charteris has set his imprint too deep upon us. We served his pleasure. We are not any longer the boy and girl who loved each other."

She waited in the rising twilight with a yet averted face. The world was motionless, ineffably expectant, as it seemed to him. And the disposition of all worldly affairs, the man dimly knew, was very anciently prearranged by an illimitable and, upon the whole, a kindly wisdom.

So that, "My dear, my dear!" he swiftly said: "I don't think I can word just what my feeling is for you. Always my view of the world has been that you existed, and that some other people existed—as accessories—"

Then he was silent for a heart-beat, appraising her. His hands lifted toward her and fell within the moment, as if it were in impotence.

Anne spoke at last, and the sweet voice of her was very glad and proud and confident.

"My friend, remember that I have not thanked you. You have done the most foolish and—the manliest thing I ever knew a man to do, just for my sake. And I have accepted it as if it were a matter of course. And I shall always do so. Because it was your right to do this very brave and foolish thing for me. I know you joyed in doing it. Rudolph. . . you cannot understand how glad I am you joyed in doing it."

Their eyes met. It is not possible to tell you all they were aware of through that moment, because it is a knowledge so rarely apprehended, and even then for such a little while, that no man who has sensed it can remember afterward aught save the splendor and perfection of it.

AND YET ANNE LOOKED BACK once. There was just the tall, stark shaft, and on it "John Charteris." The thing was ominous and vast, all colored like wet gravel, save where the sunlight tipped it with clean silver very high above their reach.

"Come," she quickly said to Rudolph Musgrave; "come, for I am afraid."

VI

And are we then to leave them with glad faces turned to that new day wherein, above the ashes of old errors and follies and mischances and miseries, they were to raise the structure of such a happiness as earth rarely witnesses? Would it not be, instead, a grateful task more fully to depicture how Rudolph Musgrave's love of Anne won finally to its reward, and these two shared the evening of their lives in tranquil service of unswerving love come to its own at last?

Undoubtedly, since the espousal of one's first love—by oneself—is a phenomenon rarely encountered outside of popular fiction, it would be a very gratifying task to record that Anne and Rudolph Musgrave were married that autumn; that subsequently Lichfield was astounded by the fervor of their life-long bliss; that Colonel and (the second) Mrs. Musgrave were universally respected, in a word, and their dinner-parties were always prominently chronicled by the *Lichfield Courier-Herald*; and that Anne took excellent care of little Roger, and that she and her second husband proved eminently suited to each other.

But, as a matter of fact, not one of these things ever happened. . .

"I have been thinking it over," Anne deplored. "Oh, Rudolph dear, I perfectly realize you are the best and noblest man I ever knew. And I have always loved you very much, my dear; that is why I could never abide poor Mrs. Pendomer. And yet—it is a feeling I simply can't explain—"

"That you belong to Jack in spite of everything?" the colonel said. "Why, but of course! I might have known that Jack would never have allowed any simple incidental happening such as his death to cause his missing a possible trick."

Anne would have comforted Rudolph Musgrave; but, to her discomfiture, the colonel was grinning, however ruefully.

"I was thinking," he stated, "of the only time that I ever, to my knowledge, talked face to face with the devil. It is rather odd how obstinately life clings to the most hackneyed trick of ballad-makers; and still naively pretends to enrich her productions by the stale device of introducing a refrain—so that the idlest remarks of as much as three years ago keep cropping up as the actual gist of the present! . . . However, were it within my power, I would evoke Amaimon straightway now to come up yonder, through your hearthrug, and to answer me quite honestly if I did not tell him on the beach at Matocton that this, precisely this, would be the outcome of your knowing everything!"

"I told you that I couldn't, quite, *explain*—" Anne said.

"Eh, but I can, my dear," he informed her. "The explanation is that Lichfield bore us, shaped us, and made us what we are. We may not enjoy a monopoly of the virtues here in Lichfield, but there is one trait at least which the children of Lichfield share in common. We are loyal. We give but once; and when we give, we give all that we have; and when we have once given it, neither common-sense, nor a concourse of expostulating seraphim, nor anything else in the universe, can induce us to believe that a retraction, or even a qualification, of the gift would be quite worthy of us."

"But that—that's foolish. Why, it's unreasonable," Anne pointed out.

"Of course it is. And that is why I am proud of Lichfield. And that is why you are today Jack's wife and always will be just Jack's wife—and why today I am Patricia's husband—and why Lichfield today is Lichfield. There is something braver in life than to be just reasonable, thank God! And so, we keep the faith, my dear, however obsolete we find fidelity to be. We keep to the old faith—we of Lichfield, who have given hostages to the past. We remember even now that we gave freely in an old time, and did not haggle. . . And so, we are proud—yes! we are consumedly proud, and we know that we have earned the right to be proud."

A little later Colonel Musgrave said:

"And yet—it takes a monstrous while to dispose of our universe's subtleties. I have loved you my whole life long, as accurately as we can phrase these matters. There is no—no *reasonable* reason why you should not marry me now; and you would marry me if I pressed it. And I do not press it. Perhaps it all comes of our both having been reared in Lichfield. Perhaps that is why I, too, have been 'thinking it over.' You see," he added, with a smile, "the rivet in grandfather's neck is not lightly to be ignored, after all. No, you do not know what I am talking about, my dear. And—well, anyhow, I belong to Patricia. Upon the whole, I am glad that I belong to Patricia; for Patricia and what Patricia meant to me was the one vital thing in a certain person's rather hand-to-mouth existence—oh, yes, in spite of everything! I know it now. Anne Charteris," the colonel cried, "I wouldn't marry you or any other woman breathing, even though you were to kneel and implore me upon the knees of a centipede. For I belong to Patricia; and the rivet stays unbroken, after all."

“Oh, and am I being very foolish again?” Anne asked. “For I have been remembering that when—when Jack was not quite truthful about some things, you know,—the truth he hid was always one which would have hurt me. And I like to believe that was, at least in part, the reason he hid it, Rudolph. So he purchased my happiness—well, at ugly prices perhaps. But he purchased it, none the less; and I had it through all those years. So why shouldn’t I—after all—be very grateful to him? And, besides”—her voice broke—“besides, he was Jack, you know. He belonged to me. What does it matter what he did? He belonged to me, and I loved him.”

And to the colonel’s discomfort Anne began to cry.

“There, there!” he said, “so the real truth is out at last. And tears don’t help very much. It does seem a bit unfair, my dear, I know. But that is simply because you and I are living in a universe which has never actually committed itself, under any penalizing bond, to be entirely candid as to the laws by which it is conducted.”

BUT IT MAY BE THAT Rudolph Musgrave voiced quite obsolete views. For he said this at a very remote period—when the Beef Trust was being “investigated” in Washington; when an excited Iberian constabulary was still hunting the anarchists who had attempted to assassinate the young King and Queen of Spain upon their wedding-day; when the rebuilding of an earthquake-shattered San Francisco was just beginning to be talked of as a possibility; and when editorials were mostly devoted to discussion of what Mr. Bryan would have to say about bi-metallism when he returned from his foreign tour.

And, besides, it was Rudolph Musgrave’s besetting infirmity always to shrink—under shelter of whatever grandiloquent excuse—from making changes. One may permissibly estimate this foible to have weighed with him a little, even now, just as in all things it had always weighed in Lichfield with all his generation. An old custom is not lightly broken.

PART X

IMPRIMIS

"So let us laugh, lest vain rememberings
Breed, as of old, some rude bucolic cry
Of awkward anguishes, of dreams that die
Without decorum, of Love lacking wings
Yet striving you-ward in his flounderings
Eternally,—as now, even when I lie
As I lie now, who know that you and I
Exist and heed not lesser happenings.

"I was. I am. I will be. Eh, no doubt
For some sufficient cause, I drift, defer,
Equivocate, dream, hazard, grow more stout,
Age, am no longer Love's idolater,—
And yet I could and would not live without
Your faith that heartens and your doubts which spur."

—Lionel Crochard. *Palinodia*

I

So weeks and months, and presently irrevocable years, passed tranquilly; and nothing very important seemed to happen nowadays, either for good or ill; and Rudolph Musgrave was content enough.

True, there befell, and with increasing frequency, periods when one must lie abed, and be coaxed into taking interminable medicines, and be ministered unto generally, because one was of a certain age nowadays, and must be prudent. But even such necessities, these underhanded indignities of time, had their alleviations. Trained nurses, for example, were uncommonly well-informed and agreeable young women, when you came to know them—and quite lady-like, too, for all that in our topsy-turvy days these girls had to work for their living. Unthinkable as it seemed, the colonel found that his night-nurse, a Miss Ramsay, was actually by birth a Ramsay of Blenheim; and for a little the discovery depressed him. But to be made much of, upon whatever terms, was always treatment to which the colonel submitted only too docilely. And, besides, in this queer, comfortable, just half-waking state, the colonel found one had the drollest dreams, evolving fancies such as were really a credit to one's imagination. . .

For instance, one very often imagined that Patricia was more close at hand nowadays. . . No, she was not here in the room, of course, but outside, in the street, at the corner below, where the letterbox stood. Yes, she was undoubtedly there, the colonel reflected drowsily. And they had been so certain her return could only result in unhappiness, and they were so wise, that whilst she waited for her opportunity Patricia herself began to be a little uneasy. She had patrolled the block six times before the chance came.

And it seemed to Rudolph Musgrave, drowsily pleased by his own inventiveness, that Patricia was glad this afternoon was so hot that no one was abroad except the small boy at the corner house, who sat upon the bottom porch-step, and, as children so often do, appeared intently to appraise the world at large with an inexplicable air of disappointment.

"Now think how Rudolph would feel,"—the colonel whimsically played at reading Patricia's reflection—"if I were to be arrested as a suspicious character—that's what the newspapers always call them, I think—on his very doorstep! And he must have been home a half-hour ago at least, because I know it's after five. But the side-gate's latched, and I can't ring the door-bell—if only because it would be too ridiculous to have to ask the maid to tell Colonel Musgrave his wife wanted to see him. Besides, I don't know the new house-girl. I wish now we hadn't let old Mary go, even though she was so undependable about thorough-cleaning."

And it seemed to Rudolph Musgrave that Patricia was tired of pacing before the row of houses, each so like the other, and compared herself to Gulliver astray upon a Brobdingnagian bookshelf which held a "library set" of some huge author. She had lost interest, too, in the new house upon the other side.

"If things were different I would have to call on them. But as it is, I am spared that bother at least," said Patricia, just as if being dead did not change people at all.

Then a colored woman, trim and frillily-capped, came out of the watched house. She bore some eight or nine letters in one hand, and fanned herself with them in a leisurely flat-footed progress to the mailbox at the lower corner.

"She looks capable," was Patricia's grudging commentary, in slipping through the doorway into the twilight of the hall. "But it isn't safe to leave the front-door open like this. One never knows—No, I can tell by the look of her she's the sort that can't be induced to sleep on the lot, and takes mysterious bundles home at night."

II

And it seemed to Rudolph Musgrave, now in the full flow of this droll dream, that Patricia resentfully noted her front-hall had been "meddled with." This much alone might Patricia observe in a swift transit to the parlor.

She waited there until the maid returned; and registered to the woman's credit the discreet soft closing of the front-door and afterward the well-nigh inaudible swish of the rear door of the dining-room as the maid went back into the kitchen.

"In any event," Patricia largely conceded, "she probably doesn't clash the knives and forks in the pantry after supper, like she was hostile armaments with any number of cutlasses apiece. I remember Rudolph simply couldn't stand it when we had Ethel."

So much was satisfactory. Only—her parlor was so altered!

There was—to give you just her instantaneous first impression—so little in it. Broad spaces of plain color showed everywhere; and Patricia's ideal of what a parlor should be, as befitted the châtelaine of a fine home in Lichfield, had always been the tangled elegancies of the front show-window of a Woman's Exchange for Fancy Work. The room had even been repapered—odiously, as she considered; and the shiny floor of it boasted just three inefficient rugs, like dingy rafts upon a sea of very strong coffee.

Patricia looked in vain for her grandiose plush-covered chairs, her immaculate "tidies," and the proud yellow lambrequin, embroidered in high relief with white gardenias, which had formerly adorned the mantelpiece. The heart of her hungered for her unforgotten and unforgettable "watered-silk" papering wherein white roses bloomed exuberantly against a yellow background—which deplorably faded if you did not keep the window-shades down, she remembered—and she wanted back her white thick comfortable carpet which hid the floor completely, so that everywhere you trod upon the buxomest of stalwart yellow roses, each bunch of which was lavishly tied with wind-blown ribbons.

Then, too, her cherished spinning-wheel, at least two hundred and fifty years old, which had looked so pretty after she had gilded it and added a knot of pink sarsenet, was departed; and gone as well was the mirror-topped table, with its array of china swan and frogs and water-lilies artistically grouped about its speckless surface. Even her prized engraving of "Michael Angelo Buonarotti"—contentedly regarding his just finished Moses, while a pope tiptoed into the room through a side-door—had been removed, with all its splendors of red-plush and intricate gilt-framing.

Just here and there, in fine, like a familiar face in a crowd, she could discover someone of her more sedately-colored "parlor ornaments"; and the whole history of it—its donor or else its price, the gestures of the shopman, even what sort of weather it was when she and Rudolph found "exactly what I've been looking for" in the shop-window, and the Stapyltonian, haggling over the price with which Patricia had bargained—such unimportant details as these now vividly awakened in recollection. . . In fine, this room was not her parlor at all, and in it Patricia was lonely. . . Yes, yes, she would be nowadays, the colonel reflected, for he himself had never been in thorough sympathy with all the changes made by Roger's self-assured young wife.

Thus it was with the first floor of the house, through which Patricia strayed with uniform discomfort. This place was home no longer.

Thus it was with the first floor of the house. Everywhere the equipments were strange, or at best arranged not quite as Patricia would have placed them. Yet they had not any look of being recently purchased. Even that hideous stair-carpet was a little worn, she noted, as noiselessly she mounted to the second story.

The house was perfectly quiet, save for a tiny shrill continuance of melody that somehow seemed only to pierce the silence, not to dispel it. Rudolph—of all things!—had in her absence acquired a canary. And everybody knew what an interminable nuisance a canary was.

She entered the front room. It had been her bedroom ever since her marriage. She remembered this as with a gush of defiant joy.

III

So it seemed to Rudolph Musgrave that Patricia came actually into the room that had been hers. . .

A canary was singing there, very sweet and shrill and as in defiant joy. Its trilling seemed to fill the room. In the brief pauses of his song the old clock, from which Rudolph had removed the pendulum on the night of Agatha's death would interpose an obstinate slow ticking; and immediately the clock-noise would be drowned in melody. Otherwise the room was silent.

In the alcove stood the bed which had been Patricia's. Intent upon its occupant were three persons, with their backs turned to her. One Patricia could easily divine to be a doctor; he was twiddling a hypodermic syringe between his fingers, and the set of his shoulders was that of acquiescence. Profiles of the others she saw: one a passive nurse in uniform, who was patiently chafing the right hand of the bed's occupant; the other a lean-featured red-haired stranger, who sat crouched in his chair and held the dying man's left hand.

For in the bed, supported by many pillows, and facing Patricia, was a dying man. He was very old, having thick tumbled hair which, like his two-weeks' beard, was uniformly white. His eyelids drooped a trifle, so that he seemed to meditate concerning something ineffably remote and serious, yet not, upon the whole, unsatisfactory. You saw and heard the intake of each breath, so painfully drawn, and expelled with manifest relief, as if the man were very tired of breathing. Yet the bedclothes heaved with his vain efforts just to keep on breathing. And sometimes his parted lips would twitch curiously. . . Rudolph Musgrave, too, could see all this quite plainly, in the mirror over the mantel.

The doctor spoke. "Yes—it's the end, Professor Musgrave," he said. For this lean-featured red-haired stranger to whom the doctor spoke, a pedagogue to his finger-tips, had once been Patricia's dearly-purchased, chubby baby Roger.

And Rudolph Musgrave stayed motionless. He knew Patricia was there; but that fact no longer seemed either very strange or even unnatural; and besides, it was against some law for him to look at her until Patricia had called him. . . Meanwhile, just opposite, above the mirror, and facing him, was the Stuart portrait of young Gerald Musgrave. This picture had now hung there for a great many years. The boy still smiled at you in undiminished raillery, even though he smiled ambiguously, and with a sort of humorous sadness in his eyes. Once, very long ago—when the picture hung downstairs—someone had said that Gerald Musgrave's life was barren. The dying man could not now recollect, quite, who that person was.

Rudolph Musgrave stayed motionless. He comprehended that he was dying. The greatest of all changes was at hand; and he, who had always shrunk from making changes, was now content enough. . . Indeed, with Rudolph Musgrave living had always been a vaguely dissatisfactory business, a hand-to-mouth proceeding which he had scrambled through, as he saw now, without any worthy aim or even any intelligible purpose. He had nothing very heinous with which to reproach himself; but upon the other side, he had most certainly nothing of which to be particularly proud.

So this was all that living came to! You heard of other people being rapt by splendid sins and splendid virtues, and you anticipated that tomorrow some such majestic energy would transfigure your own living, and change everything: but the great adventure never arrived, somehow; and the days were frittered away piecemeal, what with eating your dinner, and taking a wholesome walk, and checking up your bank account, and dovetailing scraps of parish registers and land-patents and county records into an irrefutable pedigree, and seeing that your clothes were pressed, and looking over the newspapers—and what with other infinitesimal avocations, each one innocent, none of any particular importance, and each consuming an irrevocable moment of the allotted time—until at last you found that living had not, necessarily, any climax at all. . . And Patricia would call him presently.

Once, very long ago, someone had said that the most pathetic tragedy in life was to get nothing in particular out of it. The dying man could not now recollect, quite, who that person was.

He wondered, vaguely, what might have been the outcome if Rudolph Musgrave had whole-heartedly sought, not waited for, the great adventure; if Rudolph Musgrave had put—however irrationally—more energy and less second-thought into living; if Rudolph Musgrave had not been contented to be just a Musgrave of Matocton. . . Well, it was too late now. He viewed his whole life now, in epitome, and much as you may see at night the hackneyed vista from your window leap to incisiveness under the lash of lightning. No, the life of Rudolph Musgrave had never risen to the plane of dignity, not even to that of seeming to Rudolph Musgrave a connected and really important transaction on Rudolph Musgrave's part. Yet Lichfield, none the better for Rudolph Musgrave's having lived, was none the worse, thank heaven! And there were younger men in Lichfield—men who did not mean to fail as Rudolph Musgrave and his fellows all had failed. . . Eh, yes, what was the toast that Rudolph Musgrave drank, so long ago, to the new Lichfield which these younger men were making?

"To this new South, that has not any longer need of me or of my kind.

"To this new South! She does not gaze unwillingly, nor too complacently, upon old years, and dares concede that but with loss of manliness may any man encroach upon the heritage of a dog or of a trotting-horse, and consider the exploits of an ancestor to guarantee an innate and personal excellence.

"For to her all former glory is less a jewel than a touchstone, and with her portion of it daily she appraises her own doing, and without vain speech. And her high past she values now, in chief, as fit foundation of that edifice whereon she labors day by day, and with augmenting strokes."

Yes, that was it. And it was true. Yet Rudolph Musgrave's life on earth was ending now—the only life that he would ever have on earth—and it had never risen to the plane of seeming even to Rudolph Musgrave a really important transaction on Rudolph Musgrave's part. . .

Then Patricia spoke. Low and very low she called to Olaf, and the dim, wistful eyes of Rudolph Musgrave lifted, and gazed full upon her standing there, and were no longer wistful. And the man made as though to rise, and could not, and his face was very glad.

For in the dying man had awakened the pulses of an old, strange, half-forgotten magic, and all his old delight in the girl who had shared in and had provoked this ancient wonder-working, together with a quite new consciousness of the inseparability of Patricia's foibles from his existence; so that he was incuriously aware of his imbecility in not having known always that Patricia must come back some day, not as a glorious, unfamiliar angel, but unaltered.

"I am glad you haven't changed. . . Why, but of course! Nothing would have counted if you had changed—not even for the better, Patricia. For you and what you meant to me were real. That only was real—that we, not being demigods, but being just what we were, once climbed together very high, where we could glimpse the stars—and nothing else can ever be of any importance. What we inherited was too much for us, was it not, my dear? And now it is not formidable any longer. Oh, but I loved you very greatly, Patricia! And now at last, my dear, I seem to understand—as in that old, old time when you and I were glad together—"

But he did not say this aloud, for it seemed to him that he stood in a cool, pleasant garden, and that Patricia came toward him through the long shadows of sunset. The lacy folds and furbelows and semi-transparencies that clothed her were now tinged with gold and now, as a hedge or a flower bed screened her from the level rays, were softened into multitudinous graduations of grays and mauves and violets.

They did not speak. But in her eyes he found compassion and such tenderness as awed him; and then, as a light is puffed out, they were the eyes of a friendly stranger. He understood, for an instant, that of necessity it was decreed time must turn back and everything, even Rudolph Musgrave, be just as it had been when he first saw Patricia. For they had made nothing of their lives; and so, they must begin all over again.

"*Failure is not permitted*" he was saying. . .

"*You're Cousin Rudolph, aren't you?*" she asked. . .

And Rudolph Musgrave knew he had forgotten something of vast import, but what this knowledge had pertained to he no longer knew. Then Rudolph Musgrave noted, with a delicious tingling somewhere about his heart, that her hair was like the reflection of a sunset in rippling waters—only many times more beautiful, of course—and that her mouth was an inconsiderable trifle, a scrap of sanguine curves, and that her eyes were purple glimpses of infinity.

THE END

A Note About the Author

James Branch Cabell (1879–1958) was an American writer of escapist and fantasy fiction. Born into a wealthy family in the state of Virginia, Cabell attended the College of William and Mary, where he graduated in 1898 following a brief personal scandal. His first stories began to be published, launching a productive decade in which Cabell's worked appeared in both *Harper's Monthly Magazine* and *The Saturday Evening Post*. Over the next forty years, Cabell would go on to publish fifty-two books, many of them novels and short-story collections. A friend, colleague, and inspiration to such writers as Ellen Glasgow, H.L. Mencken, Sinclair Lewis, and Theodore Dreiser, James Branch Cabell is remembered as an iconoclastic pioneer of fantasy literature.

A Note from the Publisher

Spanning many genres, from non-fiction essays to literature classics to children's books and lyric poetry, Mint Edition books showcase the master works of our time in a modern new package. The text is freshly typeset, is clean and easy to read, and features a new note about the author in each volume. Many books also include exclusive new introductory material. Every book boasts a striking new cover, which makes it as appropriate for collecting as it is for gift giving. Mint Edition books are only printed when a reader orders them, so natural resources are not wasted. We're proud that our books are never manufactured in excess and exist only in the exact quantity they need to be read and enjoyed.